Dead Time

Dead Time

MATT BROLLY

CANELO

First published in the United Kingdom in 2018 by Canelo

This edition published in the United Kingdom in 2019 by

Canelo Digital Publishing Limited
57 Shepherds Lane
Beaconsfield, Bucks HP9 2DU
United Kingdom

A CIP catalogue record for this book is available from the British Library.

Print ISBN 978 1 78863 417 5
Ebook ISBN 978 1 91142 044 6

Look for more great books at www.canelo.co

Printed and bound in Great Britain by Clays Ltd, Elcograf S.p.A.

To Ann and Jim Eardley

Prologue

The street was desolate.

A frigid wind ripped into his skin as he made his slow progress to the flat entrance. Cobwebs, crystallized like threads of silver, coated the bushes to the side of the building. He ran his gloved hand through the frozen string of the spider web before pushing multiple buttons on the intercom until he was admitted.

He'd been here before.

Fragments of frost dropped from his boots as he stamped them on the welcome mat, his nose twitching at the smell of damp and latent decay within the building's walls. His confidence was justified, and he smirked as he placed the balaclava over his head and skipped up the steps to the third floor.

There was no hesitation as he knocked at the door and displayed the gun to the corpulent man whose eyes flickered up and down, right to left, remembering.

He struck him before he had time to speak and dragged him inside.

'Strip,' he ordered, glad now he'd come here alone.

He ran the bath and watched him undress. The banality of it was bruising, the man shedding his clothes without objection. His pale body wobbled as he was guided towards the bathroom.

'Why are you doing this?' he pleaded.

It was a common refrain, one he'd heard before, though never directly.

Steam rose and swirled, clouding the mirror and bath-room window as hot water filled the bath. He pointed his gun to the water and the man climbed in.

A victim entering a grave of his own making.

'Do you remember us?' he said, plugging the appliance into the extension cord.

The man blinked, confused, staring at him like he was an apparition.

'Let's hope this works,' he said, throwing the object into the air.

It flew in an arc, the cord gliding through the steam like a bird's tail, and landed with a burst of sparks.

Chapter One

The shrill of the alarm reverberated around the bedroom, within seconds accompanied by the piercing wail of a child screaming. DCI Michael Lambert's left hand smashed down on the bedside cabinet in a blind and frantic search for his mobile phone. Murmuring a curse under his breath, his finger reached the screen and activated the snooze alarm. He rolled over in his bed, pleased to find no one was next to him, remaining that way for the following nine minutes entombed in the warmth of the duvet, caught between wakefulness and sleep, as the sound of the child's crying faded.

He accepted the second alarm, hitting the off button and sitting upright in bed lest he fall back to sleep. As usual he'd been late to bed and slept for only four hours, yet a quick splash of water on his face left him refreshed and ready, if not eager, to return to work.

Lambert headed a special investigation unit at the National Crime Agency. It was a year since his work on the Waverley Manor case, a complex criminal case resulting in Lambert uncovering a paedophile ring known as the Manor. Eight successful prosecutions followed the investigation, since which Lambert had been investigating an international money-laundering scheme in the City of London.

In those last twelve months, he'd moved back in with his estranged wife, Sophie, who was in the kitchen extension feeding Jane who stopped eating as he entered the room so she could turn her head and flash him a smile. Lambert returned the gesture and kissed the two-year-old girl – the girl he was learning to call his daughter – on her head, and poured a generous helping of coffee.

'Can you drop her at the childminder?' asked Sophie.

'Did you sleep in that suit?' asked Lambert, puzzled as to how his wife could look immaculate so early in the morning.

'You can take her any time after eight. I need to get in early,' replied Sophie, grabbing a set of house keys from the sideboard and kissing him, then Jane, in one controlled motion before disappearing to the front door and before Lambert had time to object.

'Looks like you and me, buddy,' he said to the still smiling Jane, who was too busy eating a bowl of muesli to reply. Lambert wiped some spillage from the girl's face, Jane continuing to eat throughout the onslaught, before answering the incessant ringtone on his mobile.

It was DS Kennedy. 'What can I do for you, Matilda?'

'Sir, you're needed at a crime scene. Suspicious death.'

'Care to elaborate?'

'That's all I've got at the moment. Summons comes from on high though. I've been ordered to meet you at the scene.'

'From on high?'

'From Glenn – I mean, Tillman.'

Lambert drank his coffee, pleased with the taste of the Peruvian beans he'd received as a birthday present. Chief Superintendent Glenn Tillman was his direct superior.

They'd worked together for years, and by this stage Lambert was rarely surprised by Tillman's actions. Tillman was also in a relationship with the much younger DS Matilda Kennedy, a secret only Lambert was privy to. 'Do you have an address at least?'

'I'll text it now. Could be a bit of a trek for you. It's over in West Hampstead.'

Lambert glanced at the kitchen clock. 'That's going to take me at least ninety minutes this time of the morning, and I've got to drop off Jane. Why have we been requested?'

'Tillman's been at his enigmatic best this morning. I think his exact words were, "Tell Lambert to get his arse there immediately, no questions asked."'

Lambert murmured. 'Sounds like him. I'll leave now but I doubt I'll be there before ten.'

'I'll hold the fort, sir, and let you know when I have some more details.'

Jane didn't take kindly to being told she was off to the childminder. Lambert was thankful Sophie had already dressed her as he struggled to get her into her coat. 'No,' she said, sticking out her bottom lip and stamping her foot.

'I see more and more of your mother in you every day,' said Lambert, placing an oversized woolly hat on her head and wrapping a scarf around her before scooping the girl in his arms.

Despite her best efforts, Jane's frown morphed into a smile and she giggled as he tickled her. 'You'll have a great time at Lorraine's. All your friends will be there and Mummy will pick you up later,' said Lambert, placing her back on the floor.

Jane frowned again, a gesture at once comical and highly manipulative. There was so much of Sophie in her, as well as a troubling reflection of his other daughter, Chloe. Chloe died in a car accident when she was nine. Lambert was driving at the time, and the grief from the accident led to him and Sophie separating. He was not Jane's biological father and had only moved back in with Sophie a year ago. Times like this were still difficult. He would always blame himself for Chloe's death and feared Sophie did so too. He didn't want to spend the rest of his life looking at Jane and seeing Chloe. It wasn't fair to her, and in his darkest moments he wasn't sure it was a situation he could handle.

'Daddy?'

Lambert glanced down at Jane, surprised by the look of concern on her face. He knelt so they were at eye level. 'What's the matter, darling?' he asked.

'You looked sad, Daddy,' she said, frowning.

He'd spoken at length with Sophie about whether or not Jane should call him Daddy. Lambert had been hesitant and struggled to explain his apprehensions. Even after all this time he struggled to talk to Sophie about Chloe. Jane's biological father, a partner in Sophie's law firm, was still on the scene, but had taken a back seat since announcing a surprise marriage earlier that year, and six months ago Lambert legally adopted the girl.

Lambert grabbed Jane and kissed her, ruffling her hair and causing her hat to fall off. 'Oh, Daddy,' she said, giggling.

Lambert grabbed her again and smiled, wondering how he could ever have contemplated life without his little girl in it.

Jane made a frantic grab for him as he dropped her off at the childminder's. He hated having to leave her even though she enjoyed her time there. She offered a sullen wave as he returned to his car, and he tried not to look into his rear-view mirror as he pulled away.

As Lambert expected, the journey from Beckenham, on the border of South East London, to West Hampstead in the north of the City, was plagued by traffic. It was approaching Christmas and that, coupled with the seasonally bad weather, meant the roads were full. Temporary traffic lights lined the road out of Beckenham and he sat tapping his steering wheel, the heating on full. He thought about Jane, back at the childminder's and considered turning the car around to pick her up. How easy it would be to spend the day at home, indoors, insulated from the near sub-zero temperatures, watching mindless television and spending quality time with his daughter.

A sense of contentment had come over him since he'd moved back in with Sophie and he feared it was making him soft. It wasn't quite the same as it was before Chloe's death, but it was getting closer with each passing week. They slept in the same bedroom now, unlike the two years leading to their separation. It was still far from perfect. He missed the sense of security about their relationship. At times they tried too hard, too wary of upsetting one another, but he was in a better place than he'd once been and for that he was thankful.

The traffic eased and he made slow progress over the river, before coming to a standstill outside Victoria station for twenty minutes. It was as if every car in London had decided to take to the road at the same time. Crawling past the Winter Wonderland in Hyde Park, he viewed the towering rides and remembered the times he'd driven past with Chloe and how he'd discussed with Sophie the possibility of taking Jane there one day when she was older. In the morning gloom, without the lights, sounds and smells, the place took on a strange appearance. All mystery and excitement dissolved, and the fair had a sadness to it mirroring Lambert's melancholy mood: half desperate to get to his destination, half reluctant to find out what was in store for him.

It was an hour later before he pulled into West End Lane, an enclave of up-market cafés, restaurants and shops. He'd not heard back from Matilda so presumed he'd not been missed. He pulled in next to the police barrier tape erected on one of the side streets. The change in temperature as he left the vehicle was a shock; an icy wind blew in his ears as he retrieved his coat from the boot. A uniformed officer ran to him, about to tell him to move, before falling silent at the sight of Lambert's warrant card.

'Sorry, sir,' mouthed the constable.

'Who's in charge here?' said Lambert.

The PC gawped, confused by the question. 'They're all through there, sir,' he said.

Lambert lifted the collar of his jacket against the bitter wind and moved towards the group of officers congregating in the foyer of the apartment building. They were dressed in the white latex uniforms worn by the SOCOs: the scene of crime officers. With their hoods covering their hair, Lambert struggled to recognize any of their number. 'DCI Lambert,' he said to the gathered group, who had so far ignored him. One of the female officers who'd been standing alone walked over to him.

'Do you have some ID?' she asked, taking Lambert by surprise.

Lambert took out his warrant card. 'Who's in charge here?' he said.

'They're on the third floor. You need to put on one of these,' she said, pointing to a plastic box containing a spare suit.

With the extra layer of clothing, Lambert soon became overheated. Sweat coating his skin as he made slow progress upstairs. The door of Apartment Sixteen was ajar. Lambert recognized three of the faces in the living area. They stood side by side waiting for him to enter. All three were dressed in SOCO uniforms but none of them had their hoods pulled over their heads. The smallest of the three, DS Matilda Kennedy, smiled at him. The left side of her face, blotchy and red, crinkled as she made the gesture. The scarring on her face was the legacy of an explosion that had taken place a mile or so from their current location. Next to her was the bullish figure of Chief Superintendent Glenn Tillman who stared at him with his usual look of restrained violence, as if somehow Lambert was to blame for his being there.

If Lambert was surprised by Tillman's appearance he was shocked further to see Assistant Chief Constable Thomas Daly standing next to his boss. It wasn't the kind of welcome party he'd envisioned. Something must be amiss for two such senior officers to be at the scene. Lambert nodded at Tillman. 'Sir,' he said to the Assistant Chief Constable.

'Lambert,' said Daly. 'Good of you to make it.'

Lambert, knowing better than to blame his late arrival on traffic, ignored the Assistant Chief's ironic remark. 'What do we have?' he said.

'Go look for yourself.' said Tillman, clearly unhappy to be in the room with the Assistant Chief Constable.

Matilda pulled the hood over her head. 'This way, sir,' she said, leading him down a small hallway to a bathroom. 'Alistair Beckinsale,' she said, pointing to the bloated corpse laying in the bath. 'Fifty-four-year-old banker, recently divorced. We believe the cause of death is electrocution. When we arrived we found a digital radio, connected to the mains via an extension lead, in the bath with Mr Beckinsale.'

'I assume the bath was full at this time,' said Lambert.

'Yes, the SOCO's have drained the water. We left the body here so you could see for yourself.'

Lambert was no expert on electrocution, though he'd seen similar cases before. He checked the body, the skin of the man's shoulder blade a charred black, the smell of burning flesh still evident in the room. 'Is there any sign of a struggle?'

'No. The front door of the apartment was wide open and the bath was still running. Water was leaking into the apartment below, and fortunately the neighbour was in and came up to find this.'

Lambert studied the area: the wide-eyed corpse in the bath; the damp patches on the floor. 'Now stop me if I am being obvious here, Matilda, but have we ruled out suicide?'

'Not completely.'

'Not completely? Then why the hell am I here?'

'I think you better speak to Tillman, sir.'

Lambert sighed and walked back to the living area where Tillman was deep in conversation with the Assistant Chief.

'Recognize him?' said Tillman.

'No, should I?' said Lambert.

'Well, he recognizes you,' said the Assistant Chief, handing him a clear plastic sheath with a piece of card inside it. 'This was found in the bathroom.'

Lambert took out the card and glanced at it to see in black ink the name: DCI Lambert.

Chapter Two

Lambert held the card in his hand, checking its weight. It was standard ruled card, A6 size. The hole in the left corner suggested it had been torn from a ring binder. His name was written in lead pencil.

DCI LAMBERT

Nothing else, simply his name in capital letters, each letter perfectly drawn, the lines straight, the curves immaculate as if the writer had used a stencil. The card itself was standard stock available from countless sources. Lambert placed the card back in its plastic sheath. 'Is this it?' he said.

'First responding officer found it, and recognizing your name called head office immediately,' said Tillman.

Daly pursed his lips, a sound like escaping gas leaking from the small opening in his mouth. 'Do you know this Beckinsale character?' he asked.

'No, of course not,' said Lambert, his tone sterner than intended.

'Would you care to explain why this note is here, then?' said Daly, picking up on his insolence.

As Tillman subtly indicated, Lambert had attracted some notoriety over the last year. The Waverley Manor arrests involved a number of prominent businessmen. The national press picked up on the story, Lambert receiving some unwanted attention.

'You think this is something to do with your fame?' said Tillman, reading his thoughts and getting to the point.

'Until I find out more about Beckinsale, then I would have to presume so. Yes, maybe Beckinsale saw my name in the paper and thought he would get more attention by leaving my name at the scene.'

'Someone was seen fleeing the apartment building,' said Tillman. 'Minutes before Beckinsale's body was discovered. We have some images on CCTV.'

'You don't think this was a suicide?' said Lambert.

'Why plug the radio into an extension cord? This was no suicide. Beckinsale was coerced into that bath, I'm sure of it, and whoever we have on CCTV is the culprit. We need to wrap this up as soon as we can.'

'Who is going to be the SIO?' said Lambert.

Tillman stared hard at him, eyes unblinking. It was a classic Tillman gesture, one Lambert had experienced countless times over the years. In most officers it had the required effect of instilling fear and upping concentration levels. In Lambert, it only provoked a weary resignation.

'I'm going to be the senior investigation officer,' said Tillman. 'And by I, I mean you.' He also liked talking in riddles.

'How can I run this investigation if my name has been left on that note?'

'Because officially you're not on the investigation, I am. And you will be working with Kennedy. We want this kept as quiet as possible, you've been in the papers enough as it is. An incident room has been set up at West

Hampstead nick. It's just up the hill on West End Lane. Keep us updated.'

'Your name is on the card, so to me it makes sense that you run the operation,' said Assistant Chief Daly. 'Don't let us down.'

Lambert didn't have time to complain before Tillman walked away with Daly.

'Who found the body?' Lambert asked Matilda.

'Marcus Barnett, lives directly below Beckinsale. He's left for work now but he's given me permission to view his flat.'

'Let's go.'

Barnett's flat was a mirror image of Beckinsale's. 'There,' said Matilda, pointing to a wet patch in Barnett's bathroom. 'That's where the water leaked down. Mr Barnett didn't notice it at first because he was having a shower. It was only when he turned it off and the water kept coming that he realized something was wrong.'

'And he went straight upstairs?'

'Yep, pulled on a dressing gown and ran up. He was scared the floor was going to cave in, and then he found Beckinsale.'

'What were his actions after that?'

'He had enough foresight to turn the taps off, if that's what you're getting at,' said Matilda.

'Contaminating the crime scene?' said Lambert.

'Potentially.'

'Any neighbourly disputes?'

'Not between these two, according to Mr Barnett. We've talked to the other residents. Beckinsale was a quiet sort by all accounts, though he'd recently been voted onto the housing committee.'

'Christ, those things are always fraught,' said Lambert. 'We'll have to get them all in for questioning, starting with Barnett.'

'Sir,' said Matilda.

They waited until the body was removed before leaving. The wind had grown in intensity and hit them face on as they walked the short distance up West End Lane. The neighbourhood was in full Christmas mode, the shops adorned with tasteful festive decorations. Matilda ignored the occasional glance in her direction. Lambert had grown accustomed to the burn marks on his colleague's face and didn't notice them any more. They were part of who she was, and he would have ignored them completely were it not for the occasional stab of guilt that she was marked because of him.

At West Hampstead police station they were greeted by DI Jack Canon who showed them to a newly refurbished incident room. The room was empty. 'Tillman wants a team in from head office,' said Matilda, by way of explanation.

'So we have a potential murder case and it's just you and me working on it?' said Lambert.

'For the time being.'

DI Canon heard the conversation but didn't comment. Lambert didn't have the energy to ask him if Tillman had explained the parameters of their investigation.

'Let me know if you need some extra numbers,' said Canon, before exiting.

They spent the next hour setting the place up.

'Bickland and Croft will be here soon,' said Matilda. 'They've been researching Beckinsale back at HQ, so we should have something to get our teeth into when they arrive.'

'Let me see these CCTV images,' said Lambert.

Matilda played the grainy footage of a man leaving the Beckinsale residence in the early morning.

'Is this all we've got?' said Lambert. He zoomed in on the man's face, covered by his hoody, the image black and white and heavily pixilated.

'I'm afraid so.'

The image was next to useless and Lambert was surprised Tillman gave it such prominence. 'How do we know he isn't a resident?'

'We don't. We'll eliminate everyone one by one, but look at the way he's standing like he's trying to avoid the camera.'

Lambert sighed and retreated into a side office to begin his own research. He agreed with Tillman it was likely his name was left at the scene due to his notoriety, but there was also the possibility the assailant had something more specific in mind. He began with a simple Google search on the name Beckinsale before widening it out.

He wasn't sure if he was being obsessive, but his first search was for a link to the Manor. He searched for a link between Beckinsale and the eight wealthy middle-aged white men who'd used their money and power to devastating effect. Reluctantly, he thought back to the underground prison where he'd uncovered the remains of over ninety children. Even after the eight arrests, they were still far from uncovering the full extent of the atrocities committed by the group.

The Manor was a vast and organized underground organization with codes of secrecy almost impossible to penetrate. A specialized division had been setup to continue the work Lambert started. So it felt logical to check if Beckinsale was somehow linked to the group. His initial search proved fruitless. He was about to log into the System, his department's specialized criminal database, when three officers arrived in the incident room.

DS Bickland was sweating. Lambert noticed the sweat patches on his cotton shirt. He was accompanied by the newest member of his team, DS Gemma Croft, whom Lambert had recruited from a small investigation team in Chislehurst. Finally came the lumbering figure of Lambert's boss Glenn Tillman.

Lambert was surprised, and disappointed, to see Tillman with Bickland and Croft. He tended to work better without the involvement of his boss, and his presence usually coincided with bad news.

'A word,' said Tillman, walking into Lambert's office.

Lambert studied Bickland and Croft's demeanour for clues, wondering if they knew something he didn't, before following Tillman into the office and closing the door.

Tillman sat behind the desk. He'd removed his tie since the morning and his thick neck bulged beneath his striped shirt. 'It's not your day, Lambert,' he said.

'Do I want to hear this?' said Lambert, sitting opposite.

Tillman pushed his lower lip beneath his teeth. 'It's Peter Saunders.'

Lambert shrugged.

'He's escaped.'

Chapter Three

White noise filled the room as Lambert processed what he'd been told. 'Is this a joke, Glenn?'

Peter Saunders was one of the eight members of the Manor convicted in the last year. A drawn-out trial had resulted in Saunders receiving life imprisonment with no chance of parole. Saunders had owned a medium-sized architecture firm, hence the nickname. Although they'd failed to prove it, it was believed Saunders designed and helped build the underground prison at Waverley Manor. In the end forensic evidence had been the man's undoing, with his DNA found throughout the site. The possibility he'd escaped captivity was too horrific for Lambert to accept.

Tillman rubbed his chin, his only stress indicator. 'No. He was being moved this morning to a high-security unit in Luton. It was very hush-hush.'

'Not hush-hush enough by the sounds of it.'

'He was in a car with two prison guards and an armed officer. One of the guards was murdered. The other, by the name of John Prine, is missing along with Saunders.'

'The officer?'

Tillman shook his head. 'Gunshot to the head.'

'Didn't we have a second car following?'

'No. Everything was being monitored from headquarters.'

Lambert placed his head in his hands, the adrenaline pumping through his body making him nauseous. 'When did this happen?'

'This morning.'

'Why the hell are we only finding out about it now?'

'It's lucky we've found out about it at all. The whole operation was on a need-to-know basis. Saunders was moved as there were concerns over his safety. Only a handful of people knew. Two of them are now dead and one is missing.'

Lambert sat back in his chair. 'This can't be a coincidence, Glenn. We have a murder victim, the assailant leaving my name on a card, all at the same time a major member of the Manor escapes from prison.'

'It had crossed my mind, Lambert. That's partly why I'm here.'

'Partly?'

'You're not to get involved.'

Lambert snorted. 'Fuck off, Glenn.'

Tillman tilted his head, taking in a deep breath. 'I realize you're upset so I'll let that go.'

'What do you mean I'm not to get involved? This is my case – our case, for Christ's sake. I put Saunders behind bars.'

'Yes. That was your job. Finding out how he escaped is not.'

'Bullshit. This relates directly to me, to all of us, now more than ever.' Already, Lambert's mind was working overtime trying to connect Saunders' escape with Beckinsale's death. Did Beckinsale have prior knowledge of

Saunders? Was he a member of the Manor? The new turn of events blew the parameters of the case wide open.

'Nothing links Beckinsale to Saunders,' said Tillman, without conviction.

'Where does this come from, Glenn? Who has told me not to get involved?'

'Look, Michael, the feeling is you are too close to the case.'

This didn't sound like Tillman. He'd never seen the man back away from a high-profile case or suggest his team didn't have what it took to investigate. 'Yes, I am close to the case. I saw what those animals did, what they're capable of, and what they are no doubt doing somewhere else.'

Lambert had spent the last year pushing for the opportunity to head a special task force to investigate the Manor, but the general feeling was the Manor in itself didn't technically exist. The eight arrests were considered to be like-minded men working together. The higher echelon of the force refused to officially recognize them as a group. It meant they had to be investigated on a case-by-case basis, though Lambert hoped this would now change following Saunders' escape.

'I'll keep you updated, Michael, you know that,' said Tillman, getting to his feet to signal that was the end of the matter. 'For the time being, concentrate all your efforts onto the Beckinsale case. If you find a link between Beckinsale and Saunders then we can examine it at that time.'

Lambert read between the lines of Tillman's last statement. 'That's it, then?' he said, as Tillman stood up and moved to the door.

'That's it. No one else in your team is to know about this. Am I clear?'

Lambert glared at his boss but didn't respond. He watched as Tillman exchanged words with Bickland and Croft before leaving the incident room.

Logging onto the System, Lambert searched for details on Saunders' escape to no avail. It took thirty minutes of analysis until he determined where the incident occurred. A section of Holloway Road in north London was closed earlier that morning, and emergency services received reports of the sound of gunshots in that area at the same time. As Saunders had been travelling from Woolwich to Luton prison, it was feasible his vehicle had taken such a route. In such high-profile prison transfers, the routes were random.

Lambert pulled on his coat and was about to brave the winter temperatures when Matilda knocked on the door. 'Mr Beckinsale's partner has arrived, sir,' she said.

Lambert lowered his eyes, exhaling. 'Has she been informed of his death yet?'

'Probably put two and two together following the messages we left for her. One of the uniforms from the scene drove her here, so she knows.'

'OK. Go and talk to her. See if she's in a fit state for questioning.'

'Sir,' said Matilda, not moving.

'Well?'

Matilda stood at the edge of his desk, moving from one foot to the other. 'What did Tillman want, sir?'

Lambert pulled his shoulders back. It was not a question a junior officer should have asked. He didn't want to reprimand her but was unwilling to get involved in the domestic situation of the DS and his boss. 'That's all,' he said, returning his gaze to his laptop.

–

Matilda returned thirty minutes later. 'Sir, I wanted to say sorry for earlier...'

Lambert held his hand up and shook his head. 'How was Mrs Beckinsale?' he said, the previous matter forgotten.

'She's waiting in Interview Room Six. Daniella Bolton. They weren't married. They've been together about a year.'

'He was married before?'

'Yes, sir, we've been onto the ex.'

'Right,' said Lambert, feeling underprepared, his focus still on the Peter Saunders' escape. 'Let's get the ex in as soon as we can. Find out what the hell is going on, shall we?'

Lambert was surprised by Daniella's youth. Beckinsale was fifty-four and Daniella appeared to be at least twenty-five years younger. Matilda introduced him and he shook hands with the woman; her grip was weak, her skin clammy.

'Thank you for your time, Miss Bolton. May I call you Daniella?'

Daniella smiled. 'I can't believe this is happening,' she said.

'No, I do understand what a traumatic situation this must be. Could you perhaps tell me when was the last time you saw Mr Beckinsale?'

Daniella glanced upwards. 'I saw Alistair two nights ago. We went out for dinner. I was going to stay at his house for the night but he had to work early in the morning so I caught the Tube home.'

'And where do you live?'

'Only in Finchley.'

Daniella's voice was nearly inaudible. Her words trailed away as she spoke and Lambert leant in to hear her properly. 'How long have you been together?' he asked, keeping the conversation light, probing for any indication she was hiding something.

'About a year.'

'About?'

'It will be a year in January,' she said, as if Beckinsale was still alive.

Lambert forced a smile onto his face. 'That's quite a long time. How did you find living in separate homes?'

'It was fine. Neither of us wanted to rush things. Alistair was married before and I...' She faltered, her voice failing completely.

'Can I pour you some water?' said Lambert, lifting the jug on the table.

Daniella took a large drink of the water while Lambert waited. 'Sorry,' she said, her voice a croak.

'Don't worry, Daniella, you take your time. You were saying?'

Daniella smiled, the gesture vanishing before it fully appeared on her face. 'I'd only got out of a relationship when I first started seeing Alistair,' she said, as if confessing.

'I see. If you don't mind me asking, were you with your former partner for long?' asked Lambert, keeping his tone light.

'Ten years,' said Daniella, gazing down at the desk, ashamed by the admission.

'You must have been young when you met,' said Matilda.

'Too young,' said the woman, looking towards Matilda as if she'd found a comrade.

'What was his name?' asked Matilda.

'Will.'

Lambert and Matilda said nothing. Daniella wanted to tell them something, and they were both experienced enough to know when to remain silent.

Sensing something was wrong, Daniella became flustered, glancing around the room in confusion. 'I'm sure you already know,' she began, staring in accusation at Lambert.

Lambert's eyes widened. 'Sorry, Daniella, you have me at a loss. What do I already know?'

'About Will.'

'What about him?'

She reddened, as if realizing she'd fallen into a trap. She folded her arms, sweat forming on her brow.

'It would be easier to tell us,' said Matilda.

Daniella sighed. 'He was in prison.'

'For?' said Lambert.

'GBH, but he shouldn't have gone to prison.'

'What happened?' asked Matilda, playing good cop.

'We were out one night, some guy was talking to me at the bar and Will kind of flipped.'

'Flipped?' said Lambert.

Daniella leant towards them, pleading her ex's defence. 'It got out of hand. They were pushing each other, mouthing off, you know?'

Neither officer responded.

'Anyway, this guy strikes out at Will and they have a scuffle and Will ends up hurting him.'

'Did he have a record?'

'Will? No.'

'Then how did he end up going to prison for a simple bar fight?'

Daniella sat back, glancing at Matilda for support. When none was forthcoming, she closed her eyes. 'There was a bottle on the bar. Will grabbed it and lashed out. It was in self-defence but...'

Lambert raised his eyebrows, waiting.

'It connected with the other guy's eye and he ended up losing it.'

Lambert let out a breath as Matilda excused herself and left the room to check on Daniella's ex-boyfriend.

'So he was the jealous kind, this Will?' said Lambert, once again softening his tone.

'You could say that,' said Daniella.

'When did you last see him?' said Lambert, trying to assign as little importance as possible to the question.

The tension in Daniella's body was visible. Her back straightened as she held her breath.

Lambert waited until she remembered to breathe. 'Something you need to tell me, Daniella? It would be easier all round if you told me now.'

She shook her head, close to tears.

'OK, Daniella. Tell me about Alistair. You met him about a year ago, you said?'

'Yes.'

'Where did you meet?'

'At a bar.'

'Did he speak to you, or the other way around?'

'I can't really remember. There was a group of us and at some point we got talking.'

Daniella's demeanour had changed dramatically since the first mention of her ex-boyfriend. Lambert hadn't been convinced she'd been in mourning for Beckinsale's death to begin with but was less sure now. She acted defensively, as if she had something to hide.

'Did he ask you out, or did you ask him out?'

'Does it matter?'

'I suppose not.'

Lambert was about to continue questioning her when Matilda returned to the room. She gestured for him to leave the office so Lambert suspended the interview. 'I'll just be a minute,' he said, smiling at Daniella.

'Will Fisher,' said Matilda, handing him a printed report. 'This suggests the attack was a bit more vicious than Daniella is suggesting. The victim lost his eye as well as the top row of his teeth. He suffered a fractured cheekbone beneath the eye.'

'Let me guess, Fisher is out of jail and lives in close proximity to the young lady in the interview room?'

'Same apartment building.'

'Right,' said Lambert, opening the interview door and restarting the interview, reminding Daniella she wasn't under caution but was free to request legal counsel at any point.

'You're still in contact with Will, aren't you, Daniella?'

Daniella reddened once more, her nostrils widening as her breathing intensified.

'He must have known about Alistair. Alistair was a very wealthy man, was he not?'

'What are you getting at?'

'Help me out here, Daniella. This doesn't look good. An ex-boyfriend with a violent temper, a history of jealous rages. A rich older man. You can put the pieces together yourself.'

'Will didn't do this,' said Daniella, shaking her head, convincing herself.

'You're still in contact with Will, aren't you?' said Matilda, repeating Lambert's question.

'No,' said Daniella, a child caught in a lie.

'You live in the same building,' said Lambert.

'He didn't do it. He wouldn't do that,' said Daniella, breaking down as she began to realize the enormity of the situation.

'Are you still lovers?' asked Matilda.

Daniella cracked, beginning to cry. 'Yes,' said Daniella, through sobs.

'He knows about Alistair. Didn't mind as long as the money was coming in?' asked Lambert, handing the woman a box of tissues.

'He wouldn't kill him. He's not that crazy. I'd never let him do that to them.'

'To them?' asked Lambert.

Daniella squeezed her eyes shut, caught out again. 'Alistair isn't my only boyfriend,' she said.

Chapter Four

Lambert sighed and exchanged looks with Matilda. They had to proceed with caution. Lambert reminded Daniella she could request legal representation at any point. When she declined, Lambert decided to postpone the meeting. His mind was working overtime. He thought about Peter Saunders, hoping the assigned teams was making good inroads into his whereabouts, while considering all the implications of what Daniella was telling him.

'Let's take a break, shall we, Daniella? I'll ask one of the officers to get you something to eat and we can have another chat. I know this must be very difficult,' he said, leaving the interview room with Matilda.

Back in the incident room he updated Bickland and Croft. 'You two get to that address now and pick up this Will Fisher. If he's not there track him down.'

'That was illuminating,' said Matilda, once they'd left. 'Have you heard of Will Fisher?'

'Unfortunately not.'

'That doesn't mean he doesn't know you.'

'No, but why would he leave a note with my name on it at the scene? If it was him then it sounds like it was a crime of passion. He finally got jealous of Daniella and her numerous boyfriends. If he was acting on impulse it's unlikely he would have the foresight to write my name on a piece of card before leaving. Especially as it was stencilled.'

'He could have prepared it beforehand.'

'That suggests an element of premeditation. We'll know more when we speak to Fisher. Keep Daniella busy until he comes in. I need to be somewhere.'

If Matilda was surprised he was leaving the office at such a crucial point she knew better than to question him. 'What if she wants to leave?'

'Caution her. She's obviously pulling some scam with these boyfriends and we have enough to detain her. She can get a solicitor.'

'Will that give you time to do whatever it is you need to do?' said Matilda, raising her eyebrows.

Lambert wouldn't have let many subordinate officers get away with such a remark but he'd gone through so much with Matilda he let it go. 'I think so, Matilda, thanks for asking.'

–

The temperature had dropped even further since that morning. The wind was mercifully behind him as he walked down the hill, wishing he'd driven from the murder scene rather than walked. The area surrounding Beckinsale's house was still cordoned off and the same uniform team were stationed outside.

The young PC who'd challenged him glanced over as he got into his car. Lambert ignored him and sat in his car revving his engine, waiting for the heat to kick in. He was about to pull out into the road when there was a knock on the car door.

When he saw who it was he almost drove off. Instead, he buzzed down the window, the engine still running. Outside stood Mia Helmer. Helmer worked as a senior editor on a national newspaper, though she had taken to occasional bouts of investigative journalism when cases involved Lambert. His relationship with the woman was, at best, uneasy. He'd once come close to arresting her for interfering in his investigations and she'd never forgiven him.

'Mia,' he said.

Helmer was a diminutive woman in stature but not in confidence or ability. 'DCI Lambert. It is my under-standing a card with your name on it was found at the house of Alistair Beckinsale. Would you care to comment on why this might be, and are you treating his death as suspicious?'

'Come on, Mia, you know better than this.'

Mia brushed a loose strand of black hair from her face. 'A high-profile banker, found electrocuted in his bath, your name found close to his body. This could be front-page news. I'm sure our readers would love to hear your side of the story.'

'I would talk to our press office before releasing any fantasy stories.'

'Would you care to comment?' said Mia, ignoring him.

'No comment,' said Lambert, closing the window and driving off.

—

Traffic moved snail-like as he made his way to Holloway Road. Lambert tried to ignore the nagging doubt in his mind suggesting he turn back and place all his focus on the Beckinsale case, but he needed to see the scene where Saunders had escaped. He was disappointed Mia Helmer had so many details about the case and made a mental note to discuss the matter with the uniformed officers who'd been at the scene.

Moving through what felt like the hundredth set of traffic lights, he finally found his destination. Unlike at Beckinsale's house, nothing in the area suggested there had been an incident of any kind. Lambert parked up outside a row of shops. Leaving the car, he examined the road for any sign of a traffic incident but nothing was out of place in the surrounding area – no tyre marks or fragments of glass.

Inside the local newsagent's, he waited until the shop's only customer had left before questioning the woman behind the counter. When he showed the woman his warrant card, her face dropped. 'Back again,' she said.

'Different department,' said Lambert, playing along with newsagent's assumption.

The woman sighed and shuffled a pile of newspapers on the counter. 'How can I help you?'

'I know you've gone through this already but can you tell me from the beginning exactly what happened this morning?' said Lambert.

The woman squinted her eyes as if suspecting she was being tricked. 'Why are you questioning me again?'

'Standard procedure,' said Lambert, holding the woman's gaze.

'Well, OK. As I told your colleague, I heard all the commotion but didn't think much of it to begin with. We get horns blaring all the time, the roads are jammed with crappy drivers. I thought it was another road rage incident until I heard the shots.'

'How many shots did you hear?'

'A few. Maybe five or six?' she said, as if Lambert knew the answer.

'What happened next?'

'What do you mean what happened next?'

'After the gunshots.'

The woman shrugged. 'How the hell would I know?'

Surprised by the woman's answer, Lambert was about to ask more questions when a customer entered the shop. The young man was wearing shorts and flip-flops despite the winter chill, and his hand shook as he handed over his money for the rolling tobacco he asked for.

'Thanks, love,' said the woman as the customer left.

Lambert pulled the bolt on the door and flipped the sign to 'Closed' so they wouldn't be interrupted further.

'Hey,' said the woman.

'It'll be quicker this way,' said Lambert, ignoring her protests. 'Now tell me what you did after the gunshots?'

'I hid, of course. What would you do?'

'For how long?'

'Until your colleagues banged on my door and gave me the third degree.'

'So you didn't see the ambulances?'

'I heard more sirens,' said the woman, glancing to the ceiling. 'In fact, I said to John I was surprised everything was cleared up so quickly.'

'John?'

'My husband.'

'Where is John?'

'Cash and carry.'

Lambert sensed the conversation was slipping out of his control. 'How long passed before the shots and the officers knocking on your door?'

'About twenty minutes or so, I guess. To be fair, your lot arrived pretty sharpish after the shots.'

'So twenty minutes later the police knocked at your door. Did you manage to glimpse anything of the scene outside?'

'No, as I said, the ambulances and police cars were gone.'

Lambert frowned, perplexed as to how the scene had been cleared so quickly. It was completely against protocol. Tillman said a guard and a police officer were killed at the scene. The bodies shouldn't have been removed until the SOCOs thoroughly investigated every inch of the area, which should still be cordoned off.

'OK, thanks for your help,' said Lambert, more confused than when he'd begun questioning her.

'You should give your lady officer a call, love, you look like you're a bit out of the loop.'

'Lady officer?'

'Yes, she gave me this,' said the shopkeeper, reaching under her till and handing him a business card.

Lambert turned the card over, his heartbeat jumping as he read the inscription:

DCI Sarah May, National Crime Agency.

Chapter Five

The aroma of freshly ground coffee came as a light relief. DCI Sarah May watched the Chief Constable's PA bring the tray of drinks and biscuits to the table, and worried she would never escape the stuffy confines of the conference room at NCA headquarters.

Alongside Chief Constable Alexander Mitchell was the Governor of Woolwich Prison, Paul Guthrie; Chief Superintendent Tanner, who headed up the internal anti-corruption team, AC-10 and a senior member of MI5, Charles Partridge. It was rarefied company, yet none of the men appeared capable of making a decision.

She understood why Tanner was present. What should have been the simple transfer of a category A prisoner had turned into the cock-up from hell. One of Guthrie's guards had been murdered and one had disappeared with the prisoner, Peter Saunders. In addition, an armed police officer, DS Colin Wright had also suffered a fatal gunshot wound and Tanner was here to investigate.

It was Partridge who troubled her. That MI5 were now involved, and at such a high level, suggested her control over the situation was disappearing fast.

Sarah had been in charge of the transfer of Peter Saunders, known as the Architect, hence her being in the room. She'd been in radio contact with the men transferring Saunders and had been in the response team who'd arrived within three minutes to find the dead bodies and the spaces where Saunders and the guard, John Prine, had been. She'd spent the last two hours in the room with the four men trying to formulate a plan. Whereas her focus was on how to find Saunders, the general feel of the room appeared to be how best to keep the incident quiet.

The violence and speed of the attack on Saunders' car had been staggering, matched only by the swiftness of the clean-up operation which followed, green-lighted by the Chief Constable himself, no doubt with the approval of Tanner, AC-10 and the assistance of MI5.

'I cannot overstate the necessity of keeping this from the public,' said Partridge, who leant forward in his chair, hovering over the tray of drinks, waiting for someone to pour it for him.

'Sarah?' said the Chief.

'We've managed to contain the situation at Holloway Road, though sooner or later it's going to come to light.'

Partridge frowned as if she'd said something taboo. 'No one needs to know Saunders was the party who escaped – why would they? Only a handful of people knew Saunders was being transferred, and unfortunately two of them are dead. You didn't know this, but Saunders was to be turned over to us after this transfer.'

'What?' said Sarah, surprising herself with the vehemence of her tone.

'This Manor thing has taken on a life of its own. The perpetrators have been classified as a terrorist organization. Saunders was going to spend some time at Luton prison, under the supervision of Governor Pierson, and was then going to come under our jurisdiction.'

Sarah shook her head, glancing at Tanner who was trying his best to look anywhere but at her. The classification sounded suspicious at best, and she only guess what Partridge had meant about Saunders coming under MI5's jurisdiction, 'You realize the work our various departments have done on this, the thousands of hours of manpower, the successful prosecutions, the on-going investigations. And you're handing it over to them.'

'National security, dear,' said Partridge, giving in and pouring himself some tea.

'Did you just call me "dear"?' said Sarah, getting to her feet.

Partridge grimaced as if he'd broken wind.

'Sit down, DCI May,' said the Chief Constable, keeping his tone soft.

Sarah did as instructed, staring hard at the MI5 agent as she did so.

'Remember, we're working together on this,' said the Chief. 'Sarah, you will work with MI5 on this. Saunders was in our custody so we will conduct the investigation into his disappearance,' he continued. 'But of course we will share all information in a spirit of cooperation. How does that sound, Charles?'

Partridge narrowed his eyes in acquiescence.

'Charles is right, though, news of this needs to be contained for as long as possible. We will set up the incident room here. Sarah, you will have to keep this between those officers who know about Saunders' transportation and what transpired on Holloway Road. I'm sure we can utilize MI5's resources on this, Charles?'

'Whatever you need,' said Partridge, his face unreadable.

'Tanner, you'll make sure we are in compliance?'

Tanner nodded with the conviction of a man who knew what he was doing. Only Paul Guthrie kept quiet, clearly affected by the mention of national security.

'It's settled, then. Let's find Prine and Saunders,' said the Chief, getting to his feet.

'This could be a big opportunity for you. Maybe even the chance of a further promotion,' said Partridge to Sarah, as they left the office.

The senior MI5 operative was pencil-thin, his navy-blue tailored suit clinging to him like a second skin. He inched his face towards her as she spoke, his long nose jutting towards her like a beak.

'We lost him, we'll find him,' said Sarah.

Partridge murmured. 'Let's make a start, shall we?'

Sarah studied the man, noticing the liver spots on his face and the slight discolouration of his skin. She could tell he was the kind of man who didn't enjoy taking orders from anyone. He'd sulked when the Chief spoke to him and she imagined having a female leading the operation would be unbearable for him. She didn't trust him and already considered him an obstacle to her investigation. 'I'll get my team together. Please send over anyone you can spare.'

'Very good,' said Partridge, offering a slight bow before moving away.

Sarah's team were already working on the investigation. She'd sent DS Adams to Woolwich prison to question the guards and security personnel, and DI Stevens was working on securing CCTV images for the attack at

Holloway Road. How the hell Partridge hoped to keep the escape a secret was beyond her, but she was happy to play along with the conceit for the time being. She called the two officers and told them to make their way over as soon as they were able before turning her attention to Peter Saunders' file.

Peter Saunders had been one of eight men convicted for the atrocities committed at Waverley Manor. Of the eight, Saunders was considered the ringleader. Of the eight convicted men, only the former police officer, Jonathan Barnes, had tried to strike a deal. Information from Barnes led to Saunders' arrest. It was Barnes who'd claimed he had designed the underground corridors of Waverley Manor. Saunders denied any involvement with the organization known as the Manor, but his DNA had been found on numerous bodies within the site.

DS Adams was the first to arrive. Sarah smelt the nicotine before setting eyes on him. Twenty years her junior, Adams had been on her team for the last nine months. Diligent and hard-working, he raised his hand on seeing her – an overfamiliar gesture she didn't wish to encourage.

'What have you got for me, Adams?'

Adams repeated the gesture. 'Nothing. Only four people knew Saunders was being moved and they did little more than put him in the van. As you know, Saunders was in solitary and didn't know he was moving until five minutes before the fact.'

'We need to follow this up. Someone knew he was moving and the route they were taking. Do background searches on everyone you spoke with. Look for anything, however trivial it might seem.'

Adams stood his ground, nodding his head. Sarah held her hands out. 'What are you waiting for?'

Adams shook his head as if coming out of a trance. 'Yes, sorry, ma'am,' he muttered, finding a spare desk and unloading his laptop from his bag.

Sarah took a seat behind her own desk. She hadn't managed a run that morning and her limbs were tight. A restlessness came over her, combined with a vague sense of claustrophobia. She started a new page on her notebook with the header: 'People who knew of Saunders' transfer'. She listed the deceased guard and police officer, and the missing guard, John Prine, followed by those in the support vehicle.

She added the Governor of Woolwich, Paul Guthrie, and the four guards Adams had spoken with. To the list she added the name of the Luton Governor, Stuart Pierson. She sighed. The list was already too long to allow any kind of secrecy. She completed her research and added another five names to the list, before calling Stuart Pierson at Luton prison who agreed to meet her later that evening. It would be at least a one-hour drive at this time of the day so she packed her bags and headed for the car park.

-

Outside, she realized she was underdressed despite being wrapped in a three-quarter-length coat.

She noticed the figure lurking by the bus shelter. He watched her approach from the shelter of the bus station on the main road. He was one of eleven people waiting but something about the way he stood, and the intensity of his gaze, made her sure he was waiting for her. As she continued on her way he began to move. His physique and the way he walked were familiar to her and she began to relax. As she reached the car, she could make out his face and she managed a smile.

'Michael, what are you doing here?'

Chapter Six

Lambert was surprised by his visceral response to seeing Sarah again. They hadn't seen each other since his move back home with Sophie. It was Sarah who'd suggested he make the move. She claimed her decision was a selfish one; that at some point Lambert would regret not moving back in with his wife and child. Seeing her now, Lambert's resolve faded. With the wind battering her face, sending her hair into a tangled mess, she looked confused and disgruntled but still managed the lopsided smile he'd been smitten with.

'Michael, what are you doing here?'

Her words were almost lost in the wind.

'Can we?' he said, pointing to the car.

Sarah hesitated. They had decided not to contact each other once he'd moved back in with Sophie and, not for the first time, Lambert questioned the decision. Had the break been too severe? He'd wanted to call her on numerous occasions and had come close to contacting her, but it wouldn't have been fair on her or Sophie.

'Get in,' said Sarah, unlocking the car.

Sarah's hair fell back into place as they sat in the car, the engine running as the heating filtered through the air-conditioning ducts. Lambert's pulse intensified as Sarah turned to look at him. 'Well?' she demanded.

Lambert considered apologizing for not being in touch but Sarah wouldn't care about that. He decided to get straight to the point. 'I know about Peter Saunders,' he said.

The statement did little to ease the tension in the car. Sarah rubbed at her left eye. 'What do you know?' she said, her reaction unreadable.

'I know everything about his escape. The ambush, the dead prison guard and officer. The missing guard.'

Sarah couldn't hide her surprise this time. Her eyes widened as her hand moved to her mouth. 'I shouldn't be surprised, should I? How?'

'Tillman.'

'I might have guessed.'

'What the hell is going on, Sarah?'

'You seem to know exactly what's going on, Michael,' said Sarah, a familiar hint of mischievousness returning to her voice.

'I mean with the secrecy. The cover-up. I've been to Holloway Road.'

The lighter tone evaporated once more. 'You haven't been asking questions, have you?'

'Of course I have.'

Sarah shook her head. 'Somehow, I forgot what you were like.'

'He was my conviction, Sarah. My case. I can't believe I wasn't informed.'

'No one was withholding anything from you, Michael. We would have notified you but we have slightly bigger concerns at the moment, such as finding where the hell Saunders has gone.'

'Did you not think I might have been able to help?'

'It crossed my mind, but the escape was supposed to remain classified. I've just had a meeting with the Chief and some arsehole from MI5. How the hell did Tillman find out about this?'

'That's not the point,' said Lambert.

'Maybe not. I'm sorry he's escaped, Michael. I know what he did, what they all did, and what you went through.'

'But?' said Lambert.

Sarah smiled again. 'We've been here before, haven't we?'

'You tell me not to interfere, and I do it anyway.'

'Something like that. You can trust me to get the job done on this, Michael. AC-10 are managing things to make sure it's above board. You being involved will not fit those criteria.'

'Anti-corruption? Nothing about this fits in with procedure, Sarah.'

Sarah turned the heating down in the car. She told him about the national security concerns mentioned by the Chief and Partridge from MI5.

'National security? Something's off here,' said Lambert, shaking his head.

'Those are my orders, Michael.'

Lambert's mind was in a whirl. 'Something you should consider,' he said. He told her about Beckinsale and the card left at the scene.

'It had your name on it?' asked Sarah. 'When did this happen?'

'Not long after Peter Saunders escaped custody.'

'Oh come on, Michael.'

'Give me some credit, Sarah. I'm not suggesting Saunders had any direct involvement, but it's one hell of a coincidence, don't you think? A corpse turns up on the day one of my high-profile convictions escapes custody.'

'It could be just that though. A coincidence.'

'No doubt, but don't you think we should align our investigations?'

Sarah offered him her lopsided grin again. 'Good try. Send me over your case details.'

Lambert shrugged and smiled back. 'OK, if you promise to keep me posted.'

Sarah raised three fingers. 'Brownie promise,' she said.

They sat for a time in silence. Lambert grasped for words just out of reach. He appreciated their split had been unnatural and was still not fully resolved. A sense of denial hung over their relationship, and seeing Sarah again reinforced it.

'I need to go, Michael,' said Sarah, her voice little more than a whisper.

'Take this,' said Lambert, handing her a mobile phone. 'It's not registered. Use it in case you need to contact me off the record.

She hesitated before accepting the phone as Lambert stole one last glance at her before leaving the car for the rain-speckled darkness. He watched the car pull away, confused by how bereft he felt at her departure. They'd done little more than discuss their respective cases, but what they'd left unsaid was almost tangible. Lambert analysed her every response, searching for a gesture, a clue to how she was feeling, but their brief time together left him more confused than ever.

Matilda called as Lambert drove home. She'd arranged for Beckinsale's ex-wife to visit the station the following morning.

'How did she take the news about her ex-husband?' asked Lambert on the car's internal speaker system.

'Not well. I got the feeling she didn't really consider herself an ex,' said Matilda.

'Where are we on Will Fisher?'

'We have officers stationed outside his flat but no sign yet. We've checked out all his old haunts. He's gone underground by the looks of it but we'll flush him out.'

'That's what I like to hear, Matilda, some positivity. See you in the morning.'

'Sir.'

–

It was early evening by the time he reached home. Sophie and Jane were in the living room watching children's television. Both were dressed in nightwear.

'What are you doing up, cutie?' Lambert said to Jane, kissing her on the forehead.

Jane smiled but didn't take her eyes off the screen.

'She fell asleep when I picked her up from Lorraine's. I shouldn't have let her sleep but she looked knackered. How was your day?'

'Not over, unfortunately,' said Lambert.

'I see, another fleeting visit?'

'I'll be upstairs,' said Lambert, trying to ignore the nagging guilt he felt at having met with Sarah earlier, and his response to seeing her again.

In his office he logged onto the System and went through his old files on the Manor. He flipped through pictures of Waverley Manor, the torture dungeon he'd uncovered. Horrified by the images he'd seen hundreds of times before, he forced himself to scroll through them again, one by one. He recalled the night he'd found the underground prison, the charged atmosphere and looming sense of dread; the discoveries beneath the ground beyond the limit of his own nightmares.

He dragged his eyes away from the terrible images and clicked on a photo of Peter Saunders. The seventh arrest from the Manor group, Saunders was convicted on multiple counts of murder and manslaughter as well as numerous sexual offences. Lambert checked his anger, enraged such a man was now on the loose.

He checked the System for an update on the Saunders' escape but it was as if the incident hadn't occurred. Lambert checked through profiles of the Governor of Woolwich prison, Paul Guthrie, and the guards who would have been responsible for Saunders including John Prine, who'd vanished along with Saunders. He managed to access the prison's files but could find no mention of Saunders' transfer.

He considered calling Tillman but didn't want to alert his superior that he was investigating Saunders' disappearance when he'd been warned off. Instead, he returned his attention to Beckinsale's death. He searched through his social media presence, hoping to find a glimpse of anything linking the man to him, anything to explain why Lambert's name was found at the scene. He read Will Fisher's crime sheet once more, examining the events that put him in prison. The attack was savage though not premeditated. Murder was a different beast and Lambert doubted Fisher was the sort of person who could pull off such an act. Did he really have a strong enough motive? He knew Daniella was seeing Beckinsale, as well as the others, and was presumably reaping the benefits. So why the sudden change of heart? Daniella could be lying, and her relationship with Beckinsale could be more serious than she claimed. Finding Fisher was the priority, and he hoped Matilda's optimism about finding the suspect was justified.

He slammed the laptop shut and returned downstairs. Time had slipped away; it was past midnight. The house was deserted, Sophie and Jane having gone to bed. He poured a small glass of red wine. The alcohol tasted coppery and he emptied the contents down the sink. Collapsing on the sofa, he tried to empty his mind of the myriad thoughts troubling him. The events of the Manor had never fully left him, never would, and he felt a familiar obsessiveness returning.

His vision began to cloud, replaced by thousands of miniscule dots of fiery colour, a sign he was about to slip into unconsciousness. Lambert suffered from a self-diagnosed form of narcolepsy. The condition was episodic, usually triggered by times of high stress. Over a year ago, he'd had a CAT scan. He'd undertaken the procedure in secret and the scan failed to uncover anything physical to explain why he suffered such episodes. Since then, he'd learnt to live with the occasional blackouts. They were usually impossible to fight, and as it was too late to get upstairs he made himself comfortable on the sofa seconds before slipping into unconsciousness.

Chapter Seven

It was almost two hours before Sarah reached Luton, most of which she spent thinking about Michael Lambert. His appearance had come as a shock, personally and professionally. The last time they'd seen each other he'd decided to go back to his wife. It was Sarah who'd suggested he make the move. How could she not? Sophie had a new baby and the whole of Michael's life up to that point had been overshadowed by the terrible circumstances leading to the death of his daughter, Chloe, years before.

Sarah had tried to put Michael out of her mind during the last year, and to a certain extent succeeded. Her focus was her work and it had almost been enough, but seeing him now made everything come thundering back. They'd been through so much together. Before becoming lovers they'd worked on the infamous Souljacker case in Bristol, their shared experiences solidifying their relationship.

She felt blindsided by his turning up unannounced, and was annoyed with herself for her reaction. And the reason for him contacting her only made matters worse. Peter Saunders' escape would not remain secret for long but even she was surprised by how quickly the news had spread to Lambert. In a matter of hours, Partridge's hope that the case would remain secret had evaporated. Already she could add Tillman and Lambert to her list of people who knew about Saunders' escape, and in twenty-four hours the current list would be a tiny fraction of those in the know.

Furthermore, Lambert's involvement would lead to complications. Her warnings over AC-10 and MI5 would be ignored. Peter Saunders had been his case, and knowing what the Architect did, and what Lambert went through to convict him, she understood Michael would be watching her every move.

She was thankful Stuart Pierson had waited for her. The prison Governor met her at reception and walked her through to his office. He had the air of a man in charge, his walking stride quick and purposeful. Even at this late hour, he appeared fresh, his suit neat and pressed, his face stubble free. It was a change from the tired-looking colleagues she was used to working with.

'It's probably too late for coffee?' he said, with a hint of a northern accent. 'I could get you something stronger if you wish?'

'No thank you, Mr Pierson, I have to drive back to London.'

Pierson nodded though he looked disappointed. 'Don't let me stop you though,' said Sarah.

'It's fine,' said Pierson waving his hand. 'Terrible business,' he said, taking a seat behind his desk. 'I heard there were some fatalities.'

'It appears more people know about Peter Saunders' escape than we'd envisioned. Could you tell me which of your guards knew about Peter Saunders' planned arrival?'

Pierson opened the screen on his laptop and punched in some keys.

'As per your instructions we kept people in the know to a minimum. Only two of my guards and I knew about the identity of our new prisoner.'

'But the rest of your team knew someone was arriving?'

'Yes, they knew there was an arrival due to maximum security.' He pressed a button on his laptop activating an ancient dot matrix printer on a shelf behind him. 'Here,' he said, handing her a faded sheet with the names and addresses of the guards who knew of Saunders' arrival.

'This is an awkward question to ask, and I am sure it sounds impertinent, but would your guards share info with anyone else? Friends, spouses or even inmates?'

'These two are my best,' said Pierson. 'Very experienced, they know better than to talk. If you're looking for a scapegoat you won't find it here.'

Sarah went to answer but held her tongue a few seconds, allowing silence to descend. Pierson's defensiveness came out of nowhere and she wanted to process it before continuing. She waited until Pierson grew uncomfortable before speaking.

'We're all on the same side here, Mr Pierson, but you must appreciate my situation. Only a few people knew about Saunders' transfer and obviously one of them has talked.'

'Maybe so, but we were only given Peter Saunders' name last night. Here, I have the documentation,' he said, handing her a sheet of paper. 'We were told a category A prisoner would be arriving, but received this yesterday. It's dated and time-stamped 5.32 p.m. It's the first I or any of the guards knew that Peter Saunders was coming. As you can see, there is no mention of the route the guards would be taking, so I believe the chance of my guards speaking to outside sources and planning and arranging an elaborate escape in less than twenty-four hours are close to zero. Would you agree, DCI May?'

Sarah glared at the man. She noted the way he'd become visibly animated following his little speech. The propensity of those in senior positions to cover their backs had long ceased to amaze Sarah, but Pierson's rudeness jarred.

'May I keep this?' she said, holding the transfer papers and the names of Pierson's guards.

'My pleasure,' said Pierson, smiling as he got to his feet.

She could have told him the papers meant nothing to her, that she would continue investigating him and his guards whatever timestamps he provided, but she didn't want to give him the satisfaction of thinking he'd upset her.

'Thank you for your time,' she said, before returning to her car and the long journey back home.

–

She woke at six the next morning, sighing at the sight of her running gear, wanting to stay submerged beneath the covers. But not running for over a week left her feeling bloated and lethargic, so she struggled out of bed and got dressed.

Outside, rain pelted the pavement and wind billowed through the bare trees lining her suburban road. 'I must be mad,' she mouthed to herself, stepping out into the torrential weather. She did a short run around the block to warm up, getting her heartbeat to increase before stopping to stretch. As rain lashed at her face, she set the music on her earphones to one of her favourite playlists and set off running into the wind.

She usually loved this time of day, the desolate early morning where it was mainly her and the road, but the weather and her caseload had put paid to that. Her limbs were heavy, her clothes already soaked from the downpour. She thought about the condescending way Stuart Pierson had spoken to her last night and the fact it was twenty-four hours since Peter Saunders had escaped.

She upped the pace as she turned onto the main road, the wind now behind her, and noticed a tall slender man pretending not to check her out as she ran past him. A new track played on her iPhone, her legs responding to the faster tempo, her initial tiredness fading. It would all be damage limitation now. Whatever the Chief and Partridge said, if Saunders didn't want to be found it was unlikely he would be, and sooner or later they would have to explain the attempted cover-up.

One thing was for sure, she refused to be the scapegoat for their little games. She turned for home three miles later, her pace still strong. In spite of herself, her thoughts returned to Michael Lambert. His appearance last night had thrown her and she'd noted his reaction too: the dilation of his pupils, the rise and fall of his chest as they sat in the close confines of the car. She didn't want him to leave Sophie, and didn't believe in romantic fairy tales, but the meeting convinced her something was still unfinished between them.

Back at her house, she stripped off her sodden clothes and spent five minutes beneath the hot jets of the shower before returning downstairs to black coffee and a mixed berry smoothie. As she was leaving for work, DS Adams called. 'I'm surprised you're up,' he said, with his typical informality.

'What do want, Adams?' she said, dashing to her car as the rain began a second wave of attack on her work clothes.

'We found the escape vehicle – not too far from you, actually.'

'Send me the details,' said Sarah, hanging up. The postcode Adams sent was in north London, thirty minutes away at this time of morning, yet the discovery didn't fill her with optimism. She could only hope the car would reveal something about where Saunders planned to go next, but twenty-four hours was a long time in what was effectively a missing person's case. She entered the post-code onto the sat-nav system on her phone and, unable to help herself, checked for a message from Michael before setting off.

Chapter Eight

Lambert groaned as he woke, his neck stiff from the uncomfortable position he'd fallen asleep in. Although the blackouts were less frequent, and had no further effect on him once he woke, it was a sharp reminder that the condition was beyond his control. Only Sophie, Sarah and Tillman knew about it. He couldn't risk making it public knowledge as he feared his enemies within the force would use it as a means to oust him from his job.

Sophie and Jane were still asleep so he showered in the guest room and was changed and out of the house before they'd stirred, arriving in West Hampstead at 7.30 a.m.

Good news was waiting for him. Will Fisher had been arrested trying to board a ferry to Dover. Lambert was surprised the man had fled. It was a signifier of guilt and he looked forward to questioning Fisher later that day when the Kent force delivered him.

Thirty minutes after arriving he held the morning's debrief. With Beckinsale's ex-wife to be interviewed at nine a.m., and with Fisher en route, the work for the day was continued research into both the victim and the suspects. Lambert instructed Matilda to interview Daniella again. 'I want to know the extent of the little scam she and Fisher had going. Let's find out the names of her lovers, current and past. Who knows, if Fisher is responsible this might not be the first time he's killed someone.'

Matilda brought him over a coffee once the meeting was wrapped up. 'You need me for the ex-wife interview?' she asked. Her red hair hung loose today, and she wiped away a loose strand revealing the mottled texture of her skin.

'Yes, you should sit in. It's Fisher I'm most interested in. Let me know as soon as he arrives.'

Matilda hovered and Lambert stopped what he was doing and looked at her. 'What is it?' he asked, softly. He considered the young woman a friend as well as a colleague. This occasionally put him in a difficult position, a situation complicated by her relationship with Tillman.

'It's nothing,' she said.

Lambert held her gaze. 'OK, you know where I am,' he said, drinking his coffee and turning back to his laptop. The temperature in the office matched outdoors, the sole radiator in his office stone cold. 'Bickland, let's see if we can get some goddam heat in here,' he shouted into the main office.

Despite the positive start to the day, Lambert remained distracted by the Peter Saunders' escape. He kept glancing at his mobile, wanting to call Sarah but worried doing so would result in an official record of his interference in the case. Sarah was an exceptional officer, and if he could have delegated the investigation into Saunders' escape to anyone it would have been to her. Still, the thought of Saunders loose in the world filled him with a mixture of anger and despair which he struggled to get past.

'Nancy Beckinsale is here,' said Matilda, tearing him from his reverie.

Lambert blinked and looked up from his screen. 'She kept her married name?' he asked.

'Apparently so. We've put her in Room Four. Bickland is with her at the moment. I should warn you, she's broken down a couple of times already.'

Lambert sighed. 'Better get it over with, then.'

Nancy Beckinsale stood as Lambert entered Room Four. She was a tall, statuesque woman, not much smaller than Lambert. The thin coating of make-up on her face was smudged, a black ring of mascara around both her eyes. Her handshake was firm and she introduced herself with confidence. 'Nancy Beckinsale. Please excuse the state of me.'

'Not at all. Please take a seat. Are you OK for something to drink?' said Lambert.

Nancy gripped the mug of coffee in front of her and smiled.

'I appreciate you coming to see us. I realize this is one hell of a shock.'

Nancy went to answer but her words were lost in her throat. She took a sip of the coffee and composed himself. 'I can't believe he's gone,' she said, eventually.

Lambert studied the grief on the woman's face, searching for a suggestion of fakery. 'If you don't mind me asking, Nancy... May I call you Nancy?'

She nodded.

'How long have you been separated from Alistair?'

'About two years now.'

'You still keep your married name?' He kept his tone light, fearing either a rebuke or a fresh bout of tears.

'For work reasons. We were married for twenty-three years. It would cause confusion if I reverted to my maiden name.'

'I see,' said Lambert. 'Were you still in contact?'

'Yes, I saw Alistair every week.'

'Every week?'

'Yes, we would meet for lunch at least once a week. Our split was amicable, we parted on good terms.'

'Again, I don't want to get too personal, but it may help us to know why you decided to get a divorce.'

Nancy sniffed. Producing a handkerchief from an expensive-looking handbag, she blew her noise with considerable force. 'Excuse me. Our daughter left for university four years ago. She now works in Edinburgh. Her absence shifted something in our relationship. We decided to have a trial separation. I'd thought... hoped, it was some form of midlife crisis on Alistair's part, but soon the trial separation was a permanent thing.'

Lambert leant forward. He was keen to keep Nancy onside, and didn't wish to cause her any more grief at this stage, but there was one question he had to ask her. 'Did you know about Daniella Bolton?'

The mention of Daniella's name provoked a strong response. Nancy appeared to straighten up in her seat as if every muscle in her body tensed at the same time. 'I knew of her,' she said. 'I knew it was a midlife crisis when I found out about her. He didn't like to talk about her much but I could tell she was a money grabber. You only need to look at the age difference.'

Lambert nodded supportively. 'Did Alistair ever suggest he was scared of Daniella?'

'Of course not. She was little more than a girl. Why? You don't think she did this, do you?'

'We're simply trying to get a clearer picture at this stage.'

'You think he was murdered though, don't you?' Nancy scowled at him, and he saw beneath her grief she was strong and determined. It would have taken considerable strength to deal with the separation without such fortitude.

'Our investigations are still ongoing at this point, though we are treating his death as suspicious.'

Nancy's demeanour changed once more, the features of her face contorting in suppressed rage. 'I knew she was no good.'

'Can you think of anyone who would want to hurt Alistair? Anyone who held a grudge? Someone connected to you, perhaps?'

'To me?' said Nancy, full of scorn.

'I'm sorry to pry, but I have to ask, is there anyone else in your life?'

'There's been no one since Alistair,' said Nancy, her face softening once more. 'I honestly thought he would come back to me one day, once he'd got all this stupid stuff out of his system. I guess I'll never know now.'

Chapter Nine

Lambert was disappointed when he came face-to-face with Will Fisher. He'd studied his mug shot and pictures of the man he'd found on social media and wondered if the meeting would rekindle a memory. He was slighter than Lambert had anticipated – almost skeletal. His head was freshly shaven, a line of stubble growth pitted across his scalp. He looked malnourished, sick even, his fingers yellowed from heavy smoking. He drummed them nervously on the table, glancing occasionally at the duty solicitor for support as Lambert's eyes bored into him. Fisher had already made an impression, spitting in the face of the duty sergeant when being processed. 'Tell me again, Mr Fisher, where were you on the morning of Alistair Beckinsale's death?'

'I told you I was at home.'

'At home watching television?' said Lambert, looking at his notes.

'That's right,' said Fisher, glancing again at his solicitor, who kept her eyes focused on the officers in the room.

'But you can't remember what you were watching?'

'It was on for background noise, I was tired.'

'Tired from what? You don't appear to have worked since you left prison.'

'There's no law against it,' said Fisher. He was smiling, but Lambert saw the hardness in his eyes.

'So tell me again about the little scam you have going with your girlfriend.'

'It is not a scam I've told you.'

'No, that's right, it's not a scam it's a service. I believe that's what you called it.'

'Of sorts,' said Fisher, his words slow and laced with aggression.

'Did Mr Beckinsale realize he was receiving a service?'

'How do you mean?'

'Did he know he was one of many? Did he know Daniella was only seeing him because of the money he lavished on her?'

'It's not like that.'

'I think it's exactly like that,' continued Lambert. Fisher cowered back in his seat as Lambert placed his arms on the desk separating them. 'You've got quite the temper, haven't you, Mr Fisher? Caused quite a scene downstairs with our duty sergeant.'

'He provoked me.'

'Provoked you by asking your name?'

Fisher shrugged, remained glued to the back of his chair.

'Let's see if you provoked him enough for him to press charges against you.'

'I didn't do anything,' said Fisher.

'You spat in a man's face, but that's neither here nor there. You've obviously got a temper. That's why you went to prison. Is that what happened with Mr Beckinsale? Did it get too much for you? Seeing Daniella with all these men? When I talked to her she sounded quite devastated by Mr Beckinsale's death, as if she'd sweetened to him. Was that the case, Will? Was she going to leave you for him?'

Fisher crossed his legs and turned to the side. 'Don't talk rubbish,' he murmured.

'Don't talk rubbish,' repeated Lambert. 'You make a fine point there – why would she leave you? You with your temper and your unemployment. Why would she leave you for a sweet, caring, wealthy man?'

The last question provoked the response Lambert was waiting for. Fisher leant forward, placing both hands on the desk. 'She wasn't going to leave me, she fucking hated him. She hates all of them.'

'Yet you still let her go to them, don't you? All those men. How can you live with yourself?'

Fisher's face reddened, a thick blue line standing out on the left side of his neck. 'We needed the money,' he said, through gritted teeth.

'What? Planning a getaway, were you? A holiday in the South of France, perhaps?'

The question disarmed Fisher, whose look of anger was replaced by confusion. 'What you on about?'

'That would explain why you were in Dover, wouldn't it, Will? Trying to catch a ferry to mainland Europe?'

'Oh, I see, very funny.'

'Makes sense to me, go round to Alistair Beckinsale's house wanting to confront him, full of jealousy and rage, find him in the bath and take your opportunity.'

'I don't know what the hell you're talking about,' said Fisher.

'Then why the hell did you leave? Why the hell did you try to flee the country?'

'Oh, come off it, look at my record. It was obvious you were going to pin this on me. As soon as Daniella told me I knew I had to get out of here. And I've been proven right, haven't I? You're going to try and fit me up for this.'

Lambert pretended to be wounded by the remark. 'No one is going to fit you up. But look at it from our point of view. You're a GBH convict, you're effectively a pimp for your girlfriend, and one of her clients ends up dead.'

'It wasn't me,' said Fisher.

'I'm afraid that's not good enough.' Lambert sat back, pretended to play with his notes. Neither Fisher or his solicitor knew about the card found at the crime scene and Lambert was loath to tell them. At this point it could provide a way for the solicitor to get her client out of custody. If Fisher had left the card there, he wanted to hear it directly from the man. 'You know who I am, don't you, Mr Fisher?'

The same look of confusion swept over the suspect's face, his eyes wide and mouth agape. 'You're the detective on this case,' said Fisher.

'But you know who I am, specifically?'

'Can I ask what this is about, DCI Lambert?' said the solicitor, speaking for the first time since the interview started.

'I'm suggesting your client already knows who I am.'

'Well we all know who you are,' said the solicitor.

'Do you have any prior knowledge of me, Mr Fisher?' said Lambert, ignoring the solicitor's comments.

'What the hell do you mean?' said Fisher.

'I mean, have you seen me before?'

'No, of course not,' said Fisher shaking his head. 'What the hell is going on?'

Lambert suspended the interview and returned to the incident room with Matilda. 'If he knows me he is doing an incredible job of hiding it,' he said to Matilda.

'Maybe someone gave him the note to plant at the scene to mess with your head?'

'No, doesn't make sense,' said Lambert. 'If Fisher killed Beckinsale then it was more than likely an act of passion. He would have gone to the flat to give him a beating and things would have got out of hand. I'd be surprised if even he was stupid enough to go there with murder on his mind. It seems inconceivable he would have an accomplice. Prison has taken a toll on him – you see the way he cowers?'

'You don't think it was him?'

'Not unless I can explain why he would write my name on a card and leave it at the scene. Get on to forensics again, see if we can find a match for Fisher's prints or DNA. And have another chat with Nancy Beckinsale,' said Lambert, recalling an old case he'd worked on.

'Nancy? Why?'

'Let's find out where she was at the time of the ex-husband's death, see if she had any keys for his house. They met once a week so it's a possibility. It wouldn't explain my name being on a note, but we're grasping at straws as it is.'

Lambert watched the CCTV images from the morning of Beckinsale's death. The shadowy figure could be Will Fisher. The body types matched, and the figure moved with an awkwardness reminiscent of the man they had in custody.

Lambert recalled the electrocution case he'd worked on as a probationary officer during his first year. A man called Dominic Webster was found electrocuted in his bath, a hairdryer having fallen into the water. Lambert had attended the scene with his training officer. Initially, Webster's death hadn't been treated as suspicious. His body was found by his wife and daughter, who had appeared bereft.

However, Lambert hadn't been satisfied with the wife's testimony. A quick search revealed she had accused her husband of assault on more than one occasion. It was a pitiful story of neglect by social services. Eventually Mrs Webster confessed. Her husband's attentions had recently wandered to his daughter and, fearing for the girl, and with no support, she took things into her own hands.

Lambert retreated to his office and pulled up the System, searching for news on Sarah and the Peter Saunders' escape but there were no entries. He was still distracted by seeing Sarah. He couldn't get her out of his head, the joy of seeing her again counterbalanced by guilt. He drummed his fingers on the desk before summoning in DS Bickland. 'Inform Fisher's solicitor we will be keeping him in for another twenty-four hours.'

'And charge him for the assault on the duty sergeant,' Lambert added.

Chapter Ten

DS Adams was already at the scene. Saunders' escape vehicle was abandoned in a residential area in Crouch End, north London. The authorities were notified after the car received a ticket for being parked without a resident's permit.

'No cameras on the street,' said Adams, as Sarah walked over. 'We're going door to door as we speak. So far, no one remembers the car arriving.'

'Anyone else been here?' said Sarah.

Adams stepped towards her, closer than was comfortable. It was something she'd noticed him doing more and more. He had an issue with personal space which needed to be addressed. She only hoped he wasn't doing it intentionally. 'Such as who?' he asked.

Sarah took a step back. 'Any other teams?'

'Oh, you mean MI5. I thought you would know that. They were here before us. In fact they were wrapping things up when we arrived. One of them left his card should we need to liaise.'

Sarah glanced at the card in Adams' hand: Charles Partridge, MI5.

'You want it?' said Adams.

'No, you keep it.'

If there was anything significant to glean from the scene, MI5 would have already taken it. She considered calling the Chief Constable. She didn't understand why she'd been assigned the case if MI5 were going to undermine her like this.

'Run a search on missing cars from the immediate area,' she said to Adams. 'If Saunders dumped his car here, he may have stolen a replacement.' She doubted her own words, imagining Saunders had a car waiting for him, but wanted space from the junior officer.

She walked the length of the street. Was the location of significance? That there was no CCTV was disappointing but unsurprising. When Adams called back she assigned him a further job of coordinating research into the local CCTV cameras. Saunders would have driven past a camera at some point to reach Crouch End. The NCA had a specialized team focused on CCTV, but Adams still looked deflated at the order. He loitered on the spot. 'Get going, then,' said Sarah.

She checked with the other members of her team before returning to her car. Until she was told otherwise, she was still the most senior acting investigator on the case. If Partridge wanted to edge her out he would have to be more forceful.

She didn't have an appointment but decided it would be prudent to visit Paul Guthrie. Although the Woolwich prison Governor had been present at the meeting yesterday, she'd yet to question him. He'd explained to the assembled group the security procedure the prison had in place prior to Saunders' departure, and spoke in defence of the guard John Prine, who was now a suspect. She called ahead, and confirmed an appointment in two hours' time.

She lunched alone, her thoughts alternating between the case and Lambert. She'd moved to London after working with Lambert on the Souljacker serial killer case in Bristol. She'd been recruited into the NCA, receiving a promotion to Detective Chief Inspector. Since then, her career had stalled. In Bristol, even as a Detective Inspector, her role felt more significant. She'd been the senior investigating officer on most of her cases, and although she was the SIO on the Saunders' case her responsibility was curtailed significantly by MI5 and Partridge. It was a familiar feeling. She'd been given cases to work since joining the NCA but there was always the sense she was on trial, that someone was waiting in the wings to take over.

She knew Michael shared her concerns. After the successful Waverley Manor case, he'd made a number of significant arrests only for his investigation into the Manor to be taken away from him. Although they'd had no contact in that time, she knew it still rankled with him. Ever since she'd met him, he'd always appeared to be on the brink of leaving the police force and she wondered how much longer he would stay.

She read her case notes as she ate her lunch, squirming at the details of Peter Saunders' role at Waverley Manor. The atrocities were well known to her, but reading about the sheer scale of the abuse, and the number of bodies found beneath the grounds, still made her shiver. Whether or not Saunders was responsible for the design of the place, what was beyond doubt was that the man's DNA had been found in every corner of the site.

Lambert's notes were in the file. It must have been a major blow to see the man escape from prison.

Reading further into Lambert's notes, she was reminded of Barnes' final warning. That Waverley Manor was only the beginning; that similar sites existed throughout the UK.

The thought was too much to take in at the moment. She turned her attention to her notes on John Prine, the escaped guard. Prine had worked at Woolwich under Guthrie's supervision for over ten years. Married, with three grown-up children, he had an impeccable record. So what had made him help Saunders?

In such cases the answer usually boiled down to two possibilities: money and coercion. Checks had already been run on Prine's bank accounts and showed nothing out of the ordinary. His family were safe, but that didn't rule out the possibility Prine had been blackmailed regarding their safety. A third possibility was that Prine was a member of the Manor, and helped Saunders due to group loyalty. Partridge had arranged for Prine's house to be searched and had questioned his family. Sarah read through the transcripts. The family had endured the worst type of questioning at the worst possible time. While fearing her husband was dead, Mrs Prine had been questioned over her husband's sexuality and potential links to the Manor. It was a tough but necessary line of questioning, one eliciting the same response in all three family members. One of incredulity and anger.

–

Paul Guthrie greeted her warmly at his office in Woolwich prison. Sarah was wary following her meeting with Stuart

Pierson in Luton. Guthrie's handshake was weak, his palm coated with sweat. 'Please take a seat. Can I get you a drink?' he asked, all smiles.

'I'm fine,' said Sarah. 'Thank you for seeing me on such short notice.'

'My pleasure. Anything I can do to help. Obviously we need to find Saunders and bring him back to face justice for what he did to James, and your officer of course, but we also have the additional worry of our guard John Prine. John is a valued member of our team. I realize in these circumstances you need to treat him with suspicion but we are looking forward to him returning to our team.'

Guthrie appeared to be out of his depth, talking before being questioned. It wasn't just that he lacked the alpha male persona of Stuart Pierson – she'd worked with many effective senior personnel who she would describe as introverted – it was more that he was trying to present himself as something he wasn't. He'd mentioned Prine before she'd asked the question, trying to be assertive but coming across as needy.

'Tell me about James Donnelly and John Prine. How long had they been supervising Peter Saunders?'

'Saunders was on our secure unit. John is a senior guard and leads the unit, James was his subordinate.'

'Of the two, who would have had most interaction with Saunders?'

'Donnelly, though he would have been well known to John Prine.'

Guthrie was still smiling, trying to appear calm. 'Why were they chosen to transfer Saunders?'

'We always use our senior officers for such transfers. John has done the same thing hundreds of times and, as I said, Donnelly was one of his main guards.'

Sarah pictured the van driving through central London. 'Your officers aren't armed, are they?'

'No,' said Guthrie. 'They receive significant training for combating armed violence. And, of course, there was the armed officer present.'

Sarah closed her eyes, thinking about her deceased colleague DS Wright. 'I have to ask, Mr Guthrie. Why do you think our officer and James Donnelly were shot and John Prine survived?'

For the first time since she'd arrived, Guthrie became defensive, but it was minor in comparison to his counterpart in Luton. 'I really wouldn't know, DCI. I imagine that is your area of specialization. If I was to hazard a guess, I would think the officer was eliminated because he was carrying a firearm. As to why John survived and James didn't, I have no idea. I only hope John is still alive now.'

It was a fair assessment, and again Sarah came back to thoughts of coercion and finance. 'Would you be able to show me the procedure you have in place for transferring prisoners?' she asked, waiting for the same rebuke she'd received from Pierson.

Guthrie softened. 'I'll get one of our guards to show you. It was a pleasure meeting you again.' They shook hands, Guthrie's palm damper than before, and the Governor led her to the waiting area.

Ten minutes later, a guard by the name Hudson showed her around the complex. Hudson's gut hung over his dark trousers and his breathing was laboured. He showed her to the maximum-security ward where Saunders had been held. 'We've got another one of that lot here,' he said. 'Used to be one of your lot.'

He was talking about Jonathan Barnes but she ignored his cheap insult. 'How did you find John Prine?' she asked.

'A good officer, well respected,' said Hudson, as if reading from a script.

'What about Saunders? You ever interact with him?'

'Here,' said Hudson, opening an empty cell. 'This is where Saunders resided. To answer your question, our interaction with the prisoners here is minimal. We drop their food off. Check they're still alive.'

Sarah stepped into the cell. It contained a single bed, and a desk attached to the stone wall. There were no photos, no belongings she could see.

She asked Hudson about this and he shrugged his shoulders. 'Saunders had to earn the right to belongings. He had some books but we've cleared his room now.'

'He ever say anything to you?'

'Not really. He was polite, and because of that I was polite back. He knew who was in charge and respected it so we tolerated him. It's easier if you treat them as humans, less grief.'

They walked the route Saunders would have taken to a holding area where he would have embarked the transfer vehicle.

'The officer would have met him here?'

'Yes, we would have run final checks on the vehicle before he left. Only then would the driver be handed the official route.'

Sarah thanked the prison guard, still no wiser as to how the ambush team knew the route Saunders was taking.

Chapter Eleven

The forensics' reports came in early the next day. Lambert was in his office searching through the System for the non-event which was Peter Saunders' escape. Matilda had met with Nancy Beckinsale late yesterday afternoon and persuaded her to provide her fingerprints to eliminate her from the crime scene. The forensic report showed no trace of Nancy Beckinsale or Will Fisher being found at the scene of Alistair Beckinsale's death.

Lambert stared hard at the report, searching for a reason to charge Will Fisher for Beckinsale's death. He had motive, coupled with the fact he'd tried to flee the country. It was sufficient grounds for a charge. Lambert still had five hours to decide and wasn't in any rush to do Fisher any favours.

Tillman chose that moment to make an appearance. Without knocking, he entered the office and sat down.

'Ah, the SIO,' said Lambert, not hiding his sarcasm.

Tillman was out of breath, the shirt covering his huge bulk damp with sweat. 'Do we have enough to charge Fisher?' he said, ignoring Lambert's taunt.

'We have the foundation of a case. He clearly had motive, and the fact that we picked him up in Dover will help our case but the forensic reports came in and there are no signs of him at Beckinsale's house, and of course there's the anomaly of the note left at the scene. There's no explanation for that, and a half-decent defence lawyer would use it to their advantage.'

'You're sure you've never met Fisher before?'

'I would have remembered,' said Lambert, picturing the skeletal frame and nicotine-smeared hands of the suspect.

'What about the girlfriend?'

'We have her prints at the scene but she has an alibi. She was at work, she's a nurse at the Royal Free, from six a.m. that morning.'

'So we're at a bit of standstill,' said Tillman, with more than a hint of accusation.

Lambert was used to such a pause in a case. There was rarely a quick fix, and this case had more anomalies than normal. Despite everything, they couldn't yet prove it was anything more than a suicide. Only the open door and grainy CCTV image suggested otherwise. Lambert said as much to Tillman, who shook his head.

'You really think that?' said his superior. 'The front door was open, and if you're going to commit suicide, why do it in such a manner?'

Lambert had dealt with numerous suicides in his years as an officer. He'd investigated people taking their own lives in countless elaborate ways which didn't make sense.

'Maybe he was trying to get my attention, left a note so I could look into what happened to him.'

Tillman shook his head. 'No way, this was an attack.'

'OK, but I don't feel we're ready to charge Fisher at this point. We'll have to release him and assign some officers to watch him.'

'And in the meantime?' said Tillman.

'We'll keep up our research on Beckinsale and see if there is something in his past we're yet to uncover.'

Tillman was about to stand when Lambert stopped him. 'What's the latest on the Peter Saunders' escape?'

Tillman sighed. 'That's none of your concern.'

'Cut the bullshit, Glenn. I should have been involved from the beginning.'

'Well you're not involved now, and let me give you a massive piece of advice. Steer clear. I can see this going belly-up, it's been handled poorly.'

'Who's in charge?' said Lambert.

Tillman shook his head, smirking. 'Fuck off, Michael You know very well DCI Sarah is in charge. You must think I'm stupid – I know you've been in contact with her.'

'I spoke to her once,' said Lambert, unsurprised Tillman knew. 'But I've had no update since. What's happening?'

'They found the getaway car, no prints other than Saunders' and the missing guard, John Prine. It was dropped in a dark zone, no CCTV images, no idea what vehicle they took next or where they went.'

'He could be anywhere,' said Lambert, wondering if Sarah had any more relevant information for him.

'Exactly. As I said, steer clear. They're not going to find him, and if you get yourself involved you're going to take the fair share of the blame.'

Lambert linked his fingers together and rested his chin on them. 'I'm going to have to release Fisher at four p.m.'

'Fine,' said Tillman, getting to his feet, 'Make sure we have someone on him. And for Christ's sake, take away his bloody passport.'

Lambert waited until Tillman left the outer office before taking a burner phone from his trouser pocket and calling Sarah.

–

Sarah was already there, waiting for him. Lambert was overcome by déjà vu as he entered the coffee shop by Leicester Square underground station. He checked with Sarah before ordering a black Americano.

Sarah offered him a warm smile, her upper lip curling in its familiar way – a gesture still unreadable to Lambert. Despite everything, a sense of temporary peace came over Lambert as he sat down opposite her.

'This reminds me of the old times, these clandestine meetings,' said Sarah.

'We can't get you in trouble now, can we?' said Lambert.

'You know I can't give you anything significant,' said Sarah, eyes peering out at him over the top of her coffee cup.

Lambert updated her on the Beckinsale case, mentioning the key players: Will Fisher, Daniella Bolton and Beckinsale's ex-wife.

'You've never met this Fisher before?'

Lambert shook his head. 'Obviously it got me to thinking that maybe it's linked somehow to Saunders' disappearance.'

'Come on, you don't think Saunders has anything to do with this? From what I can ascertain, he escaped around the same time Beckinsale was murdered.'

'I don't think he did it directly but it's interesting his escape coincided with my name being left at the crime scene.' Lambert paused, sipped his coffee. 'I hear you've found the getaway car.'

Sarah laughed. 'Now why am I not surprised to hear that?' She lowered her tone. 'In all seriousness, Michael, MI5 are all over this now. You understand the limitations this puts on what we can discuss. We shouldn't even be meeting here. If they think you're interfering they won't hesitate to take you in.'

'I'll take my chances. They're the ones who lost Saunders in the first place.'

'I don't think it works like that. Technically that will be put at my door.'

'So where are you on finding him?'

Sarah flashed her lopsided grin again. 'You don't give in, do you?'

She told him about meeting Stuart Pierson in Luton and her more cordial meeting with Paul Guthrie in Woolwich.

'For a covert operation, it appears a lot of people know about it,' said Lambert.

'That's my concern. There's nothing secret here any more, and you know how these cases work. It's been over twenty-four hours now. Saunders could literally be anywhere in the world at this point.'

'What's your next step?'

Sarah hesitated. Lambert thought she wanted to unburden herself. He was sure she trusted him but understood why she had to keep some things to herself. 'If I get my way I'll speak to the other incarcerated members of the Manor. We have them on increased security.'

'If you get your way?'

'I'm waiting for the call. I'm sure it's only a matter of time before this is taken away from me.'

—

Lambert waited fifteen minutes after Sarah left to join the throng of seasonal revelry outside Leicester Square. Snow fell from the sky as he rushed across the road to the Tube station, the ice droplets exploding into nothing as they hit the concrete pavement. At various stages of his career, Lambert had battled with the bureaucracy blighting his profession. From what Sarah told him he suspected the possibility of a cover-up meaning all the work he'd put into arresting Saunders would amount to nothing.

His mood hadn't improved by the time he returned home that evening. Sophie was already asleep. The familiar sense of being under the same roof, but somehow separate, crept over him. Chloe's death had led to his split from Sophie last time, but their busy lifestyles contributed to the decline in their relationship. It was a cliché of his job that it was close to impossible to have a proper relationship, but couple that with Sophie's high-profile position and it became even harder to live a normal life. Already the case felt like it had priority. He'd barely seen either Sophie or Jane since the morning he'd dropped his little girl to the childminder's. Was this a life he could sustain without damaging his relationships once more?

Exhausted, he succumbed to the lure of alcohol, pouring a large dose of vodka from the freezer. The drink was a departure from his normal tastes. He'd learnt the freezer trick from Matilda and the coldness of the liquid followed by the blast of heat was a welcome relief. He took the drink upstairs to the spare room and sipped it while undressing. A centimetre remained in the glass when he collapsed into sleep.

He woke to the soft trill of his mobile phone, noticing five missed calls from DS Matilda Kennedy as he pressed answer.

'Sir, where are you?' said Matilda, breathless on the other end of the line.

'I was asleep.'

'Sir, you better get up. There's been another one.'

—

The snow was heavier than yesterday, had settled on the ground overnight. Lambert made quick progress to Catford in south-east London, driving down streets still familiar to him, streets he'd once walked on the beat during his probation. As he approached the flashing beacons and cordoned-off area he knew his growing sense of dread was well placed.

It was the same tree.

He glimpsed the body as he left his car. The broken and battered corpse took him back to the end of his probationary period and his first serious case as a fledgling detective. He pushed through the uniformed cops to Matilda who was shielding herself from the snowy down-pour. Frozen blood pooled around the twisted body, lying at an unnatural angle against the large oak tree at the side of the junction.

'Seventeen-year-old boy, Lance Jenkins. Parents are on their way,' said Matilda, handing him a plastic sheath with a piece of A6 card within. 'Your name was pinned to his jacket.'

'Cause of death?'

'The pathologist is with him now. First thought was a road traffic accident but with the position of the body it appears unlikely. As you can see, the tree is fifteen metres from the road. The boy could have been knocked off his bike and landed there but it appears the body has been arranged in a specific way. Furthermore, there appears to be a lack of blood at the scene as if he'd bled out elsewhere.'

Lambert moved towards the remains of the racing bike. The frame was bent out of recognition, both wheels crushed into abstract shapes.

'You OK, sir? You look a bit pale.'

Lambert's body vibrated from the continuous jets of adrenaline shooting into his system. 'This has happened before,' he said.

Chapter Twelve

It was no coincidence; the body was there for his benefit. That was why his name was pinned to the boy's jacket, on a piece of card identical to the one found at the Beckinsale house.

'Sir, I don't understand.'

'One of my first cases as a rookie detective. Dead boy, seventeen, hit-and-run. His body was found by this tree,' said Lambert, staring at the mangled cycle like it was a mirage.

'Definitely this tree?'

'I wouldn't forget, Matilda. We thought it was a simple RTA but it turned out to be anything but.'

'Did you find out who was responsible?'

Lambert recalled the haunted eyes of the victim's parents. 'It was his aunt,' he said, as if doubting his words. The woman cried in front of me like it was her son she'd lost, but she'd run him down. It was almost wrapped up at one point. I'd become suspicious of a comment she'd made about the boy's mother and it had stuck with me. Turned out the aunt was unable to have children of her own and her jealousy turned her beyond sour. She later claimed she didn't mean to kill the boy. She got manslaughter. She's probably out by now.'

'Jesus,' said Matilda, processing what she was being told. 'What the hell does it all mean?'

The pathologist approached. Lambert was surprised to see it was Lyndsey Harrington. 'This isn't your patch, is it?' said Lambert.

'No, but your lovely Chief Superintendent decided I needed to get out of bed in this early winter morning. I appreciate you providing these bodies for me, Lambert, but could we do something about the timing?'

Lambert was in no mood for Harrington's borderline humour. 'What do we have?'

'What we don't have is a road traffic accident. At least not one occurring here. The body has lost a lot of blood, which is not present. He has been moved from his place of death. The cause of death would appear to be from a heavy impact, a blunt force instrument to the back of the head.'

'His arms and legs broken too?' said Lambert.

'Those injuries are post-mortem,' said Harrington. 'The poor lad has been laid out in a particular way. As you can see the angles of his bones are unnatural. The breaks appear deliberate, like the killer made them exactly so he could arrange the boy like this.'

'Thank you, Lyndsey,' said Lambert, walking over to the boy's body.

'Lance Jenkins,' said Matilda, crouching on her knees as they studied the corpse. 'Do you remember the name of the original victim?' She was trying to be tactful but failing.

'Thomas Powell. He was seventeen as well. See his left arm there,' said Lambert, pointing to Lance's arm which was bent backwards at the elbow, almost doubled up on itself. 'Powell's arm was exactly like that. It's one of the many things I haven't forgotten about the case.'

'I'll make an order for the files,' said Matilda, leaving Lambert alone with the victim.

Lambert wouldn't have been surprised if every bone in Lance's body and been arranged in a perverse copy of Thomas Powell's death. He'd come across copycat killers before but this was something new to him: a re-enactment of a murder, a hit-and-run some twenty-five years on.

Tension gripped Lambert as he pondered why someone would do this, go to so much trouble to replicate the killing. It was more than a simple question of getting his attention. It was narcissistic, especially considering the mutilated body of the teenager in front of him, but someone was targeting him.

As snow fell on the vacant eyes of Lance Jenkins, Lambert blamed himself for the tragic sight in front of him. Whoever did this to the boy wanted him to feel this way, to feel responsible for the deaths of Lance Jenkins and Alistair Beckinsale. Lambert had initially dismissed the similarity of Beckinsale's death to the electrocution case he'd worked on as a first-year beat copper, but now accepted it was more than mere coincidence.

He considered who would want to do this to him and regretted how easy it was to create a long list within seconds. Lambert had made enemies from the first day he'd started as a police officer. He'd put away hundreds of people, and upset countless more during his career. Although the actions of the killer were specific and vindictive, there were still countless possibilities. His immediate thought was the Manor, his most recent significant case. Until his investigation into Waverley Manor, no one had even heard of the group's existence. Lambert exposing their network was reason enough to invite retribution, and again he was forced to consider Saunders' escape was too coincidental.

But it was just one potential avenue to explore; experience warned him not to be blinkered to other possibilities.

He considered the most immediate facts. For one, whoever was responsible had detailed knowledge of these old cases. The files were accessible, and accounts of the two previous deaths were in the public record, but the detail of the two cases suggested an intimate knowledge of the original cases. He needed to check if any of the files had been accessed recently and, heaven forbid, if other case files had also been searched. It was unlikely this was the last they'd heard from this killer.

Secondly, this case ruled out Will Fisher as a suspect. He'd been released earlier that day but had been kept under surveillance.

A large hand clasped him on his shoulder. The weight, and overfamiliarity of the gesture, meant it could only belong to one person. 'Glenn,' said Lambert, turning to see a dressed-down version of his superior.

Tillman tightened his grip. He was wearing jeans and what appeared to be a bomber jacket. Both items were not usual Tillman attire. Tillman chose not to notice Lambert's scrutiny. 'Kennedy tells me you've been here before,' said Tillman. 'Shall we go somewhere warm?'

Lambert followed Tillman to his car, the interior fresh with the smell of fast food and Tillman's sweat. 'So we're here because of you?' said Tillman.

Lambert told him about Thomas Powell and the similarities with the boy currently slumped against the tree.

'You're sure this is the same location?'

'You can check but everything is the same. The age of the boy, the type of racing bike, and the way his body is arranged. There's more, Glenn. It didn't occur to me at the time, but Beckinsale's death could also be a recreation. Once when I was still on probation I attended a murder scene where there was an electrocution.' He told Tillman about the Webster case. 'I didn't see the parallel at the time, it's not the only electrocution case I've worked on, but now I don't think it was a coincidence.'

Tillman sighed. 'So in both old cases we have a victim killed by a family member. Does that mean anything to you?'

'I've considered that. That part could be coincidence, might not be. Until a couple of hours ago I didn't realize we were dealing with a serial killer.'

'Someone who intends to recreate every case you've ever worked on?' said Tillman.

Lambert shuddered at the thought. 'There's plenty that's been missed out, even between these two cases. The killer is being selective, either highlighting these cases because they mean something to them, or because they were the cases he has access to. I'll investigate if the past and present cases are linked somehow. I need to get some sort of handle on what is going on here.'

The windows of Tillman's car steamed over and he switched off the car's heating. 'You took the words out of my mouth, Lambert. Your journalist friend is going to have a field day with you. Hates you, doesn't she?'

One of many, thought Lambert. Mia had become an enemy during his investigation into a serial killer known as the Watcher. The wife of one of Mia's journalists, Eustace

Sackville, had been the first of the killer's victims. Mia had interfered in his investigations to the extent Lambert had almost arrested her. In Lambert's eyes, her sole mission from that day onwards was to discredit him, and now she had an ideal opportunity. 'Professional loathing, nothing more. Look, Glenn, I'm not ruling out the involvement of the Manor in this. It's still too much of a coincidence for me that Saunders escaped just as this began to happen. I need access to his case.'

Tillman sighed, the gesture exaggerated. 'Good luck with that,' he said. 'As far as I can ascertain, MI5 are effectively totally in control now. We're less than bit players.'

The words echoed what Sarah May had told him. 'We still have people working on it, Glenn.'

Tillman smiled. 'Yes, but you're not one of them.'

Lambert was used to his superior being obstinate. He wasn't beyond changing his mind but sometimes needed a little persuading. 'If the Manor has something to do with this then denying me access will only lead to more deaths like Lance here.'

At the best of times, Tillman struggled with his temper. Lambert saw the anger in his eyes now, the slight change of colour to his cheeks. 'Who exactly do you want to speak to, Lambert? It's not as if they have a head office.'

'Barnes,' said Lambert.

Tillman sucked in his breath. A former Detective Chief Inspector, Barnes had been arrested by Lambert and Tillman, the first major arrest in the Manor case. Barnes had subsequently been attacked in prison and accused Tillman and Lambert of being responsible. 'I don't think that's a good idea at the moment, do you?'

'Someone needs to speak to him, Glenn.'

Tillman laughed. 'Someone?' he repeated, understanding Lambert meant Sarah May.

'Let DCI May speak to him. She can question him over Saunders and slip Beckinsale and Jenkins into the conversation.'

'I'm making no promises,' said Tillman, opening the car door and signalling the end of the conversation.

The snow had stopped falling and coated the ground like a second skin. The SOCO's blurred into the background in their white suits as they finished their various jobs marking the crime scene. Lambert glanced about for Matilda and instead was drawn to the slight figure of another woman. 'Jesus,' he said, feet crunching through the snow as he walked over to the area cordoned off by police tape.

The journalist, Mia Helmer, was deep in conversation with one of the uniforms. She held a handful of hair in her right hand which she twirled whist smiling at the police officer who stood rigidly to attention as Lambert approached.

'Mia,' said Lambert.

'DCI Lambert. What have you got yourself into? A second victim. This one with your name pinned to them. Do you think the killer did this in case you misplaced his calling card?'

'No comment at this time, Mia. You know the normal channels,' said Lambert, as the uniformed officer took the opportunity to make himself busy.

'The normal channels are a bit congested at the moment, Michael, and I think we both know why.'

'Surprise me,' said Lambert, already tired by the conversation.

'A little incident over in Holloway. Shots fired, by all reports. Yet no official comment from the NCA. What can you tell me about that?'

Lambert was used to bluffing to the press and didn't reveal his surprise that Mia had stumbled upon news of Saunders' escape. 'I have no idea what you're talking about,' he said.

'But your friend does, doesn't she, Michael?'

'You've lost me, Mia. Now, if you don't mind.'

Lambert walked away, concerned by how much Mia claimed to know.

'Don't worry, Michael,' called Mia. 'I'll let Sarah know you were asking about her when we speak.'

Chapter Thirteen

Lambert called Bickland and Croft who were still in West Hampstead and told them to return to head office. He'd decided to disband the incident room in West Hampstead, and to run the Beckinsale case concurrently alongside the Lance Jenkins case from headquarters.

Lance's parents arrived as the sun came up. Lambert was thankful Harrington and the SOCOs had finished their work on the body and that Lance had been moved to the back of the ambulance to await transfer. The look of shock and disbelief on the faces of Mr and Mrs Jenkins was all too familiar. They were caught in a waking nightmare and Lambert struggled to offer them any meaningful words. He'd been in this position countless times before, and the only truth was that their lives would never be the same again.

Matilda held Mrs Jenkins upright as her legs failed her, while Lambert studied Mr Jenkins' studied detachment. He could almost see the man's thought patterns as he moved swiftly to and fro through the stages of grieving, only to return granite-like to denial. 'No,' he started muttering to himself, as his son's body was covered up again. 'No,' he continued, his voice strained and increasing in volume until Lambert instructed one of the uniforms to restrain him as gently as they could.

The parents would have to be questioned and, remembering the Thomas Powell case, it was too early to rule them out as potential suspects. Unfortunately, grief was not a guarantee of innocence.

He left Matilda in charge and drove into the NCA headquarters in central London. The place was already bustling with people and Lambert received a number of glances as he made a quick detour to the canteen to top up his caffeine intake. News spread fast in this place and everyone would know about the second victim. He ignored the questioning looks and took his coffee to the office on the fifth floor. The open-plan space where his team worked was deserted, everyone either in Catford or West Hampstead. Despite this, Lambert shut the door to his office, happy to be cocooned within its four walls.

He fired up his laptop and loaded the System. His first search was the Thomas Powell case but that, and the Dominic Webster case predating it, had not been entered onto the database. Many older cases were not digitized and he would have to order paper files. For the time being he searched for newspaper articles featuring Thomas Powell and found what he was looking for, a full article by the journalist, Eustace Sackville. The article credited Lambert for his investigation. A picture showed Powell, young and fresh-faced, smiling towards the camera, no concerns about his immediate future in his bright eyes. Lambert was sure there would be a picture of Lance Jenkins online by the end of the day. Lambert continued reading the article and confirmed the name he recalled.

Catherine Williamson was Thomas Powell's aunt on his mother's side. In typical journalistic style, her picture showed her at her worst. Bleary-eyed one Christmas, her arms draped over her sister as they stood smiling in front of the family Christmas tree. After Lambert found her car, deserted in a lock-up in Lewisham, she'd admitted killing Thomas. At first she'd claimed it was an accident but she broke down in the interview and admitted she'd wanted to hurt the boy. Lambert remembered the interview clearly. That a woman would kill her sister's child because of jealousy had dumbfounded the then naive Lambert. He'd experienced crimes of passion in his first two years on the force, and too many cold-blooded murders, but Powell's death was something different. It was not the premeditation, but the pointlessness of the motive which always stayed with him. It turned him into a hardened cynic overnight and in hindsight it probably benefited his investigative career.

Through the System he found an address for both Catherine Williams and Thomas Powell's parents. He entered them into his phone and sought a feasible reason why they might be linked to Lance Jenkins' murder.

The team gathered in the main office and Lambert held a debrief, assigning roles to each individual detective. He explained the cold cases which might have some bearing on the Beckinsale and Jenkins murders. 'Nothing suggests they are anything but copycat murders at this stage, but we'll look into the old cases and examine the connections. Chief Superintendent Tillman pointed out that the two cold cases were committed by family members so we should consider this angle with the present cases. Matilda, I want you to interrogate Mrs Beckinsale further as well as Daniella Bolton. Search deeper into Beckinsale's family history and see what you can unearth. Bickland and

Gemma, you need to speak to Mr and Mrs Jenkins today and then expand your scope to the rest of the family.'

He informed the team about his plans to talk to the family of Thomas Powell and wrapped the meeting up.

'What about the Dominic Webster case?' asked Matilda, breaking from the group.

'That reminds me. Could you get the files for that and the Powell case before interviewing Jenkins? Leave them on my desk,' said Lambert, pulling on his coat and heading out of the office.

-

An elderly lady wearing a discoloured housecoat answered the flat door. Lambert had traipsed eleven floors of staircase, the lift in the sixties-built block being under repair. The woman stared at him for the briefest of moments before she started shaking.

'Mrs Powell?' said Lambert, taking a step back lest he scare the woman.

'Detective Lambert, I can't believe it's you.'

Mrs Powell led him down a narrow hallway, the walls covered in a rich, flower patterned wallpaper, to an immaculate living area. Lambert gazed at the pictures of Thomas decorating the walls, forever aged seventeen. 'I can't believe you're here,' said Mrs Powell. 'Take a seat, I'll fetch some tea.'

Lambert complied, surprised to find a sleeping cat snuggled deep behind one of the dark cushions on the sofa. The cat looked up at him with a dismissive sneer before returning to sleep.

It was impossible not to feel guilty. The last time he'd seen Mrs Powell was at the Old Bailey on the day her sister was sentenced for manslaughter. Mrs Powell remained calm during the sentencing, stoic as her husband watched proceedings through tear-drenched eyes. She'd hugged Lambert that day and thanked him for his work. He hadn't known what to say at the time and wasn't sure what he would say if faced with the same situation now.

She returned with a tray of tea and placed it on the table in front of him. 'Mr Powell?' said Lambert.

'Ah, you didn't hear,' she said, pouring the tea. 'He never recovered, I'm afraid.'

Lambert frowned, regretting not doing his research. 'When?' he said, taking the offered cup of tea.

'Five years after Thomas. He did his best but he couldn't face life without him. I found him in the bath-room, empty bottle of pills and gin by his side. He didn't even drink,' she said, as if the very thought was ridiculous.

Lambert closed his eyes. 'I'm sorry,' he said, trying to comprehend what the woman's life would have been like. Widowed, bereaved of her son, and her sister in jail.

'Things like that happen all the time. I have a good life here. I'm a bit lonely but I get out. I can't complain, Detective Lambert. Now how can I help you? I don't imagine you're here under pleasant circumstances.'

'I'm afraid not,' said Lambert, drinking the milky tea.

He told her about Lance Jenkins while wondering if burdening her with such knowledge was fair to the woman.

A tear fell from her eye. She rubbed it away and smiled at him, embarrassed by the show of emotion. 'The exact same place?'

'I'm afraid so. Lance was seventeen. The way… the way his body was arranged, it was identical to Thomas.' Lambert bit his lip as he waited for Mrs Powell to respond.

'Those poor folks.'

'If you don't mind me asking, Mrs Powell?'

'Catherine?'

'Yes.'

'She's still about. Comes here once a year and begs forgiveness,' said Mrs Powell, with such venom that Lambert looked away.

'I have an address for her,' said Lambert, showing her the address on his phone.

'I believe that's where she lives. You think she did this?'

'I don't know. I need to speak to her but wanted to talk to you first.'

'Thank you, Detective Lambert. You were always such a polite young man. Tell me, do you have children?'

Lambert hesitated, unsure how to respond. 'I have two daughters. One passed away some time ago now,' said Lambert, surprised to hear himself unburdening.

Mrs Powell moved towards him, gripping his hands. 'I can see the sadness in your eyes. How old is your other daughter?'

'Eighteen months.'

'You treasure her, Detective Lambert. Never forget your other daughter, but make sure you treasure your little girl.'

–

Lambert walked down the stairs of the apartment block dazed by his meeting with Mrs Powell. She'd asked him if he thought her sister had anything to do with Lance

Jenkins' murder. Catherine Williamson was in her sixties and he couldn't believe she had the will or inclination to plan and carry out a re-enactment of a crime she'd committed twenty-five years earlier.

Matilda called as he made his way across the icy patch of concrete separating the building from the car park. 'Sorry, sir, you're not going to like this,' she said.

At first Lambert feared a third copycat killing but what Matilda told him was only slightly more palatable. 'Mia Helmer's been up to her old tricks again. The Lance Jenkins case is featured in the afternoon edition of her rag.'

'Can't say it comes as a surprise, Matilda. Did she mention Beckinsale?'

'Yes. Though most of the article was devoted to you.'

'Marvellous. Have you managed to speak to Mrs Beckinsale yet?'

'I'm at her place of work now.'

'OK, keep me updated.'

Lambert stopped at a newsagent's on his way to Catherine Williamson's house and picked up a copy of Helmer's paper, putting it in his car for later study. Mrs Powell's estranged sister lived only two miles away. He pictured her tragic yearly visits to her house, part of him pleased Williamson's prison sentence effectively continued long after her release.

Williamson lived in a ground-floor flat in a more modern set of council-built buildings than her sister. Her husband had divorced her following the death of her nephew but, like Nancy Beckinsale, she'd kept her ex-husband's name. Lambert hadn't called ahead. He wasn't sure what he hoped to achieve by meeting Williamson again after all this time. The chance of her being involved in Jenkins' murder was so remote. Was it simply ghoulish curiosity driving him on?

Outside the building, Lambert pressed the button for Williamson's flat. There was no response and, after trying again, Lambert pressed a number of the other buttons until he gained entry to the building. No central heating greeted him as he entered, only the smell of damp and a cold draught whistling through the hallways. He opened a fire door and moved along the corridor, a squabbling man and woman stopping their argument long enough for him to pass, until he reached Williamson's door. 'Mrs Williamson,' he called, banging the door. 'I'm from the police. This is important.'

Lambert placed his ear to the door, the sound of shuffling feet coming from within. A minute later the door opened and an elderly woman thrust her head through a thin opening. 'You got ID?' said the woman.

Williamson was the younger of the two sisters but looked twenty years older than Mrs Powell. Her pale white face was caked in poorly applied make-up and a limp cigarette drooped from her mouth.

Lambert showed her his warrant card and waited for her to recognize his name but her glance was cursory and she handed it straight back. 'May I come in?' he said.

'What's this about?' said Williamson, holding firm.

'It's about your sister.'

This resulted in a murmur of interest. 'I don't have a sister.'

'It's about her son, Catherine. Don't you not remember me, Catherine? I'm Detective Lambert.'

Williamson looked at him for the first time, her hands shaking as she sucked on her cigarette. 'You,' she said, a billow of smoke drifting towards Lambert.

'May I?' said Lambert, not waiting for an invitation as he barged past the woman.

The interior of Williamson's house was in stark contrast to her sister's. The floor was cluttered with various pieces of furniture piled high with old newspapers and takeaway cartons. The walls were bare save for a cheap pine-framed mirror, and a patch of damp spreading from the corner of the window to the light bulb in the centre of the ceiling. On the sideboard was a full glass of white wine, a thick smear of red lipstick on the rim of the glass.

Williamson followed his gaze. 'It's six p.m. somewhere,' she said, moving towards the glass and drinking.

'How did it all work out for you, Catherine?' said Lambert.

'Very funny. I do OK.'

'Was it worth it? Taking that young boy's life? Ruining your sister and brother-in-law's life?'

'I did my time,' said Williamson, lighting another cigarette. 'Now what the hell do you want?'

Lambert was glad Williamson was still doing time. Some things could never be forgiven, and if Williamson's penance was living the rest of her life lonely and drunk in this hovel of a place, it was the least she deserved. He'd already found out everything he needed to know but told her about Lance Jenkins anyway.

'I'm sorry to hear that,' she said, sounding genuine.

Out of procedure he asked her for her whereabouts during the periods of the two deaths, and wasn't surprised when she said she'd been at home.

'Have you seen anything suspicious in the last few days? Anyone speak to you about what happened to Thomas?'

She flinched at her nephew's name, dragging hard on her cigarette. Lambert could tell she was remorseful but was unable to muster any sympathy for her. 'Why do you go and see her?' he asked. 'Your sister?'

Williamson tried to fix him with a stare but couldn't keep her head still. Her whole body trembled and the wrinkles on her face formed into a snarl. 'Don't you understand, I have to go and see her? I have to beg her forgiveness every year. It's what she wants.'

–

Lambert was pleased to reach the fresh air outside. Williamson had spat the last words at him, as if somehow she was the victim here. Lambert sat in the car staring at Williamson's building and regretted his decision to see her. The sight of her and the recollection of the Powell case acted as a catalyst, and memories from the time flooded back to him. He'd been a different man. He'd joined the police for what he believed were the right reasons. His best friend had been brutally murdered at university and he'd signed up to make a difference. Had he achieved that? It sounded naive to him now; that young man full of passion and purpose. Yes, he'd put away more than his fair share of villains but replacements came along every single day. The world was not a better place than the day he'd joined the force, and it had been ridiculous to expect any different.

He grabbed the newspaper from the back seat and read Mia Helmer's hatchet piece. He almost admired the way she sprinkled the article with fear. She reported the deaths of Beckinsale and Jenkins, and questioned what a serial killer obsessed with the famous police detective Michael Lambert would do next. The piece mentioned in brief Lambert's work in capturing members of the Manor as well as two other notorious serial killers. The word famous was not one he liked to see connected with his name, and that was the exact reason Helmer put it in her article.

Though she did raise a salient question. What would the killer do next?

Chapter Fourteen

Eyes followed her as Sarah May made her morning run. This was nothing new in itself – she noticed the occasional admiring glance, especially the ones lingering too long – but this was something different. She found she was running faster than normal, as if being chased by an invisible foe. Such bouts of paranoia were not uncommon. She'd been attacked while running once and it made her extra vigilant. The streets were almost desolate this time of the morning and no threat was visible, yet the feeling remained.

She risked a glance as she rounded the corner into her road. There was no one and she continued the short distance home, increasing her pace until she was sprinting as she did at the end of every run. Hands behind her head, sucking in lungfuls of cold air, she refused to panic as she surveyed the quiet backstreet and took her house key from her jacket. Reminding herself she wasn't being anxious, only vigilant, she entered the warmth of her house, taking one last look before closing the door behind her.

Beneath her shower she made a mental list of the day's tasks. The extra paranoia stemmed from the pressures involved in the Saunders' case. Partridge and MI5 were doing their best to marginalize her involvement to the extent that her role was close to being defunct.

Partridge had assumed control and was delegating actions to her. That afternoon she had a meeting with Peter Saunders' wife while Partridge and his team were tracking a potential sighting of Saunders in Scotland. It was her first experience of working with the security service. Michael had worked in a joint task force with them in the past and warned her they were insular, but she hadn't been prepared for the disdain they showed her. Partridge saw her as a necessary impediment to his job and would have her taken off the team in a heartbeat had he not agreed to work with the NCA on the prison escape.

She put both her phones into her jacket as she changed and considered calling Lambert. Only when she saw him leaning on her car outside did she acknowledge her subconscious telling her there were other reasons for wanting to see him.

'This is a pleasant surprise,' she said, wondering if he'd been the reason she'd felt eyes on her during the run.

'Sorry, I should have called but thought I'd pop by on the off-chance.'

'You looked tired.'

'Tell me about it. I've just left a crime scene. It's happened again, Sarah.'

He told her about Lance Jenkins and his theory that someone was recreating the cases of his early career.

'Let's get in the car,' said Sarah, appreciating how cold it was now she wasn't running.

'Your suspect from the Beckinsale case was released prior to this incident?' asked Sarah once they were inside.

'Fisher? He's not responsible. Whoever did this was highly organized and professional. Jenkins wasn't killed at the scene. He was dumped there along with his bike.

His body was arranged to look identical to the murder of Thomas Powell, a case I worked early on in CID. This is not the work of one person. Anyway, we had eyes on Fisher at the time.'

Sarah pre-empted what he was about to say. 'You think this is the work of the Manor?'

'How can I rule it out? What do we know about the Manor? We know they use outsiders to do much of their dirty work. I think maybe this is what happened this time. Have you read the papers recently?'

Sarah had read the report by Mia Helmer the previous day. 'Not the best reading.'

'I think they're trying to discredit me somehow. They love to fuck with people, so why not me? I was partly responsible for bringing some of them to justice.'

He was being modest about his role in arresting the members of the Manor but she understood his thinking. 'Can you think of anyone else who would want this to happen to you?'

Lambert smiled. 'I have plenty of enemies but this would appear the most logical explanation. And it could be a distraction.'

'From the Saunders' escape?'

'Yes.'

'That part of the plan may have backfired,' said Sarah. She explained about Partridge and how her role was being diminished. 'I'm not sure if Partridge and MI5 even know about your cases.'

'They'll know. I'm only surprised they haven't spoken to you about them yet. You won't be seeing Partridge today if he's in Scotland?'

'I guess not.'

'Mind if I tag along to your meeting with Mrs Saunders?'

After all this time together, she couldn't tell if he was joking. 'Sure, that would go down well. She would recognize you from the trial.'

'So? If they're responsible for Beckinsale and Jenkins, this might put the wind up them that we are onto them.'

'And if they're not?'

'No harm fucking with them at any rate.'

She would have welcomed the company but declined. 'You know you can't, Michael. The orders are that you're not involved at any point. If they find out you were snooping around in Holloway Road and that I took you along to see Mrs Saunders then my career would be on the line.'

'Worth a try,' said Lambert.

She wanted to tell him to get some rest but knew he wouldn't. He would need to solve the riddle of Beckinsale and Jenkins before he even considered resting, and she imagined finding Saunders would now also become an obsession.

'There is one more thing,' said Lambert.

'Why do I not like the sound of that?'

'I spoke to Tillman last night. I suggested I should interview Jonathan Barnes.'

'I hope he told you that was ludicrous?'

'In so many words. But I think he may know something. Have you spoken to him yet?'

'No, do you think I should?'

'Tillman has arranged a meeting for you this morning,' said Lambert, looking apologetic.

'How convenient. How long have I got?'

'Ninety minutes.'

–

Although slightly put out that Michael and Tillman had arranged the appointment without consulting her, Sarah accepted their motives were good. The fallout from Jonathan Barnes' imprisonment across the NCA and the Metropolitan Police had been devastating. Trusting your fellow officers was a cornerstone of being in the police. You didn't always like who you worked with, but you should be able to trust them, so to find out that one of your colleagues, a senior detective, could be responsible for such atrocious crimes was hard for many of her colleagues to accept.

Woolwich was the fourth prison Jonathan Barnes had been incarcerated in since his conviction. Sarah scanned his file as she waited in the holding area, noting Barnes had initially been in Luton under the supervision of Stuart Pierson.

'DCI May, we meet again.' A firm, jovial voice greeted her and she stood to shake the hand of Governor Paul Guthrie.

'Mr Guthrie,' she said, again noting his limp handshake.

'You should have said yesterday that you wanted to speak to Barnes.'

'If only I'd known. Is he ready?'

'Yes, we have arranged a room for you. He's not the most talkative of fellows. Here.' Guthrie handed her a list of privileges he was prepared to offer Barnes should he prove to be cooperative.

'Thank you, sir,' said Sarah, who hadn't been told any such privileges were to be discussed.

'It's my pleasure to help, though I'd rather limit what we offer someone like Barnes. Please let me know if I can help any further.'

Once again, Sarah was struck at the differing attitudes of Guthrie and Pierson. Whereas Pierson was unhelpful to the point of being obstructive, Guthrie couldn't do enough for her. She wasn't sure who she trusted less.

The same guard, Hudson, guided her to the interview room. His stomach appeared to droop even further over his waistband today as he opened the reinforced door where Barnes was waiting. 'Be warned, he's not very pretty,' whispered the guard, with a smile failing to reach his eyes.

A year ago, Jonathan Barnes had been the same rank as her in the Met. Now all he had to look forward to was a life in prison full of pain. He didn't look up as she entered the room. His hands and legs were cuffed, a steel chain linking them to a holding iron in the stone floor.

Sarah had primed herself to view the injuries to the man's face but nothing could have prepared her for the sight before her. Her first thought was that the man's face had slipped. The left side of his face drooped towards his chin, the skin melted away. He'd lost the sight in his left eye, and the mottled skin glared back at her – lifeless. Barnes had suffered a so-called napalm attack in prison. The makeshift acid, a mixture of boiling water and sugar, had been poured over his head, scalding his scalp where random tufts of hair now grew from the broken skin. During the attack he'd swallowed some of the substance, so when he spoke his words were garbled.

'DCI May. Lambert's bitch,' he said, as Sarah sat down.

They'd never met but she wasn't surprised he knew her. 'That's not a very pleasant way to start a conversation, Jonathan,' she said, ignoring the insult.

'What do you want?' The words came as a growl. It sounded as if each utterance caused pain to the man.

'I'm here to discuss Peter Saunders.'

Barnes' right eye flickered in recognition but he didn't answer.

'You may or may not be aware that Peter Saunders has escaped custody.'

'I'd heard.'

'I'm here to ask for your help, Jonathan.'

Barnes made a low cackling sound Sarah took for a laugh. 'Why would I help you?'

'You know how this works, Jonathan. I've met with the Governor. There's a certain set of privileges you could be entitled to if you cooperate.'

'What, like some adequate painkillers?'

'If that's what you want.'

'How about prosecuting the people who did this to me?' said Barnes, with a sneer.

'I can't help you with that. There was a thorough investigation as far as I understand.'

'Thorough,' said Barnes, as if saying the word for the first time.

Sarah handed him the list of preapproved privileges. Barnes glanced at them with his good eye without responding, which Sarah took for acceptance.

'You knew Peter Saunders?'

'I knew of him.'

'In what capacity?'

Barnes repeated the strange gargling noise he'd made earlier. 'You think I'm going to incriminate myself?'

Sarah hadn't meant to try and catch him out, and as he was facing life in prison with no chance of parole in the next forty years it hardly mattered if he incriminated himself. 'He was convicted for his part in Waverley Manor, as you know. Can you think of anyone who would help him escape?'

'Can't you?'

'We have our leads, Jonathan, but if you had anything more specific?'

Barnes went blank, possibly lost in thought. 'Everyone I know who could help him is in prison now.'

'You're referring to the other members of the organization known as the Manor?'

'Am I, now?'

'If you're not going to help, Jonathan, we might as well call this off.'

Barnes hesitated but she could tell he was interested in the offer of privileges. 'I can't tell you what I don't know. Have you spoken to his wife?'

'I am seeing her later today.'

'I would suggest keeping an eye on her. She may lead you to him. Aside from that…' He stopped talking as if he'd lost track of his thoughts and Sarah wondered if the attack had resulted in any lasting psychological damage to the man.

'Jonathan?'

He shook his head, staring at her like he'd never laid eyes on her before. 'Aside from that I don't know.'

She wanted to wrap things up there. Barnes was either a great actor or didn't know anything. But she'd promised to help Michael. 'There was one more thing,' she said. She told him about the deaths of Alistair Beckinsale and Lance Jenkins.

Barnes couldn't hide his glee. 'So he did send you. I thought as much. Coward. Sending someone to do his dirty work just like when he did this.' Barnes pointed to his face, the mottled skin and blistered lips. 'He did this to me, and I'm glad he's got what's coming to him. I only hope whoever is responsible takes him next. Nothing could make me happier.'

Regretting having said anything, Sarah couldn't resist responding. 'You do remember why you're here, don't you? The things you did…'

'Don't give me that. Lambert and Tillman did this to me. They broke the law, they're as guilty as I am.'

Sarah banged on the door. 'Guard,' she said, taking and ripping up the privilege sheet she'd handed to Barnes.

–

Michael was waiting for her outside. 'Anything?'

She shook her head. 'I'm not sure Barnes has adapted well to prison life. The only sensible thing he said was that I should see Saunders' wife.'

'Damn. It was unlikely he would talk. How did he look?'

Sarah sensed the question within the question. She liked to think Michael wasn't responsible for the attack on Barnes. She had no pity for Barnes but hoped Michael hadn't resorted to such retribution. 'Not great.'

'Is he still accusing me of being responsible?'

'I'm afraid so.'

'You don't believe him, do you?'

Sarah studied Lambert's eyes. She knew what he was capable of, what he would do to protect the people he loved, but at the moment she was convinced he wasn't lying. 'No,' she said. 'No I don't.'

'Good. You'll let me know how it goes with Anna Saunders?'

'Of course.' There was so much she wanted to discuss, but the timing was wrong. 'You keep me updated too,' she said, not knowing what else to say.

–

Saying goodbye to Michael proved harder than she'd anticipated. Although she'd never put him completely out of her mind, she was surprised by the depth of her feelings now he was back in her life. She wanted to question him over his relationship with Sophie, but couldn't bring herself to do so. She couldn't be the sort of person who would break up a family. Shaking her head, as if she could empty it of conflicting thoughts, she headed towards her next destination.

The opulence of the Saunders' residence came as no surprise. Anna Saunders lived in a row of Georgian buildings in the heart of Maida Vale. Sarah circled the area four times before finding a parking space. She walked through the beginning of a new snowstorm, envious of the customers warm inside the boutique coffee shops and wine bars on the high street.

Anna Saunders didn't hide her disdain as she answered the door. 'I'm not sure why I have to waste my time further, but you may as well come in,' she said, by way of introduction.

Sarah followed her across polished wood flooring to what she presumed was the space she used as an office. Anna Saunders sat behind a glass-topped office table and invited Sarah to sit opposite as if she was attending an interview.

'Thank you for seeing me, Mrs Saunders,' said Sarah. Still wearing her large overcoat, she was overdressed in comparison to Saunders who was lightly wrapped in jeans and pullover. Sarah noticed her manicured nails, the hint of a tan on her exposed skin.

'Yes. Now exactly what do you want?'

'I have to ask, Mrs Saunders,' said Sarah, forcing a smile, 'when was the last time you saw your husband?'

Saunders face morphed into something Sarah could only describe as a snarl. 'The day he was wrongly convicted for those heinous acts.'

'You think he was innocent?' said Sarah, unable to hide her incredulity. Only that morning she'd read the evidence against the man. The fingerprints and DNA found at Waverley Manor.

'He was innocent, DCI May. You know as well as I do that people get framed for this sort of thing all the time. Peter made some enemies. I am sure of this as I am sure he will be proved innocent one day.'

Anna Saunders' protestations echoed those of Jonathan Barnes. 'Yet you never visited him in prison?'

Saunders snarled again, grimacing like she'd swallowed something foul. 'No, dear. We agreed I shouldn't visit. It's not the sort of place that…'

Sarah raised her eyebrows, waiting for the woman to finish.

'Let's just say I wouldn't have felt comfortable in such a place.'

'No, I suppose not. So did you plan to ever see your husband again? He was sentenced to a minimum of thirty-five years. It was highly unlikely he would ever see freedom again.'

Saunders shifted in her chair and folded her arms.

'Or did you expect to see him again? Was his escape planned in advance?'

Saunders sat back. 'I told your colleagues, and I'm telling you now, I have no knowledge of my husband's so-called escape and if you wish to continue this line of questioning I will be forced to call my solicitor.'

'So-called?' said Sarah, ignoring the threat.

'I know what happened to Jonathan Barnes. Horrifically mutilated while in a secure unit of prison. Reportedly on the orders of two police officers.' Saunders whispered the last sentence, leaning in towards Sarah in confidence.

'And you think?'

'I think it is within the realms of possibility that his escape was staged. I believe my husband may have been murdered or kidnapped by the police.'

Sarah was impressed with the woman's diversion tactics but ignored the implausible comment. 'Did you and your husband know Jonathan Barnes?' she asked.

'Of course we bloody didn't. The whole thing was an elaborate set-up. Look at the men you arrested. All powerful men – rich men with the exception of your police friend. Someone wanted them out of the way so they could benefit from their absence, just as Chief Superintendent Tillman and DCI Lambert no doubt benefited from Barnes going to prison. That's where the real crime lies. That's where you should be investigating. That's the real travesty of justice.'

It was classic conspiracy theory, and Anna Saunders either believed it or at least chose to believe it. Denial was a natural reaction to discovering what her husband was capable of. Sarah had seen it countless times before, the disbelieving spouses finding out the truth about the person they'd trusted for a lifetime.

She changed her line of questioning, playing to Anna Saunders' theories. 'OK, if that's true help me find Peter. I'm not here to condemn anyone. If Peter is in danger I'd like to find him.'

'Find him so you can send him back to prison.'

'If you think he is in danger, surely he would be better off under our supervision? If he truly thinks he has a case to fight then his legal team can put together an appeal. At the moment he is a fugitive from justice.'

Saunders crossed her arms once more.

'Where do you think he is, Anna?' asked Sarah.

Saunders kept her arms crossed and offered the slightest shake of her head.

'Is there anywhere he would feel safe? A special holiday destination perhaps?'

Saunders eyes darted upwards, suggesting she was thinking about the question.

'If we find him, I will arrange for a private visit. How's that, Anna? It will be in a prison environment – there's nothing I can do about that – but we can arrange for it to be just the two of you. You wouldn't have to wait in those horrendous waiting rooms. I could personally escort you. You could see he was safe, that he was being looked after.'

Anna Saunders shivered, her eyes watering. 'You could do that?' she asked, for a second revealing another side to her personality. The lost and broken side, the one failed by her husband.

'You have my word, Anna.'

Anna looked down at the glass table. 'I remembered something the other night. Something he said on our honeymoon. We'd been talking about disappearing at the time, you know the sort of silly things you talk about. What we would do, where we would go. He told me about this place he'd discovered as a child. It was a farmhouse in Norfolk. Funny I should have thought about that, really. I'd been surprised at the time. He'd never struck me as the outdoor type, and he wasn't. We never visited the countryside in all the time we were married, except that one time. He'd been taken there as a child, you see, before...'

'Before?' said Sarah.

'Before his parents died. He was nine when they died and I think that place was forever entwined with his memory of them.'

'Do you know where this place is, Anna?'

'Yes. Yes,' she repeated, her eyes reddening as she began to cry. 'He took me there once.'

Chapter Fifteen

Lambert should have handled the conversation with Sarah better. She'd been waiting for him to speak, to say something beyond what was important to him and the case, but he'd failed.

At the time, his thoughts were overwhelmed with Jonathan Barnes. The last time he'd seen the man had been the day of his sentencing. Lambert watched every second of the case, obsessed about the prosecution missing any detail. He could picture Barnes now. He'd remained passive for the whole case, only showing a hint of emotion during his cross examination where he'd glared at Lambert, and stared forlornly at his wife and two teenage children.

After speaking to Sarah, he knew he had to come here. Back to where it all began.

Waverley Manor.

Lambert pushed through hedges and loose branches dusted with frost, where once he'd fought his way through almost impenetrable foliage. It was growing back, and he was pleased nature was trying to cover the site, to hide the gruesome secrets hidden within.

A hundred metres from where he stood was a trapdoor, once hidden, leading to an underground chamber with levels upon chilling levels. It was empty now – the

SOCOs had spent months within its depths, had dug up the surrounding area until every body was accounted for – but the place would never lose its dread. The dungeon and tunnels below were cleaned but not yet cemented over, though every fingerprint and DNA trace had been excavated from within. Trees had been planted over the surrounding area. It was changing, and one day soon Waverley Manor would be no more. It was already difficult to pinpoint the exact area, and if Lambert hadn't spent those nights within its depths he would have struggled to locate the site's entrance.

He stood there now, his boots trampling down the frozen foliage. The trapdoor was different to before, had been replaced by the Met. It was chained up so Lambert couldn't access its depths without a set of bolt cutters.

Reminiscing was a form of punishment. He'd hoped being here would trigger a memory, or an idea would form and begin to unravel, would explain what the hell was going on. Even now, it was difficult to grasp what had occurred here, and despite the successful prosecutions he would never fully know.

Barnes, Saunders, and other members of the Manor had used the place as a grotesque playground. Despite his years of investigating the kind of crimes which would make most people physically sick, it was hard to comprehend the extent of the misery which had occurred in this spot. The sheer inhumanity staggered him to this day and the horror of what he'd seen was only exceeded by what he was forced to imagine.

Snow began to fall, and to the casual eye the white dusting on the ruins and evergreens would appear picturesque. But he could smell what lurked beneath. A thousand thoughts swarmed through his mind. He could no longer feel his toes, his fingers stinging beneath his leather gloves. He took one last glance and retreated back to his car a little faster than he'd approached.

–

His mood was not lifted by the debrief back at headquarters. On the crime board, pictures of Lance Jenkins and Alistair Beckinsale were connected to the two older cases of Thomas Powell and Dominic Webster. On the periphery of the board were photos of Will Fisher, his girlfriend and Nancy Beckinsale, but their images were there almost as an afterthought.

Lambert conceded they had no credible suspect at present. No one with a motive to see both Beckinsale and Jenkins dead, let alone the wherewithal to get the job done.

'I'm sure you're aware now that Peter Saunders has escaped during a prison transfer,' said Lambert to the group. It was still not official but the talk in the building over the last couple of days had been about little else, and Lambert was beyond caring about breaking procedure.

'We had heard, sir,' said DS Bickland with his West Country drawl. 'You think this has some bearing on these cases?'

'Honestly, Bickland, I have no fucking idea. All I can say is Saunders escaped the day Beckinsale was killed. I don't believe he is a credible suspect but I would not rule out the Manor's involvement.'

'But who exactly are the Manor? As far as I can see they're a group of perverts who have a tenuous link to one another. I'd thought they were all in prison,' said Croft.

Croft had been transferred to Lambert's team during the Waverley Manor case and she'd worked out so well that he'd made the transfer permanent.

In part it was a good question. The Manor was not an organization in a traditional sense and many considered it no longer existed following the arrests. Lambert knew different but had to be careful airing his views. 'Someone broke Saunders out. He was transferred under category A security. It would have taken meticulous planning. Furthermore, there has been no sign of Saunders and one of his prison guards, John Prine, since his escape. He has disappeared with literally no trace.' Lambert missed out the confidential part about the dead prison guard and police officer.

'OK, let's say the Manor are responsible for springing Saunders. Why target Beckinsale and Jenkins? Why the links to your old cases?' said Matilda.

Lambert glanced at the officers for inspiration.

'A distraction?' suggested Bickland.

'Have we checked if Jenkins and Beckinsale are linked some way to the Manor? I imagine it's difficult to link them but we could check if they had similar… interests,' said Croft.

'Worth a shot,' said Lambert. 'Get on with that, Gemma. Everyone else, more research on all four cases,' he said, pointing at the board. 'Matilda and Bickland, your focus is on Powell and Webster. See if anything was overlooked first time around. It could be we've missed the one thing linking those two cases. If we find that, we find the link to the current cases as well.'

Lambert spent the rest of the afternoon on the System running cross-checks on the four victims, the various suspects, and everyone ever linked to the Manor. It was a haphazard approach but one which often proved fruitful. Data scrolled across his screen and he absorbed it all, trusting something would eventually click. He accessed his old notes on Powell and Webster, momentarily nostalgic for old paperwork and his former naivety.

The Powell case had been a turning point for him. His extra diligence had led to Williamson's conviction. He wondered what her life and her sister's would be like had he not pursued it with such vigour. Would Williamson have helped her sister through her grief, forever encumbered with her guilt? Both women would probably be better off, not lost in different versions of their own private hell, but Lambert couldn't dwell on that. Speculating on future recriminations was not his role, finding who was responsible: 'hunting the bad guys' as his first detective supervisor told him, was his only job. And it had seemed so much easier then.

The internal phone buzzed and Lambert shut the computer. 'Yes?'

'DCI Lambert. We have an Inspector Duggan for you in reception. He's from—'

Lambert frowned. 'I know where he's from. Tell him to wait, I'll be down in five minutes.'

–

Inspector Duggan worked for AC-10, one of the Met's anti-corruption units. They'd come across each other on numerous occasions, and one thing Lambert could count on was that Duggan couldn't be trusted.

'Sergeant Duggan,' said Lambert, mistaking his rank on purpose.

Duggan got to his feet, his movements slow and calculated. As always he was immaculately dressed in a tailored suit and crisp shirt. Clean-shaven and hair cut with military precision. 'DCI Lambert,' he said. Lambert could tell he wanted to correct him, to announce his recent promotion to Inspector, but to his credit Duggan didn't respond to his provocation. 'May we speak?'

'Is this official business?' asked Lambert.

'Of sorts,' said Duggan, as evasive as usual.

'This way. I'm using Interview Room Three,' said Lambert to the duty sergeant, who waved his pen in response.

Lambert had no time for pleasantries. 'What can I do for you, Duggan?' he said, taking the first seat in the room so Duggan had to walk past him.

'I'll get straight to the point. There are major concerns about the articles in Mia Helmer's newspaper. I wanted to give you the heads-up, see if I can help sort out this mess.'

Lambert had been forced to work with Duggan in the Waverley Manor case. It had been an uneasy alliance at best and they hadn't spoken since. Duggan wasn't there to do him any favours. 'You shouldn't believe everything you read in the papers, Duggan. Even you know that.'

Duggan's smile revealed impossibly white teeth. He held the grin a beat too long. 'It's not just the papers though, is it DCI Lambert? I've read the files on the cases of Lance Jenkins and Alistair Beckinsale. Your name appeared on a card at both crime scenes. In the case of Lance Jenkins it was pinned to the deceased.'

'Correct.'

'So Mia Helmer has a point, does she not?'

Duggan was yet to discover the potential copycat links to Jenkins and Beckinsale and Lambert wasn't about to inform him. 'Are you really going to sit there and tell me you take the side of a journalist? A bloody dubious journalist I might add. All she ever prints is conjecture. She has a personal vendetta against me, Duggan, and for the life of me I cannot understand how this concerns anti-corruption.'

Duggan held his hands up. 'As I said, I'm here as a colleague. You know how these things work though. Should you really be working on a case where you're linked to the murder scene? Is this good practice?' asked Duggan, managing to combine condescension and smugness in every word.

'Chief Superintendent Tillman is the SIO and he decided I was the best fit for the case.'

Duggan visibly winced at Tillman's name. He'd investigated Tillman at least once and had come off second best. 'You think that's advisable?'

'I think it advisable I take my orders from my direct superior, don't you, Duggan? Now, as your senior ranking officer, may I make the suggestion that you kindly fuck off?'

Duggan's mask slipped. 'Have it your way, Lambert, as always. But be warned,' he said, leaning in close. 'You're being watched. One more slip-up and it won't be just me you answer to.'

Lambert grimaced, leaning back from Duggan. 'A little advice, Sergeant. Floss.'

DI Duggan clenched his fist but didn't respond as he exited the room.

Sophie was working late so Lambert picked up Jane from the childminder. She was usually hyper at this time of day and cried most of the way home. 'Did Lorraine give you any dinner?' he asked her, once they reached home.

'Yuck,' said Jane.

'Yuck?'

'It was yuck,' said Jane, as if he was stupid.

'What did she give you?'

'Meat,' said Jane, screwing up her face in disgust.

'What sort of meat?'

'I dunno.'

'Unidentifiable meat, hey? Would you like something else now? A sandwich perhaps.'

Jane nodded and began pushing a baby doll in her toy pushchair.

'Well, what do you want?' said Lambert, chasing after her as she raced the pram down the corridor into the living room.

'Sandwich,' said Jane, with a hint of impatience.

'What would you like in it?' said Lambert, mimicking her voice.

'Hummus, of course,' said Jane.

After eating they caught the end of children's television; Lambert intrigued by the surreal images entrancing his daughter. 'Bedtime,' he said once the show ended.

'Mummy.'

'She'll be home soon. I'll get her to kiss you when she's back.'

Jane looked unconvinced but was happy to be carried to her room. Lambert read to her for five minutes before she fell asleep.

Downstairs he began defrosting some food from the freezer. He was annoyed with himself for being so affected by Duggan's visit earlier that day. He'd expected to draw some attention but having AC-10 involved helped no one.

He ate alone, a single glass of red wine accompanying his dish of bolognaise. Sophie barely said a word to him when she returned. She looked exhausted, eating her food perfunctorily and refusing his offer of wine. 'I'm going to bed,' she said once she'd cleared her plate.

'Lovely to see you too,' said Lambert.

'I'm sorry. Busy day,' she said, kissing him on the head. 'I'm off tomorrow. I promise to give you some attention then,' she added, teasing him.

'Sleep well.'

The wine made him drowsy but he was too wired for sleep. He retreated to his office and uploaded the System, scrolling through the day's notes. Replaying everything he knew about the four cases over and over, his mind became overloaded until nothing was making any sense. He switched on the digital radio, tuned to 6 Music, the electronica pumping through the speakers intriguing but far from relaxing. He was about to turn it off when he heard a second underlying tone to the music which didn't make sense.

'Jesus, I must be tired,' he said to himself, realizing the tune was from his burner phone.

'Yes,' he said, answering.

'Michael. It's Sarah. If you're not busy can we meet? And maybe bring some overnight gear.'

Chapter Sixteen

Lambert agreed to meet Sarah in the car park of a twenty-four-hour supermarket close to the Blackwell Tunnel. He packed in a hurry, leaving a note in the kitchen for Sophie explaining his departure. It wasn't the first time he'd left in such circumstances during their marriage and in the past it had led to arguments. Lambert was thankful Sophie was now off for most of the Christmas period, though he feared he would have some questions to answer when he returned.

Sarah texted him her exact location and he found her car with little effort in the darkest corner of the car park, sheltered beneath a broken street lamp. Sarah's face was illuminated by the dim glow of her mobile phone. Lambert left his car, checking out of habit he wasn't being watched, and opened the passenger-side door.

'What's all the mystery?' he said, sitting down next to her.

Sarah told him about her meeting with Anna Saunders.

'I met that woman once and can't say I was particularly impressed. She was in denial, blaming everyone but herself,' said Lambert.

'That was my first impression and overall I think it's a correct appraisal. However, she let her guard down at the end. I could tell the experience got to her. How wouldn't it? She misses Saunders and I genuinely believe she doesn't know anything about his escape.'

'If that's true, I'd be surprised if she wants him found.'

'I'm not so sure. I don't think he's been in contact and that bothers her. She's worried about him.'

Peter Saunders was a pure psychopath. Lambert doubted he had any real feelings for his wife, not in the conventional sense. In his experience, men like Saunders took partners to create a veneer of normality. Like all of Saunders' victims, he would have dropped his wife without a second thought and would never have risked contacting her. Lambert also understood such men could be charming, had the ability to create replicas of them-selves people could love. Lambert had convicted men who came from seemingly perfect families, with wives and children who couldn't believe what their spouse or father was capable of. If Anna Saunders was in denial it was because her husband created a character she had fallen in love with – a character far removed from his true self.

Sarah told him about the farmhouse Saunders visited first as a child then on his honeymoon.

'You think he actually went there as a child?'

'Who knows, but I'm sure he went there with Anna.'

'I take it I'm here because you haven't told Partridge.'

'There's no fooling you, Michael.'

'Why haven't you told MI5?'

'For one they are in Scotland, trawling the area of the family holiday home.'

'And for two?'

'Frankly, I just don't trust them.'

They took Sarah's car. Where once they'd been so relaxed in each other's company, Lambert sensed a growing tension. To break the silence, he told her about the visit he'd received from the newly promoted Inspector Duggan.

'What did he want?'

'You know him, likes to stick his nose in where it's not wanted. Claims murmurs from above are that I shouldn't be working on the case, that I'm too closely linked. He's been reading too much of Mia Helmer's work.'

Sarah smirked. 'He's got a point.'

'He probably does but I'm not walking away now. Unless Tillman decides otherwise.'

'Really? You follow orders now?'

Lambert paused. 'Well, if he has a compelling reason I might. Until then, I consider it my case and I told Duggan as much. He kept going on about that bloody journalist as if he was working for public relations.'

'She doesn't like you, does she?'

'She doesn't appear to, no.'

Lambert turned to face Sarah and matched her smile.

'How's Jane?' she asked.

'She's good. A little cutie.'

Lambert wondered if she would ask about Sophie and was glad when she began fiddling with the car radio, settling on a golden oldie channel.

'What the hell is this?' said Lambert, as a power ballad from the eighties came on.

'Some people like to enjoy their music, Michael. We don't all listen to the dour stuff you do.'

'Dour?' said Lambert, pretending outrage.

Sarah turned the volume up. 'Dour,' she repeated.

The roads were clear and they made good time along the A12 and M11. 'It's a different world here,' said Lambert, as a sign heralded their entry into Norfolk.

'It's not for us big city types, then?'

'You'll be OK,' said Lambert. 'You're from Bristol, you share the culture.'

Sarah frowned. 'I think you're being prejudiced against country folk, Michael. And be careful, I've told you before, I was working in Bristol when you met me, but I'm from London.'

'So you say.'

They reached their destination fifty minutes later. The roads had long become single track. With no street lighting, Sarah slowed her pace, taking her time on the winding country lanes.

'Could we not have waited until the morning?' said Lambert.

'I've already waited too long to report my conversation with Anna Saunders. I'll need to tell Partridge by the morning. Why not see if we can find Saunders before then?'

They parked half a mile from their destination, Sarah worried that if Saunders was there he would see them approach.

'I gave up my lovely warm house for this,' said Lambert, grabbing his coat and hat.

'You're not going to moan all the way there, are you?'

'Not all the way. Sarah, you don't really expect to find him, do you?'

'Stranger things have happened, Michael, you know that. You should have heard Anna talking about the farm-house. I had the sense she was confessing.'

'If she was confessing, she may have warned him we're coming.'

'We better get a move on, then.'

The house appeared in the shadows, an opening in the hedges leading to a stone pathway. Sarah checked her GPS signal. 'This is it,' she said.

With only the illumination of the moon in the clear sky they made their way towards the derelict building. There was no evident sign of occupancy, no vehicles in the driveway or light behind the windows. In the daylight Lambert imagined the area would be picturesque. The building had an impressive structure and grounds, even if the exterior had seen better days. Not that he would have considered living there; such remote solitude was not for him. He needed the hustle and bustle of city life and such isolation would be too much after a couple of days. He followed Sarah towards the front door and matched her action of taking out her expandable baton.

If Peter Saunders had fond memories of the farm-house, he must have been sorely disappointed when he returned. The interior was nothing more than an empty shell. Nothing remained of the original features, not even the carpets. After forcing the front door, they walked across the bare floorboards, Lambert's torch revealing the occasional trace of faded graffiti on the walls.

Upstairs, the windows were either cracked or missing. Only the bathroom was intact, sporting a seventies-style avocado-coloured bath suite. Lambert turned the taps but nothing but air fell from the openings.

After securing all the rooms, they spent the next thirty minutes searching every inch of the building for signs of recent occupation. 'If he's been here he's cleaned up after himself,' said Lambert. It had always been a long shot but he understood the disappointment on Sarah's face.

The sun came up and they watched the surrounding fields slowly come to life. 'Strange no one has done this place up. It's a lovely spot,' said Lambert.

'From the land registry records it's been owned by the same people for fifty years. Didn't get any response yesterday. I've left messages at their last recorded address.'

'What were the names?'

'The Hurst family.'

The name meant nothing to him. He gazed out at the grassland and was reminded of his time at Waverley Manor. Was it coincidence that brought him here the day after he'd visited the site? Waverley Manor was less open than the farmhouse, but who knew what lay beyond the woodland.

Lambert had long believed the group known as the Manor could have more secret locations similar to Waverley Manor. It had been a major part of the interrogations following the arrests but none of the men cracked, only Jonathan Barnes hinting at other sites.

'Let's take a walk,' he said to Sarah, heading off into the fields.

When they reached the woodland perimeter, Lambert realized how difficult searching the area would be. With Waverley Manor he'd had a location to work with and found the trapdoor to the underground prison within fifty or so metres from the derelict Manor itself. Here he faced acres and acres of forest.

They walked through the dense woodland area for thirty minutes, Sarah tracking their progress on her phone so they could find their way back. 'I appreciate you going to this trouble, Michael, but I think I may have made a mistake.'

They took a different route back. Lambert caught some movement through the trees and followed the sound, watching what appeared to be a wild boar disappearing into the undergrowth. Surprised such animals lived in deepest Norfolk, he was about to share with Sarah what he'd seen when sunlight bounced off an object on the ground.

'What have you got?' said Sarah.

Lambert bent down to retrieve the object. 'A tent peg.'

'Is there even room here for a tent?' said Sarah, bending down to examine the area.

'I'm sure a one-man tent would fit in this space. I'm no expert, mind you.'

'Why would you camp here?'

'To be at one with nature,' said Lambert.

'Or to escape from reality.'

They scoured the surrounding area for further signs of life but it was a job beyond the scope of two officers.

'How can I call it in? I can hardly explain I came here on the off-chance after speaking to Anna Saunders,' said Sarah.

'Not on the basis of one tent peg, no.'

'Let's work this methodically. We'll move out in increasing circles. I have some scene tape so we can mark where we've been. We can give it an hour and reassess.'

They spent the next two hours scouring the site, Lambert's clothes filthy from crawling on the ground, his hands and face scratched from too many encounters with low-lying brambles. Eventually their hard work paid off, Sarah uncovering an area where the ground had recently been dug. The earth was cold but not frozen. Sarah told Lambert to stand back as she pulled at the ground with her gloved hands. They exchanged looks and the occasional smile, both appreciating how mad their actions were. Only when Sarah uncovered the arm of the corpse did they realize their search hadn't been in vain.

They didn't want to disturb the crime scene but needed to check the identity of the body. Removing the shallow covering of earth with care, Sarah uncovered the face of the frozen corpse.

'That's not Saunders,' said Lambert.

'No, that's his prison guard.'

Chapter Seventeen

Lambert and Sarah retreated from the makeshift grave.

'John Prine,' said Sarah.

'Probably outlived his usefulness,' said Lambert.

They searched the surrounding area for camping gear. 'I guess we have to work from the assumption he came here with Saunders and they camped for some time before Saunders decided he was better off alone,' said Lambert.

'Saunders may have a rendezvous point he was aiming for.'

'Or he may still be in the woods. You should call it now, Sarah.'

'What about you?'

It would be better for both of them if Lambert's presence at the discovery of the body went unrecorded. Sarah had been careful not to let him near the gravesite and he would be unlucky if his DNA was discovered. 'We either take the risk and I head back, or we say you wanted some company and you asked me to help. It's your call. I'll go with whatever you decide.'

In the end they decided Sarah would say she came alone. 'I'll tell them I came on a hunch having spoken to Anna Saunders and I didn't want to waste their time.'

She drove Lambert to the nearest train station before calling it in. 'It was great working with you again,' said Lambert as she pulled into the car park.

'It's not too late, I'm happy to stay here and get my knuckles wrapped,' he said, noticing her agitated look.

'It's fine. You go. Take this though,' she said, handing him her burner phone. 'Just in case. I'll keep you updated, I promise.'

Lambert hesitated. He wanted to say more but was momentarily at a loss for words.

'Get going before you're missed,' said Sarah, rescuing him from his awkwardness.

–

He was back at headquarters before lunchtime. If the team were suspicious about his absence and battered appearance, they knew better than to question him. 'Matilda,' he said, walking to his office.

'Sir,' said Matilda, following him.

'Close the door.'

He told her about where he'd been with Sarah. 'This can go no further, Matilda. You can't even tell Tillman,' said Lambert, thinking Tillman was probably the last person who should know.

'You think Saunders is in that vicinity?' said Matilda, lowering her voice to a whisper.

'We'll find out more once the pathologist arrives. They'll search every inch of that land, especially if MI5 are involved.'

'How does this relate to us?'

'I'm not sure. If Saunders was with Prine it would suggest he wasn't directly involved with Beckinsale and

Jenkins but we thought that anyway. It doesn't rule out the Manor's involvement. It could still be diversionary. Do you have anything else for me?'

'Nothing linking the cases whatsoever, aside from your name being found at the scene and them being your old cases. I met with Dr Harrington this morning. She confirmed the body was moved post-mortem. The cause of death was the blow to the head and the bones were manipulated into position after Jenkins was dead, which I suppose we can be thankful for.'

'That is the smallest of blessings, Matilda.'

As she was leaving, DS Bickland popped his head around the corner. 'A word, sir?'

'Come in.'

'Maybe you should hear this too, Matilda,' said Bickland. The DS had put on weight recently and his breathing was heavy. 'I was thinking about what we discussed yesterday, searching for a link between Jenkins, Beckinsale and the Manor. As you know, neither had criminal records so I looked at it a different way.'

'What way?' said Lambert.

'I considered them as potential victims. I looked into Jenkins' history first as he is the youngest. Now I appreciate I maybe clutching at straws, looking at something that wasn't there, but one of Jenkins' primary school teachers was suspended when Jenkins was aged ten. George Forrest was never formally charged with anything but there were reports of inappropriate behaviour. He'd been alone in the boys' toilets on a few occasions, and fellow staff members were concerned by his closeness to some of the children. Basically, he'd been breaking safeguarding procedures.'

'It's an interesting lead,' said Lambert. 'You're right though, it's one hell of a leap to the Manor.'

'As I said, it was just a thought. Forrest left the profession not long after being suspended.'

'You're thinking Jenkins was somehow involved with him?'

'Worth checking.'

'You speak to the head teacher. I don't suppose you can link this teacher with Beckinsale?'

'No. Alistair Beckinsale is much older than Forrest, but it's an angle to consider.'

'Matilda?'

'I'll get the team onto it.'

–

Lambert changed into the spare suit he kept in the office. Even if Bickland's suggestion was little more than a punt it was a move forward as far as Lambert was concerned. It was unlikely Forrest would end up being linked with the Manor but asking such questions often resulted in unexpected answers and potential new leads.

He glanced at his phone and realized he'd done little else since returning from Norfolk. He'd destroyed both burner phones and Sarah wouldn't be so careless as to phone him directly, even from a payphone. Still, he wanted to hear from her. Spending last night in her company made him realize he'd never fully come to terms with their separation. The split was artificial. Sarah's affection eased once Jane was born and it was at her insistence he try again with Sophie. It didn't feel like something she would do, but had she been testing him, and he too dumb to realize? There'd been no recriminations, no prolonged arguments or fights, only a sad goodbye which never felt final. This made the current situation twice as complicated. He had a daughter now, and he loved Sophie. So why couldn't he stop thinking about Sarah?

He visited the canteen and ordered lunch. He'd managed a couple of hours' sleep on the train back from Norfolk but was still wearing yesterday's underwear. His face was rough with stubble and he was in need of a shower. Playing with the chicken dish in front of him, he drank black coffee – the canteen's only saving grace – and tried to formulate what he could do next. His thoughts were still with Sarah. He was desperate to know what was happening with Saunders, and though he was sure news would reach him if they found the escaped convict, it was difficult being out of the loop.

DS Bickland's lead made him think. Of the four victims in the investigations, it could be assumed that Thomas Powell, killed by his aunt, and Lance Jenkins, killed by unknown assailants, were innocent victims. He took out his notebook and wrote his thoughts on paper. Next to Powell and Jenkins he wrote first 'innocent', then 'victim'.

The same could not be said of Webster. Electrocuted by his daughter and wife, Webster had systematically abused both his family members for years. He wrote down Webster's name and drew a line pointing to a second word 'guilty'. Finally he wrote 'Alistair Beckinsale?'.

He had no way of knowing what it meant, if it meant anything at all, but it gave him fresh impetus. He purchased a second cup of coffee and took it back to his office where he searched for records of Dominic Webster's widow and daughter.

The pair had moved to a small village twenty miles outside Leeds. Using the System he found recent bank and work records. The mother, Kate Webster, was retired. The daughter, Eleanor Webster, worked as a teaching assistant at a local primary school.

Lambert sat back from his laptop. What good would it do to contact them now? The files were clear on what Webster had done to them, and the threat he posed, and no charges were ever brought against them. Both women would have to live with what he'd done on a daily basis and it was unlikely a visit from Lambert would uncover anything further, while it would undoubtedly cause distress.

Webster was guilty of abuse; that was evident. Was Beckinsale guilty for some unknown crime?

Innocence was subjective. Beckinsale had left his wife and taken a much younger lover. To some that would equate to some form of guilt, but it was nothing in comparison to Webster's. Beckinsale had no record, and the interviews conducted with friends and work colleagues suggested he was a good man.

Lambert went back to the beginning. On the System he dragged up everything he could find about Beckinsale. The System was still not an official application. Out of his department, only Lambert and Tillman had access. It had existed in one form or another for years, an amalgamation of police and government databases, social media back ends, and was linked to domestic and external security service databases.

A detailed snapshot of Beckinsale's life appeared on screen from his birth certificate onwards. It listed all his known addresses, from his parents' first home in East

Sussex to the flat where he was found in West Hampstead. In minutes, Lambert knew the man's exam results, his work and tax history. Although his social media presence was limited, the System accessed all the photos ever posted to Facebook, Instagram and Twitter and gave Lambert the option to view the posts Beckinsale accessed over the years.

Lambert concentrated on the discrepancies, periods of time when Beckinsale's life could not be fully accounted for. A period of a year existed between the time Beckinsale received his A level results and when he started university. A year out, possibly, but there was no record of where he'd gone. After graduating, there were three periods – of six months, two months, and eight months respectively – where Beckinsale had been out of work. Lambert made a note and continued searching, hoping something would spring out at him.

He read everything intently once and then let the file play out on the screen as he processed everything he'd read. The answer, if there was one, wouldn't necessarily come now.

Splitting the screen in two he updated his logbook. He grimaced at the irony that he couldn't enter the most significant entries. He recorded his visits to Mrs Powell and her sister but omitted his contact with Sarah and his visit to Waverley Manor. He could have added the latter but didn't want to include any link to the place in the official report. For one, it would smack of obsession; his greater concern being that it would alert the Manor he was onto them.

Something was missing; something obvious. He clicked on Beckinsale's file and returned to the beginning once more, charting the young Beckinsale's formative years, and finally found what he was looking for.

It was a long shot at best, but thinking about Waverley Manor jogged his memory. Lambert's memory was strong, if not quite photographic. He'd begun using memory techniques as a new recruit in the force. At first he'd used it to memorize the names of colleagues, suspects and witnesses. As his ability increased he'd used the techniques to memorize number plates and street names. The ability had become so ingrained he did it without thinking.

And that was why he remembered seeing the name of the village, Fairleigh, on his way to Waverley Manor yesterday. The same Fairleigh Beckinsale had moved to aged seven.

Chapter Eighteen

They came in silence – no wailing sirens or flashing lights – a dark saloon car, German make with blackout windows. Sarah May watched the car from her vantage point at the abandoned farmhouse. She'd been preparing her report for the last seventy minutes, going over the details verbatim in her head. She kept mainly to the facts. Her meeting with Anna Saunders, the woman's recollection of the farmhouse, the late-night journey and desperate scrambling in the dark until the body of John Prine was uncovered. Only, in this new version, there was no Michael Lambert.

It was a necessary risk. She could have argued his involvement away. He was a trusted officer and knew the Manor as well as anyone on the force, had been instrumental in its discovery and partial destruction. Yet the security services didn't work that way. At best, she was considered a necessary hindrance to their ongoing investigations. They marginalized her as best they could, and one thing they would not tolerate was outside help. Involving Lambert would be considered a betrayal and would lead to her being taken off the investigation, with more severe consequences likely down the line.

The car glided to a stop metres from where she stood. Sarah took a deep breath as the rear door opened.

Partridge stepped out like a dignitary, draped in a pure wool overcoat.

'DCI May. What have you been up to?' There was a hint of humour to his voice, undercut by the hardness of his gaze.

'You may want to change your shoes,' said Sarah, glancing at the man's expensive-looking brogues.

Two colleagues, neither introduced to Sarah, joined Partridge. They followed her like stalkers through the frozen grassland to John Prine's shallow grave. The three men stood on the periphery and confirmed the deceased's identification. None of them made a move to touch the crime scene.

'Tell me again, what led you to this discovery?' asked Partridge.

Sarah recounted the tale she'd told Partridge on the phone. She varied the order of the details so not to sound like she was rehashing a prepared script.

'You came here alone?'

'Yes.'

'Why didn't you wait for backup?'

'It was the middle of the night and it was little more than a hunch. Anna Saunders suggested this place was important to her husband but I didn't think that warranted a full-scale search. I wanted to see what the house was like myself before concluding how best to proceed.'

'And yet you went into the woods in the darkness?' Partridge's questioning remained neutral in tone. He wasn't accusing her of anything directly but she sensed the undercurrent of distrust.

'I was here. The house was derelict. I didn't want to come away empty-handed.'

'Quite. Well you certainly haven't done that, DCI May. What do you think happened?'

Sarah was surprised by the question. She wondered if Partridge was humouring her, or was genuinely interested in her opinion. 'It would appear Prine outlasted his usefulness.'

'You think Saunders did this?'

'Possibly.'

'Why would he do that?'

They both knew Saunders' chances of remaining at large would increase being alone. Saunders wouldn't have any hesitation in dispatching Prine if it benefited him, and Sarah imagined loyalty was not something he worried about. 'We can presume it benefited Saunders this way. However, take a look at his right leg.'

Partridge smiled but didn't look. 'I noticed the discolouration,' he said. 'Prine injured his leg and was put down like a lame horse.'

'Possibly.'

'OK, good. We'll change our search parameters. I have a team on the way. We'll scour the woodland for Mr Saunders with the hope he hasn't absconded beyond its scope.'

'And the body?' asked Sarah.

Partridge smiled once more, the humour not reaching his eyes. 'You leave that to us.'

Within the hour, the area was overrun with MI5 agents. Two helicopters scoured the sky, as a specialist team examined then removed the body of John Prine.

Sarah folded her arms, watching events unfold. She was largely ignored by Partridge and his team despite having found the body. She consulted a map of the local area, searching for potential escape routes.

If Saunders ran to the farmhouse due to its familiarity, where would he go next? She moved her finger along the map until she hit water. Had Saunders hid in the woodland until he had time to reach the sea? The coastguard had been put on high alert the day Saunders went missing, but resources were not unlimited and not every stretch of water could be monitored. Sarah imagined Saunders scrambling through the woods after killing Prine to a rendezvous point, escaping across the Channel to the European mainland. Interpol had been alerted, but Saunders could be thousands of miles away by now.

The clouds opened and hailstones fell from the sky like bullets. The agents took shelter, some in the building of the farmhouse, others beneath the trees. Sarah took the opportunity to retreat to her car. Once the engine was warmed up, she switched on the heating and her body began to thaw. She glanced idly at her phone, searching for a message from Michael despite knowing he wouldn't, and shouldn't, contact her.

Her time and ability was being wasted. Partridge had already arranged for Anna Saunders to be interrogated again so she couldn't even explore that avenue of investigation. She checked the map again on her phone, and searched for the closest stretch of shoreline where Saunders could conceivably reach. Then, with nothing else to do, she released the handbrake and set off.

Chapter Nineteen

Lambert considered the various connections before summoning Matilda.

'Sir?' Matilda appeared harried, the scar tissue on her face darker than usual.

'Alistair Beckinsale. His parents are alive?'

'Yes, I spoke to them myself. Elderly couple, but still have their wits about them. Beckinsale's wife is still in contact with them. Naturally, they were devastated. He was one of six children. Third to pass away.'

'The other two?' said Lambert, alert to possibility.

'A younger sister died from cancer aged thirty-two. Elder brother, took his own life aged twenty-eight.'

'Brother's name?'

'Richard.'

'How much older than Alistair was he?'

'Sixteen months, I think. I'll confirm.'

Matilda stood by the door and waited for him to respond. 'You visited the Beckinsales?'

'Yes,' said Matilda, suspicious. 'You'd slipped out for the afternoon as I recall,' she added, recalling the day Lambert visited the escape site on Holloway Road.

'Fairleigh?'

'That's right.'

'The area seem familiar to you?'

Matilda was momentarily confused. 'You mean Waverley Manor?' she asked, lowering her tone.

'Yes.'

'It's about fifteen miles away. What are you thinking, sir?'

Lambert was unable to answer the question. 'Let's pay Mr and Mrs Beckinsale another visit. You show me the way.'

–

It was the last Friday before Christmas, not the best day to be travelling anywhere.

'Could be a white Christmas,' said Matilda, weaving a slow route through the city traffic.

'Let's hope so,' said Lambert, his words laced with sarcasm. He hadn't thought about Christmas in the last few days. He'd yet to buy anything for Sophie and Jane, and was thankful his department had a Secret Santa, meaning he would only need to contribute one present purchased from the local off-licence like the majority of his colleagues.

'Not in the seasonal cheer yet?' said Matilda.

'Yet?'

In many ways he was more comfortable in the car with Matilda than he was with Sarah. The tension was absent, and although he would never assuage the guilt he felt for the horrific injuries the woman suffered under his command he was at total ease in her company. She was one of a very small number of people he trusted implicitly.

They'd called ahead but were an hour late by the time they reached the picturesque village. The drove along Fairleigh's one main street past a church, two pubs and a newsagent's. Judging by the car parks, the pubs were enjoying a fine seasonal trade. Matilda continued driving until the street was out of sight, the single lane reminiscent of Lambert's visit the night before to Norfolk.

Preparing himself for a similar isolated house, he was surprised when Matilda turned into another road with a cluster of houses scattered over a half-mile area in a random order. The houses competed with one another for the most outlandish Christmas decorations. Sparkling lights covered every inch of the brick buildings, some with illuminated statues on their front lawns. Father Christ-mases, snowmen, one house even had a sleigh and full complement of miniature reindeers.

Matilda pulled up outside the only undecorated house. 'Not the best Christmas present,' said Lambert, looking at the Beckinsale residence, drab in comparison to its sparkling neighbours.

Simon Beckinsale greeted them at the front door. In his seventies, the man towered over Lambert, a shock of silver hair on his head. 'I saw you pull in,' he said, surprising Lambert with the strength of his handshake. 'Please come in.'

Geraldine Beckinsale was waiting for them inside. She sat next to a small wood fire and looked up at them as they entered the room but didn't move.

'Please, take a seat, you've had a long journey. May I get you something to drink?' said Mr Beckinsale.

'We're fine,' said Matilda. 'How are you, Mrs Beckin-sale?'

'I'm OK,' said Mrs Beckinsale, an empty glass by her side.

'Please, take a seat,' said Mr Beckinsale.

The grief covered the room like a shroud. Geraldine Beckinsale was trying to drink the pain away, Simon Beckinsale doing his best to deny it had ever happened. Lambert had sat in such rooms on too many occasions. It was a travesty for your children to die before you, whatever your age.

'We're very sorry to come here again,' said Matilda. 'I can only imagine how difficult it is for you. We need to ask you some more questions, then I promise we will leave you to your grieving.'

Mrs Beckinsale stared at the fire as if she could see something within the dancing flames. Her husband's forehead furrowed as he glanced at his wife.

Matilda glanced at Lambert who nodded back at her. The questions would not be easy to ask or answer. 'I realize this is the last thing you'd wish to answer at the moment, but we'd like to talk about your other son, Richard.'

Lambert noticed Mr Beckinsale's neck tensing as Matilda mentioned his other son's name.

'Why would you need to know about him? He passed away years ago,' said Mr Beckinsale, his gaze flitting from Matilda to his wife and back again.

'The coroner's report was suicide,' said Matilda. Her words were soft, kind, but the comment angered the husband.

'What's your point?' he said.

'I don't mean to upset you, Mr Beckinsale. Richard was only a year or so older than Alistair, wasn't he?'

'Eighteen months,' said Mrs Beckinsale, not taking her eyes from the fire.

'Yes, Mrs Beckinsale, eighteen months. Richard left no note, did he? Did you notice a change of behaviour at the time? Did he mention any concerns to you?'

'You told us Alistair's death was suspicious, that it wasn't suicide.'

'No, we don't think it was suicide,' said Lambert.

'Then why are you asking about Richard?'

Lambert hated putting them through the ordeal, especially for what was little more than a hunch, but he needed to get to the truth. 'Did something happen to Richard? Maybe something in his childhood?'

The whole of Geraldine Beckinsale's body tensed as if she was momentarily paralysed. Mr Beckinsale turned away and silence descended over the small room, broken by the crackling of burning wood. Matilda appealed to Lambert but he shook his head, waiting for a revelation from the parents. It was Geraldine Beckinsale who finally broke the silence.

'For heaven's sake, Simon, tell them,' she said.

Water pooled in Mr Beckinsale's eyes and he placed his head in his hands. 'I don't know what to tell you,' he said, after sitting that way for two minutes.

'Just tell us what you know,' said Matilda.

'That's the thing. We don't really know. Those boys were as thick as thieves. From the day Alistair was born, Richard doted on him, and as they grew older they couldn't be separated.' Mr Beckinsale's smile at the reminiscence disappeared a second later, as if the memory had kept them alive for that brief period of time. 'And the secrets. They loved their secrets, didn't they, Geraldine?'

Mrs Beckinsale ignored her husband. She reached for her empty glass and continued to stare at the fire.

'Yes. Anyway. The secrets. Thick as thieves, I tell you. They would disappear for hours on end, in the hills. Go for their little adventures. They formed some kind of club like that book, *Swallows and Amazons*. No river, of course, but that didn't stop the adventuring.'

Mrs Beckinsale began crying and her husband was on the verge of tears. 'Anyway, that stopped.'

'What stopped?' said Lambert.

'The adventuring.' Beckinsale took in a deep breath and held it. Lambert was about to ask if he was OK when he realized it was a large sob. 'It was different times,' he said, unsure. 'We shouldn't have let them play on their own, really, but they were boys, and they wanted to go out on their own, and they had each other...' His words faded as Mrs Beckinsale began crying harder.

'What happened, Simon?' said Matilda.

'We don't know, but one night they never came back.'

'They disappeared?'

Mr Beckinsale bit his lip. 'For the night. They'd left the previous morning. They took small rucksacks with provisions and promised to return late afternoon. I'm afraid we didn't start taking notice until it got dark.'

Lambert hadn't read about such an incident on the System but that wasn't surprising given how long ago it had occurred. 'Did you tell the police?'

'We did. We searched the hills as best as we could with torches and were about to start again in the morning when they turned up.'

'What happened?'

'Richard had injured his leg. He was hobbling quite badly, being carried by Alistair. The boys apologized, they'd gone further than anticipated and decided to shelter for the night when it got too dark. We were just delighted to have them home. The police accepted their version of events and we got on with our lives.

'At first we thought their reluctance to go out was a response to the incident but then their behaviour changed. Richard's especially. He became withdrawn. His leg was fine by this point but he never left the house except for school and he stuck to Alistair like glue.

'We should have done more but we were at a loss. We asked them what was wrong, spoke to them both on an individual basis but they would clam up.' Mr Beckinsale stood and moved to his wife. He tried to touch her but she shrugged his hand away.

'Did you ever find out what happened?'

Mr Beckinsale closed his eyes. He appeared shorter than before, his body hunched as if old age had chosen that moment to attack him. 'Richard never got over it, you see. As they became older, they grew apart. They were close but not as close as before. Alistair started going out. He played football, had girlfriends. Richard stayed at home, only leaving the house for school. He refused our help and we didn't know any better. As an adult he was hospitalized for clinical depression. He never told me what happened but he said there had been some men.'

Geraldine Beckinsale whimpered at the last statement. She left her seat and retreated to the kitchen where she filled her glass with brandy, hitting back the shot in one go.

'He was having counselling and we hoped he was getting better. He appeared more responsive when we saw him, and then…'

'Did you ever speak to Alistair about this?'

'He refused to talk about it. I tried to speak to him on numerous occasions, especially when Richard was hospitalized. It was as if he'd completely blanked it out. He didn't live with it any longer, and we weren't about to make him relive it.'

'You never went to the police?' said Lambert.

'I'm ashamed we did not, Detective Lambert. I wouldn't have known what to tell them. I just know that whatever happened to the boys that day led to my little boy killing himself.'

Lambert stood and thanked Mr Beckinsale for his time, all the time wondering if the events of that day had also led to the murder of the man's other son.

Chapter Twenty

Lambert grabbed some sleep as Matilda drove back to London. Having not slept for over twenty-four hours he decided it would be prudent if she took the wheel. His eyes snapped open eighty minutes later as they reached headquarters.

Matilda appeared to have spent the time formulating questions. 'Are you going to let me know what you're thinking, sir?' she asked, as he righted himself into position.

'You'll have to tell me if I'm being obsessive.'

'Of course.'

Lambert paused, formulating the words in his mind. 'What if Lance Jenkins and Alistair Beckinsale are both former victims of the Manor? We now know something happened to Beckinsale in those woods and we have a tentative link with Jenkins' old teacher, George Forrest.'

'Tentative is putting it mildly, sir.'

'Maybe, but you can see what I'm getting at. It wouldn't even be a consideration if Saunders hadn't escaped but with that, and the Beckinsales' proximity to Waverley Manor, it's something I don't think we can rule out. First thing tomorrow, we speak to Forrest.'

Matilda dropped him back at the car park so he could collect his car. He kept his window partly down as he drove home so the cold air could keep him awake. As he entered the roundabout leading to Croydon Road, he thought he glimpsed a familiar car, an Audi estate heading up the high street. His eyes moved towards the number plate but he didn't have time to focus as the car disappeared around the corner. The car was the same colour and make as that driven by AC-10's Inspector Duggan. Was he under surveillance? At that moment, he didn't have the energy to worry. He drove the short distance to his house, cursing that all the parking spaces were taken. He parked on an adjacent road, his legs heavy as he trudged through the iced pavements towards his house.

'I remember you. Michael Lambert, isn't it?' said Sophie, repeating a familiar tease as he entered the living room.

'The one and only. What's for dinner?' he said, pushing his luck.

'Whatever you can find to make,' said Sophie, returning to the novel she was reading.

Lacking the energy to cook, he made a sandwich and returned to the living room. 'What you reading?'

Sophie frowned. 'You left last night and haven't been back since.'

'I'm sorry, it's one of those cases. Too many directions. I'm trying to rein it in, get some control, but I can't at the moment.'

'I've read the paper, Michael.'

With everything else that had occurred since last night, he'd given little thought to Mia Helmer. 'I didn't know you read that rag.'

'It's not a joke, Michael. Two murder victims, and your name at the scene. Is someone trying to set you up?'

'No, of course not,' said Lambert, trying to keep the conversation light.

'How the hell are they letting you investigate this? Surely you should be kept away, if you're implicated?'

Lambert finished his sandwich. His throat was dry, the sandwich devoid of flavour. 'I'm not implicated, Soph. My name was written on a card found at the scenes. Someone wants me involved and I'm the best person to find out who is responsible.'

Sophie's eyes widened. 'You always think you're the best person for the job.'

It was a recurring argument. Once he was involved in a case he would never let it go. It became obsessional and he ended up absorbing all the pressure and responsibility that went with it. 'I'm going up to the office,' he said, lacking the energy to argue further.

'Remember my mother is coming tomorrow for Christmas,' shouted Sophie, as he made his way upstairs.

His first action was to check the System. He was desperate to find out how Sarah May was faring in Norfolk but as expected there was no report. Next he began searching for mentions of Alistair and Richard Beckinsale during the period where they'd gone missing as children. He cross-checked that with other disappearances in the local area during the period but found nothing significant.

They already had an address for George Forrest, and Lambert spent the next few minutes checking the man's details on the System. He'd left Lance Jenkins' school eight years ago. The governing board had received a number of complaints about his conduct but hadn't dismissed him. It appeared some form of agreement had been made as

Forrest continued working as a supply teacher for three years before changing careers and retraining as an IT consultant.

Lambert's eyes began to droop and he lay on the small bed in the office, and considered if Forrest could be a member of the Manor. Every thought he'd ever had about the Manor played in his head and he feared he was reaching for answers that were not there. Forrest didn't fit the profile of the other members of the Manor. He'd been a primary school teacher and now made an average income in his new role. As for Alistair Beckinsale, it couldn't be denied something happened to him as a child but the only real connection he appeared to have to the Manor was the proximity of his family home to Waverley Manor.

As he fell asleep, Lambert juggled conflicting thoughts. First that his obsession with the Manor, and the disappearance of Peter Saunders, had distracted him from the true nature of the investigation into the deaths of Lance Jenkins and Alistair Beckinsale. And second, this was exactly what the Manor wanted him to think.

–

George Forrest worked as an IT consultant in Euston and commuted in every day from Bushey in Hertfordshire. It was Sunday and Lambert could only hope the man was at home. He didn't want to call ahead, and the journey was relatively short from headquarters. He picked up Matilda from her flat. Lambert never asked, and was never told, about Matilda's ongoing relationship with Tillman. It was best for everyone that way, but waiting for her in the car he was unable to resist searching for a sign that Glenn Tillman had stayed the night.

Matilda skipped down the steps outside her apartment building, her red hair billowing behind her. 'Sorry, sir,' she said, collapsing in the passenger seat.

Lambert ignored her characteristic dishevelled appearance and set off for Hertfordshire. Banks of snow covered the pavements as waves of sleet and freezing rain fell from the sky. There was little sign of the festive season as they traversed the grey roads and it was hard to conceive Christmas was only two days away. 'What do you have planned for Christmas?' he asked Matilda, realizing he hadn't considered time off for his team.

'You tell me, sir. My family live up north so I don't think I'll get to see them.'

She sounded resigned rather than hopeful and Lambert wondered if she planned to spend time with Tillman over the Christmas period. Unless something spectacular unfolded in the next twenty-four hours, he decided he would let the team go home early on Christmas Eve and to return on the twenty-seventh. Nothing much would be achieved in the interim and he would rather have the team rested and focused.

The sleet intensified as they reached the outskirts of Bushey, where Forrest lived in a terraced house. Lambert was surprised by the green and open space surrounding Forrest's home.

'The IT business obviously pays better than teaching,' he said, as Matilda opened the wrought-iron gate leading to Forrest's front door. Lambert peered through the front windows as Matilda knocked on the door. The living room was sparse and well presented. A minimalist

Christmas tree stood in one corner, decorated in alternative lines of purple and silver tinsel. A maroon chesterfield sofa faced a fifty-inch television hanging from the uncovered brickwork of the wall.

'Sir,' said Matilda.

Lambert turned back and saw a man moving towards the gate. Dressed in running gear, he was wearing earphones and had yet to notice them. The figure matched the photo in Forrest's file. Six feet one, grey hair now accompanied by a matching beard, Forrest stooped as he opened the gate, pulling his earphones off as he caught Lambert's eye.

Forrest tensed, his back straightening as he glanced from Lambert to Matilda and back again. 'Mr George Forrest?' said Lambert.

Forrest glanced at them both again, assessing the threat, before closing the iron gate and running away.

Chapter Twenty-One

Matilda acted first, Lambert impressed with her agility as she used her arms to spring over the gate. She called Forrest's name as she ran after him across the road to the local park, informing him she was from the police.

Following Matilda, Lambert scanned the park, searching for an exit, and glanced back to see a German shepherd had appeared and was joining in the chase. Lambert laughed at the absurdity as the dog ran between Lambert and Forrest, trotting next to Matilda at times, as if he was running in a pack. A teenage boy shouted frantically at the dog, who bounced from one runner to the next, tail wagging at the game.

The dog affected Forrest more than Matilda. He stumbled as the dog caught up with him again, losing his stride until Matilda was on him. Then Forrest stopped running and bent over, leaning on his knees as he caught the breath duly knocked out of him by Matilda who had charged into him.

Lambert caught up and watched as Matilda cuffed the man. 'I would have kept up but I'm wearing these,' he said to Matilda, pointing at his shoes, as the dog danced around them barking.

'Yeah, yeah,' said Matilda, dragging Forrest to his feet.

'DCI Lambert. This is my colleague, DS Kennedy. You are George Forrest, I presume?'

Forrest was still out of breath. Patches of red stained the pale skin of his cheeks and neck. 'What is this?' he muttered, not meeting either officer's gaze.

'Why don't you tell us, Mr Forrest?'

'Am I under arrest? You haven't read me my rights.'

The teenager appeared carrying the dog's leash. 'Sorry,' he said, grabbing the dog by its collar and clicking the leash into place, while trying not to look at the cuffs holding Forrest in place.

'Police, get going. Now where were we?' said Lambert, as the boy led the dog away. 'Oh yes, your rights. It's up to you, Mr Forrest. We can either go to your house and discuss why you decided to run from two police officers, or we can take you in and charge you. What would you rather?'

'Can I see your ID?' asked Forrest, his voice faltering.

'You think we're lying?' said Lambert.

'No. It's just...' Forrest stammered, and shrugged his shoulders.

Lambert took out his warrant card and held it in front of Forrest. 'OK?'

'Thank you.'

They escorted him across the park in cuffs to his house. 'Keys?' asked Matilda, as they reached the front door.

'Right-hand jacket pocket.'

Lambert retrieved the keys and opened the door, dragging Forrest through to the living room with the Christmas tree. 'Sit,' he said, pushing Forrest onto the Chesterfield sofa.

'These are hurting,' said Forrest, looking at the cuffs.

'When I'm convinced you won't run again, I may take them off. Now tell me, why the hell did you run like that?'

'I wasn't sure who you were.'

'Who were you expecting?'

Forrest looked sheepish. He failed to meet Lambert's gaze, his eyes turned towards the ground. 'No one,' he murmured. Lambert edged nearer as Matilda began searching the house. The fear and confusion was evident in Forrest. Sweat dripped down his blotchy skin, catching in his beard.

'You used to be a teacher, didn't you?' said Lambert. He'd crouched down on his haunches so he was close to eye level with the man.

'Yes, I used to,' said Forrest still staring at his shoes.

'Look at me, George,' said Lambert reaching towards Forrest and thrusting his chin upwards. 'You were at St Mary's, is that correct?'

Forrest tried to nod, his head held in place by Lambert's firm grip.

'It didn't end well for you there, did it?' Lambert let go of the man and sat in the single armchair opposite. 'Why did you leave St Mary's, George?'

Forrest's head began to fall again. 'Look at me,' insisted Lambert, raising his voice. 'Why did you leave St Mary's?'

'I left my job, nothing more than that. Now, will you release these cuffs? They're digging into my skin.'

Lambert ignored the protests. 'You were asked to leave, George, we both know that, let's not waste each other's time.'

Forrest's face fell into a dismissive snarl. 'It was a misunderstanding... Parents are like that nowadays, you run the risk every day you go to school.'

'But there were complaints. Inappropriate behaviour.'

'I wasn't inappropriate,' said Forrest.

'But you were asked to leave?'

'It was thought best, but I didn't lose my teacher status,' he said proudly. 'I did a bit of temping before moving into IT and there was no problem whatsoever.'

'You learn from your mistakes, George, is that you're telling me?'

'No, not at all. As I said the complaints at St Mary's were not upheld and there was a good reason for that. I didn't do anything wrong.'

Lambert had heard the same phrase from too many suspects in the past to take it seriously from the man in front of him.

'Why did you run, then?'

Forrest tried to shrug, his movement restricted by the handcuffs. 'I didn't know who you were...' he repeated. 'You were looking in my front window. I thought you might be burglars.'

'It's broad daylight, George. My colleague was knocking on your door, there were people walking along the street, there's no way you thought we were burglars. You were spooked by something. Either you knew we were police or you were fearful of something else.'

Forrest turned his gaze to his feet as Matilda appeared by the living room door. She beckoned Lambert over, a newspaper in her hand. She'd opened it to a report about Lance Jenkins. The paper was not Mia Helmer's and there was no mention of Lambert.

Lambert threw the newspaper at Forrest. 'You knew Lance Jenkins, George, didn't you?'

Forrest closed his eyes as if doing so could rescue him from the situation. Lambert was getting fed up with his lack of response and grabbed the man by his tracksuit top, shoving him back into the sofa. Forrest grimaced and complained again about the handcuffs. 'Did you used to teach Lance Jenkins?' asked Lambert, inches from Forrest's face.

'Yes, so what? He was a pupil and I'd read about him in the paper, that's why I kept it. I was sorry to hear about what happened to him.'

Lambert kept his pressure on the man's chest. 'You were sorry to hear he'd been brutally murdered?'

Forrest turned his face away, trying to distance himself from Lambert.

'What are you into, George? What will we find in this house if we search through it?'

'Let me go...' pleaded Forrest, shrinking into the leather of the sofa.

Lambert pushed him back and released his grip. 'Who are you expecting, George?' he repeated.

'No one, I told you,' said Forrest, sounding uncertain.

Lambert left the man on the sofa and went into the hallway with Matilda.

'Shall we take him in?' she whispered.

Lambert shook his head. He wasn't finished with Forrest yet. He'd learnt from Tillman that sometimes lines had to be crossed. He would never go as far as his boss but sometimes procedure was too restrictive. Whether the Manor were involved or not, Lambert had two deaths connected to him and if he didn't get a handle on things soon another would follow.

Forrest rocked on the sofa, every few seconds grimacing as if remembering where he was. Lambert gave him a couple more minutes before walking behind the sofa. He grabbed Forrest's handcuffs, tightening them so they pinched the man's skin, the metal rubbing against the bone of his wrists.

'This can go two ways, George,' he whispered in the man's ear. 'Personally, I don't think this has anything to do with you. You're caught up in something beyond your control. We don't have to make it official, we can even offer protection if you think that's what you need. But let me tell you this, George, if we bring you in, which is the second option, we will not rest until we discover everything about you. This house will be stripped and searched to the smallest detail. We will check your computer, your social media records, we will speak to your employers, we will find what we are looking for. But it doesn't have to go that way. You tell me why you are running, who you are scared of, and that never needs to happen.'

Lambert exerted more pressure on the man's wrists. He fought the guilt, convinced Forrest was hiding something. Matilda watched on. He couldn't tell if she disapproved but she'd yet to object so he turned up the pressure, forcing a yelp of discomfort from Forrest.

'I don't know who they are,' said Forrest between sobs. 'I hadn't heard from them in years and I thought they'd forgotten about me.'

Lambert released the man and moved to the other side of the sofa so he could face him. 'Tell me, George,' he insisted.

'When I saw what had happened to Lance, I thought they might be coming for me next. That's why I ran.'

'Who are "they", George?'

Forrest looked up in him with a hint of defiance. 'This isn't on the record?'

Lambert shook his head.

'I didn't do anything wrong.'

'Just tell us, George.'

Forrest was still crying. 'I used to be into things I shouldn't have. I used to go to some groups and met with like-minded individuals.'

Lambert closed his eyes, nauseous at the thoughts Forrest's words conjured in his mind.

'I'm not going to incriminate myself,' said Forrest.

'Just go on,' said Lambert.

'I got friendly with a couple of guys. They were nice at first but then...'

'Then?'

'They began to threaten me.'

'Threaten you how?'

'Physically, mainly. They were big guys and I'm not into the violent stuff. They told me I'd be safe if I helped them.'

A wave of adrenaline hit Lambert, his hands shaking. 'Help them with what, George?'

'They were threatening me,' insisted Forrest. 'You don't know what it's like, I feared for my life.'

'What did they ask you to do?' said Lambert.

'They were looking for recommendations.'

Lambert glanced at Matilda who appeared poised to attack.

'To be clear, this was when you were teaching at the school?'

'Yes.'

'What sort of recommendations, George?'

Tears flowed from the man now, giving him the countenance of a puffy-skinned child. 'St Mary's was a poor school in a deprived area. They wanted to know about the children in my class, the boys especially.'

A wave of rage came close to consuming Lambert at these words. He gripped the leather armchair, when all he wanted to do was rain blows down on the man sitting opposite him.

'What did they want, specifically?'

Forrest looked up at him and what Lambert saw in his face went beyond defiance, it was as if the man had resigned himself to his fate and was at last showing his true colours.

'They wanted to know which boys wouldn't be missed.'

'And you helped them?' said Lambert, under his breath.

'I told them all about Lance Jenkins,' said Forrest, with a smile.

Lambert stood and smashed his elbow into the side of the man's head. He was about to strike him again when Matilda grabbed his arm.

'I won't repeat any of this,' said Forrest, blood drooling from his mouth.

'You won't have to, you sick fuck,' said Matilda, showing him her phone. 'I taped the whole thing.'

Chapter Twenty-Two

Sarah May stopped the young waiter and asked for another coffee. Barely a teenager, his trousers appeared as if they were painted onto his thin legs; they only reached his lower shins, below which he didn't appear to be wearing socks. I must be getting old, she thought to herself, considering how ludicrous she thought the boy appeared. He returned a few minutes later and placed a piping hot Americano onto the table in front of her. He smiled, a line of acne spots appearing on his brow.

She let the coffee cool, and returned her gaze to outside the window. She was in St Albans, her eyes fixed on the restaurant opposite and more specifically to the man within.

After leaving the John Prine murder site, she'd spent a fruitless day searching the ports of Norfolk. She interviewed the local residents but due to the season and treacherous weather there'd been very little boating activity. She'd tried to check in with Partridge, who'd ignored her calls, so she'd returned to headquarters.

Her team allocation had dwindled to just her and Adams, everything else being taken over by MI5. Together they'd worked through everything, even Adams coming to the realization they'd been marginalized. In the end she'd told him to work on something else while she worked through the few leads left to her.

She checked through the files of DS Wright, the officer killed at Holloway Road, and read the brief reports offered by Partridge's team. From Woolwich prison, she drove the route taken by the team via Holloway Road. It wasn't a logical route, but that was beside the point. The route was purposely random, chosen to avoid predictability. Whatever way she looked at it, she always reached the same conclusion. Someone had tipped off those responsible for attacking the van.

This was the reason for her sitting in the café now, staring out at the occupant of the restaurant. The list of people who knew of the transfer was limited and centred mainly on the staff of the two prisons, Woolwich and Luton. AC-10 were investigating the armed response unit who'd assigned DS Wright, so that left her with the prison staff and specifically the two governors, Guthrie and Pierson.

Pierson was the less experienced of the two. He'd only been at Luton for five years as opposed to the decade plus Guthrie had been at Woolwich. Furthermore, his defensive behaviour when they'd met had raised her suspicions, and when she looked further into his files her concerns increased.

It was probably a coincidence – there were only a limited number of prisons containing category A prisoners in the UK – but all eight of the men prosecuted for the events at Waverley Manor had done time at Pierson's prison, including Peter Saunders, who had originally been incarcerated there, and Jonathan Barnes.

The revelation intensified her interest in Pierson. She'd been following him for the last forty-eight hours and he was now in the restaurant opposite. He was dining with the third different woman Sarah had seen him with in that short period of time. The first of the three, a blonde woman in her twenties, had spent last night in his apartment, and a second had visited him in his home an hour after the first woman left. Now Pierson was on a third date. It made Sarah exhausted just thinking about it.

Not that his dating rituals meant much. Other than discovering Pierson was something of a player, her surveillance hadn't revealed anything of relevance. She watched him now, deep in conversation with Girlfriend Three, a pretty brunette lady in her late forties, and wondered if she was wasting her time. She finished her now lukewarm coffee, and was about to leave when Girlfriend Three got to her feet.

The move was dramatic and Pierson froze. Knife and fork in hand, he sat as if in shock, a shock intensifying as the woman poured a drink over his head.

Sarah placed some money on the table, grabbed her coat and left the coffee shop in time to see Girlfriend Three run from the restaurant. She was obviously in some distress, the make-up on her face smudged from crying. Sarah pretended to tie her shoe as Pierson followed her outside.

'Don't do this,' said Pierson, as if addressing a child.

The woman rounded on him, tears replaced by a fierce look, and she ran at Pierson, fists held out in front of her. Pierson was taken aback. He tried to fend off the attack but the woman was persistent. She followed him as he retreated, raining more blows on him as the tears began to flow.

Sarah trailed after them, trying to hear the exact words of their heated conversation. From what she could tell, it sounded like the woman had discovered the existence of Girlfriends One and Two. The woman told Pierson in no uncertain terms what he could do with his explanations and walked away.

Sarah followed her to a car park behind the shops where she watched her climb aboard a dirt-covered, thirty-year-old Land Rover. She took a note of the number plate and was about to instruct Adams to check it when her phone rang.

It was Partridge. She looked at his name on her screen for four rings before deciding to answer.

'May.'

'Ah, good, DCI May. I need to see you immediately. How long until you can reach NCA headquarters?'

Sarah glanced at her watch. 'Probably within two hours,' she said.

'Try and make it nearer to one,' said Partridge, hanging up.

–

She didn't get as far as her office. Partridge greeted her at the entrance to the NCA headquarters. He was sheltering beneath an umbrella, a smug smile on his face as if he could somehow control the weather.

'Please follow me, DCI May,' he said, walking towards the car park without waiting for a response.

167

He held the back door of the car open for her and she held his gaze for a second before climbing into the back seat.

Partridge shook off his umbrella and joined her, smoothing his suit down. 'That's better,' he said, smiling at her like she was a simpleton. 'Long time no see, DCI May.'

Whose fault was that? She'd left numerous messages for him since they'd last met, all unreturned. She knew what was about to happen and was determined not to react or make it easy for the man.

Partridge jutted out his beak-like chin, annoyed she hadn't responded. 'You have an update for me, perhaps?'

'As you know, my team has been reduced to DS Adams and me. We've been working on the escape angle itself, assessing those who knew Saunders was being moved.'

'Quite so. And where were you today when I called?'

Something about the way he asked her told Sarah he already knew. 'I've been following Stuart Pierson for the last forty-eight hours,' she said.

'Any particular reason for doing so?'

She explained that the eight convicted members of Waverley Manor all spent some time at Pierson's prison.

'Still, strange decision to spend all your time on him.' Partridge tilted his head, his eyebrows raised. The look was condescending and it took all of Sarah's strength not to say something.

'We've spoken to Governor Guthrie and the guards at both prisons. I've been denied access to the family of DS Colin Wright, as you well know. I had to justify my time somehow.'

'Yes, very good,' said Partridge. 'Thing is, we've had teams on Guthrie and Pierson all this time.'

Sarah glanced at Partridge's driver who sat motionless, staring forward. 'Then why the fuck didn't you tell me?' she said, growling at the MI5 agent.

'Yes, quite. I agree there has been some poor communication between our teams. I'm afraid in my experience this often happens. We all want the same thing, naturally, but sometimes we can end up working against one another.' He lifted his hands up and pulled them apart to demonstrate his thinking.

'Why don't you get to the point?' said Sarah.

'Very good. It is with regret I have to inform you that you and your department are no longer part of the investigation into the escape of Peter Saunders.' He stared at her, wide eyed, as if she hadn't heard.

It was expected but grated. 'This is absolutely ridiculous. I've been working non-stop on this with absolutely no cooperation from your team and now you're taking me off the investigation? May I remind you I found John Prine. Where would we be without that lead?'

Partridge pursed his lips and nodded like she was a child he was trying to understand. 'We appreciate everything you've done, DCI May, and I will be passing on my thankful comments to your superiors. However, the case is receiving a lot of attention and it has been decided that it would be simpler, and more effective, if we contained it.'

More effective, thought Sarah. 'Why did you have us on board in the first place?'

Partridge's lips formed into a smile which instantly faded. 'Well, exactly. Thank you for your help, DCI May.

I'm sure I don't need to remind you not to interfere from here on in. Consequences for you could be severe.'

Sarah left the car, shutting the door with controlled aggression. Not only had she been taken off the case, she'd been threatened as a parting shot. Holding her phone, she considered calling the Chief Constable, but what good would that do? She would come across as a whining child, which helped nobody. The Chief would have been part of the decision process. It would have been easier to accept the dismissal had it come from him rather than MI5 directly, but it was done now. The hardest part was the joy she'd seen in Partridge's face as he dismissed her. She'd never really been a part of the investigation in the first place, hadn't received any credit for finding the body of John Prine, and had been kept at arm's length all along, yet the man had taken a perverse joy in letting her go.

She called DS Adams to tell him the bad news before returning home and packing. It was nearly Christmas, time she took some annual leave.

Chapter Twenty-Three

They drove Forrest back for questioning. He began complaining that they'd promised he wouldn't be implicated, but a single glare from Lambert was enough to silence him.

'What were the names of these men who asked you to recruit boys for them?' asked Lambert as he drove, the very question filling him with rage.

'I'm not saying anything further without a solicitor,' said Forrest.

Lambert breathed in through his nose. 'You understand two people are dead?'

Forrest didn't answer.

'These men, did they belong to some sort of organization?'

Lambert studied Forrest's reaction in his rear-view mirror, caught the twitch in his right eye.

'I don't know what you're talking about.'

'You said you read about Lance Jenkins?'

'Yes.'

'Then you would have read about me? You know what happened at Waverley Manor, the arrests I made?'

'I guess so.'

'So you know the men who were prosecuted belonged to a group called the Manor.'

'A so-called group,' said Forrest.

Lambert's foot pressed harder on the accelerator. 'They exist, George. And I think you know that. The two men who coerced you, did they belong to the Manor?'

'How would I know that?'

Lambert increased his speed, Matilda giving him a nervous glance as he hit sixty. 'You feel safe, George?'

'Not really, no.'

'Not from me, you cretin. From them. They've killed Lance Jenkins. You introduced him to them.'

'I never said that.'

'There are some things you don't know about this case, George. But let's just suppose the Manor are involved. That they killed Lance for whatever demented reason. Wouldn't that make you scared? It would scare the hell out of me.'

Forrest considered the question. 'I don't know if they were from the Manor.'

'But you'd heard of the name at the time – what was this? – nine years ago?'

'I'd heard the name but it was just hearsay, an urban legend.'

'An urban legend,' repeated Lambert, shaking his head. 'When was the last time you spoke to them?'

'Not since I left the school.'

'Bullshit.'

'I swear. Look, I've tried my best to get out of this. I don't like the way I am. I didn't want to help them in the first place, but I had no option.'

Lambert overtook a car, the driver blaring his horn as Lambert sped by. He was doing 70 mph now, the single

172

road rushing towards them, his driving fuelled by his rage. Matilda rested her hand on his arm.

'You always had a fucking choice,' he said, easing his foot off the accelerator.

–

Chief Superintendent Glenn Tillman's feet were on Lambert's desk. He was leaning back on Lambert's chair, hands behind his head. 'You've been busy,' said Tillman.

Lambert switched on the light in the room. 'We've been exploring all angles.'

'Sit,' said Tillman, taking his legs off the desk, the almost permanent look of hostile agitation on his face. 'Would you like to tell me what some IT consultant from Bushey has to do with this current investigation?'

'George Forrest used to teach Lance Jenkins,' said Lambert.

Tillman looked incredulous, holding his hands out in front of him as if he wanted to strangle Lambert.

'So do you think he's a credible suspect? Did he murder Lance Jenkins and Alistair Beckinsale?'

'No, but that's not the point.'

'Would you kindly like to tell me what the point is, then?'

'Well, for one, Forrest is guilty of something that much is evident. The local CID are trawling his house now and I am sure they'll find something.'

Tillman frowned. 'That has nothing to do with us. Our job is to find the person who killed Jenkins and Beckinsale, who left your name at the crime scene, lest we forget.'

'Somebody recruited Forrest,' said Lambert.

'Recruited?'

'I have it on tape. Maybe it would be easier just to listen to that.'

'Just give me the bullet points,' said Tillman, adjusting the knot of his tie.

Lambert explained about the men who'd recruited Forrest when he'd been a teacher to find young children.

Tillman turned away. 'And in your head you linked this to the Manor?' he said.

'Why the hell not? He's admitted as much, just not in so many words,' said Lambert, raising his voice.

'People are starting to talk, Lambert.'

'Since when did that bother you, Glenn?'

'It bothers me when they're threatening to take the case from us. You do realize how this affects you? Your name being at the crime scene? And then you're making random, seemingly unrelated arrests.'

It wasn't always easy to please his boss, yet Lambert was disappointed with his response. 'Let's just go over the facts for a second, Glenn. From our discussions with Alistair Beckinsale's parents and now Lance Jenkins' ex-teacher, it's conceivable both Jenkins and Beckinsale were previously victims of some form of abuse. If that's true, and considering Peter Saunders has just absconded from prison, I believe it's a fair jump to at least entertain the idea the Manor are somehow involved.'

Tillman surprised him with his angry response. He pushed himself from the desk, spittle flying from his mouth as he spoke. 'You need to change your approach, Lambert,' he bellowed.

Lambert studied his superior officer. He was used to these mini outbursts but was confused as to why Tillman would react this way. To Lambert it was the logical conclusion that the Manor were potentially involved. 'What is happening with the Peter Saunders' investigation, Glenn? Is there something you're not telling me?'

'They found the body of John Prine, Saunders' prison guard, in a shallow grave in Norfolk. Though I'm sure you already know that. I'll pass on this information to them but you're not to get involved. MI5 have a bee in their bonnet about this. You've worked with them before, Lambert, you know what they're capable of. It's not like pissing off me or the Assistant Chief. You piss these guys off and you'll find yourself in prison or worse.'

'Surely we're after the same thing,' said Lambert, though he doubted his own words. Lambert wanted to catch the criminals, those responsible for the deaths of Beckinsale and Jenkins, those who ran or worked for the Manor. He got the impression the security services had different priorities, including hiding the fact Saunders ever escaped in the first place.

'We need some answers soon,' said Tillman, moving to the door. 'If Forrest is not responsible forget about him. Find out who killed Beckinsale and Jenkins before it's too late.' He stormed out, as adept at making an exit as he was making an entrance.

Lambert switched on his laptop and made a last-minute attempt at ordering Christmas presents. His choice was limited if he wanted deliveries before Christmas day. He considered getting vouchers for Sophie but she would be upset if she didn't have something to open. He remembered a jewellery brochure she'd left in the house. In retrospect it was a significant hint. He snapped the laptop shut and headed home, hoping he could find the brochure and that the shop would still be open.

His phone rang as he left the office building, the number withheld. He accepted the call, a voice announcing, 'It's me.'

Lambert got into his car. 'Sarah, how are you?'

'Not so great actually. I've been taken off the Saunders' case.'

'How come?'

'MI5 have taken over completely. They felt the attention the case was attracting meant they should handle it themselves. I sensed it coming. After you left the farmhouse I was grilled about John Prine. I'm not sure Partridge fully accepted my answers about me being alone. He as good as told me to leave the site. I've spent the last day working the two prisons. I'm finding it very difficult to trust any of them at the moment.'

She told him about the two Governors, and Pierson's public fallout with Girlfriend Three, Lambert laughing at her description.

'Partridge told me they already had Pierson under surveillance, which is ludicrous. I don't trust Partridge, or any of them, but what else can I do? My only recourse is to go to the Chief Constable and I think that would be unwise,' said Sarah.

It was a difficult situation. MI5 were prone to closing ranks, and Lambert understood Sarah's reluctance to take things higher. 'Where are you now?'

'I've washed my hands of it. I'm heading back home for Christmas. Let Partridge and his team take care of it if that's what they want. They're obviously trying to keep this quiet and I'm a threat to that.'

'You think Pierson and Guthrie have been told to keep quiet too?'

'It would be in their best interests. Partridge basically threatened to take my badge if I continued.'

'Frustrating,' said Lambert, but it was more than that. He'd been convinced the Saunders' case and his own were linked from the beginning and this increased his suspicions. 'Look, if I have to I'll call you on your usual number.'

'OK.'

'And Sarah?'

'Yes.'

'Happy Christmas.'

Chapter Twenty-Four

Michael wished her a happy Christmas, and Sarah chided herself for feeling cheated by the words. He'd paused before speaking and for a second she'd been convinced he was going to suggest they meet up. And despite her better judgement, she would have accepted the invitation. It was good to finally admit to herself she'd felt his absence over the last year. Although things hadn't run smoothly during the last couple of months of their relationship, she'd been able to depend on him. The baby changed everything and that was unavoidable. Her best course of action at the time had been to forget about him, and although she may have missed him she'd done a pretty good job of not having him in her life. Why, then, only days after seeing him again, was she feeling like this?

She walked to the buffet carriage of the train and ordered a red wine. She hadn't taken leave for over ten months, and this enforced break couldn't have come at a better time. She could put the stress of work, and thoughts of Michael Lambert, behind her. Back in her seat she raised her plastic beaker of wine and toasted her resolution. She glanced at her phone and considered calling him back.

Instead, with a smirk, she placed the phone in her bag and took a deep drink.

She caught a taxi from Bristol Temple Meads train station. A sense of nostalgia came over her as the car drove through old haunts where she'd worked as a detective, despite having only visited the city a few months ago. It was a reaction to the disappointment of the Saunders' case, and a general disillusionment with working for the NCA. She'd been part of something when she'd worked for the serious crimes' squad here. In London, she was just another ambitious officer looking to make her mark.

Her parents greeted her like they hadn't seen her in years. She hugged them both as they fussed over her, her father taking her case, her mother offering tea and food. They'd retired to Bristol, in part to be closer to her. Each time she returned to their house she experienced a stab of guilt, as if somehow she'd abandoned them.

'You back for long?' asked her father as they sat down for dinner.

'A few days,' said Sarah.

'We'll have to get to the shops tomorrow and get you something for Christmas,' said her father, teasing.

'Oh, stop it, Jeff,' said her mother.

'Look, don't let me stop you, Dad. If you want to buy me some extra presents, be my guest.'

'Not having the best of times at the moment?' asked her mother, not bothering with any preamble.

'Just finished a tough case.'

'And you don't want to talk about it, do you, Sarah,' said her father, filling her glass with wine.

'Thanks, Dad,' she said, receiving a frown from her mother, who clearly wanted to hear more.

The food made her drowsy and she thanked her parents and headed upstairs to the spare room. The contentment she'd experienced at dinner soon evaporated. She tried to sleep but was restless, unable to relax in the change of environment. Try as she might, her mind kept returning to the case. She pictured DS Wright, the gun wounds which had taken his life on the Holloway Road, and John Prine, lying in the shallow grave in Norfolk. She thought about Anna Saunders and her reluctance to see her husband in prison, the prison Governors Guthrie and Pierson, and the bizarre incident of the multiple girlfriends. Charles Partridge's smug face appeared in her memory, raising her blood pressure. She tried to accept being sidelined. In her many cases as SIO she'd had to reassign personnel and made many unpopular decisions, so why did this feel so unfair?

She glanced at her phone. She wanted to call Michael for numerous reasons – to hear his voice and get the latest details on his case and Saunders. She'd only been in Bristol for a matter of hours, and already her early nostalgia for the place was fading.

Switching on her laptop, she loaded her case notes. It was Christmas Eve tomorrow but she couldn't think about stopping. Despite having told Adams he was off the case, she sent an email to the DS, instructing him to check the plate of the rusted Land Rover belonging to Pierson's Girlfriend Number Three. Partridge didn't use the same System as her so she was unable to gather any updates about the Saunders' case.

It was the secrecy she hated. She slammed her laptop shut and returned to bed, sometime later falling into an uneasy sleep.

Lambert's mother-in-law greeted him at home when he arrived back an hour later. 'Nice of you to join us,' she said, blocking his path as if he was a salesman pitching for business. She didn't seem prepared to allow him entrance to the house.

'Happy Christmas, Glenda. Do you mind if I come in? It's freezing out here.'

Glenda didn't move. She kept her arm against the door frame staring at Lambert like he was a mirage.

'Don't blow this,' she said.

'I haven't got time for this now, Glenda.'

'Michael, this is important. This is your last chance with Sophie, you must realize that.' She looked behind her to check her daughter wasn't listening. 'She tells me you've been working late all week, that your work patterns have been returning to how they were before.'

'I'm working on a very big case, Glenda, what do you expect me to do?'

'So I've read. You still need to make time for your wife.'

Lambert's head hung low. 'I'm doing the best I can. I take Jane to the childminder when I can,' he said, realizing how feeble the statement was.

'She needs more, Michael. I can tell you're falling back into the same old patterns and look where that got you.'

'May I come in now?' he said, more sternly than before.

Glenda stepped aside. 'Just think on it, Michael,' she said, as he walked past.

Lambert didn't respond, pleased to see Jane was still up.

'Daddy,' she screamed, as he entered the kitchen. She was sitting at the kitchen table eating. Lambert spun her around, to squeals of delight.

'Put her down, Michael, you'll make her sick,' said Sophie.

'Will you be sick?' Lambert asked Jane.

'Maybe,' said Jane, laughing.

'I better put you down, then.' He placed her back on the chair and stole one of the boiled potatoes from her plate.

'Daddy,' she said, with a warning tone.

'Remember, you're making the grown-ups' dinner tonight, Michael,' said Sophie. She pointed to a plate of steaks on the kitchen side table. Lambert usually cooked on Christmas Eve and was about to protest about having to do so a day earlier when Glenda walked into the room, her glass brimming with gin.

'Okey-dokey,' he said. 'How do you take yours Glenda – raw?'

'Your husband is a wit, Sophie. Medium rare please.'

'How do you take yours, Jane?'

'Daddy, I've already eaten,' said Jane, stuffing her face with the remains of her dinner.

–

While Sophie and her mother bathed and put Jane to bed, Lambert alternated between cooking dinner and scanning the house for the jewellery brochure. He managed to find it seconds before Glenda returned downstairs, shoving it into the back of his trousers as he threw the first of the steaks onto the griddle.

'I'm sorry if I came on too forceful earlier,' said Glenda, joining him by the cooker. 'Believe it or not I want the best for you – not just for Jane and Sophie.'

'It was raw you said,' said Lambert, putting the second of the steaks on.

'Very funny,' said Glenda, smiling. 'I know you do your best for them and you always have, but sometimes there have to be compromises.'

While he appreciated the sentiment, she only knew a fraction of what his job entailed. The things he'd gone through and the things he'd seen. 'We are working on it, Glenda, and I promise I'll do my best to make it work this time.'

'That's all I ask,' said Glenda, placing a hand on his shoulder. 'Now, for heaven's sake, don't burn my steak.'

The meal went well, Lambert opening the bottle of red wine left on his office desk from Tillman. 'Why don't you two go relax in the living room?' he said, when the meal was finished. 'I'll put these away.'

Sophie looked at her mother and shrugged her shoulders. She placed her hand on Lambert's forehead. 'Are you feeling OK, honey?'

'Go before I change my mind.'

Lambert switched on the digital radio and filled the dishwasher, helping himself to the dregs of the wine bottle. He'd forgotten the tranquillity of occasional bouts of domesticity. Filling the dishwasher, scrubbing the pans and cleaning the work surfaces while indie pop blared from the speakers helped take his mind off the case. Every time his mind wandered back to George Forrest or the Manor he banished the thought by finding another job to do until the kitchen was spotless.

Sophie and her mother were watching television in the living room: a mindless Christmas quiz special. The room smelt of tinsel and pine from the Christmas tree. Michael poured some more drinks and slumped down next to Sophie. 'I could get used to this,' he said, sipping the small measure of brandy he had poured himself. He wasn't used to such normality, and surprised himself further by laughing at the lame jokes on the television. 'I must have had too much to drink if I find this funny,' he said.

Glenda retired not long after and Lambert's eyelids began to droop. 'Carry me to bed,' he said to Sophie.

'Let's carry each other,'

Tillman called as he began climbing the stairs, hand in hand with his wife. It lacked professionalism not to answer but he couldn't bring himself to accept the man's call. He placed the phone back in his pocket, convinced Tillman would call back if it was important.

The alcohol made him drowsy and he was asleep within seconds of Sophie switching the bedroom light out. His sleep was uneasy, filled with images of Waverley Manor and running German shepherd dogs. When Sophie grabbed hold of his arm seemingly minutes later, Lambert swiped it away.

'Michael,' she said, ignoring his protests.

He turned towards her, his eyes adjusting to the darkness. 'What is it?' he said.

'Can't you hear, Michael? Someone is knocking at the door.'

Lambert shook his head, getting his bearings. The sound, a solid thud against the wood panelling of his front door reverberating through the house. He jumped out of bed and grabbed his dressing gown and looked out of the window.

Parked in the middle of the road, stopping traffic in both directions, were four police cars, blue lights flashing in the darkness.

Chapter Twenty-Five

Lambert opened the window and peered out, searching for a familiar face amongst the silhouetted figures gathered outside his front door. He recognized one of their number and turned to look at him. He knew Chief Superintendent Tanner from his dealings with anti-corruption; a short stout man, reminiscent of Tillman save for the complete lack of hair on his scalp, Tanner headed up AC-10.

'Lambert, will you get down here?' he shouted up. 'It's frickin' freezing.'

'It's the middle of the goddam night,' said Lambert.

'Now, DCI Lambert, or we'll be coming in.'

'Give me five minutes to get changed,'

Tanner offered him a short nod. Lambert had no idea what Tanner wanted but as they'd arrived in such numbers it was likely they were going to take him in and he was loath to appear at any police station wearing only his dressing gown.

'What is it?' asked Sophie, as he changed.

'A misunderstanding. A bloody inconvenient one, but a misunderstanding nonetheless. I imagine it is something to do with the case. I'm going to have to go in for a bit.'

'Why? Do they think you've done something wrong?'

'It's anti-corruption so I assume so. Don't worry, they have nothing on me.'

'Do you want me to call someone? Glenn? Or a solicitor? I can get one of my team down there straight away.'

'It's fine. I'll get one of the union reps if needs be, but this is going to blow over. It's that idiot, Tanner. He loves making a show.'

Glenda stood on the landing wrapped in a dressing gown. 'Is everything all right?' she whispered, as Lambert and Sophie left the room.

'Go back to sleep, Mum, it's fine. Michael has just been called into work.'

'And you must think I was born yesterday,' said Glenda. 'I've seen the flashing lights and I heard what they said about breaking in if he didn't go downstairs.'

'This doesn't concern you, Glenda,' said Lambert.

Downstairs, he kissed Sophie goodbye and told her not to worry before opening the front door.

Tanner was about to speak but Lambert interrupted him 'May I shut the door first, sir?'

'By all means,' said Tanner, who was flanked by two AC officers Lambert recognized but whose names he couldn't recall. He noticed the tension in their bodies, ready to confront Lambert should he choose to run. 'You're going to have to come with us, son,' said Tanner.

Lambert glanced at the three men blocking his way. 'Are you going to tell me what this is about?'

Tanner's front teeth jutted out over his lower lip. 'Let's discuss this back at the station, shall we, or do I need to cuff you?'

Lambert considered pressing his point. He wasn't under arrest, but something had happened to make them come out in such force and he had little option but to do as instructed. He glanced at the officers, puzzled by the open hostility shown towards him. 'Why would I run?' he said.

'Fantastic,' said Tanner. 'You won't mind if these two officers escort you to the back of my car, then?'

One of the officers attempted to place his hand on Lambert's shoulder. Lambert stopped and glared at the man. The officer looked at Tanner who shook his head. Taking his time, Lambert climbed into the back of the car. The two officers sat either side of him on the back seat. 'Buckle up,' said Tanner with a grin, sitting behind the wheel.

'You going to tell me what this about now?' said Lambert, as Tanner started the car.

'Why spoil the surprise? Sit back and enjoy the view, DCI Lambert. We'll be there before you know it.'

Lambert's limbs were heavy. He'd only been asleep for ninety minutes and the alcohol still lingered in his bloodstream. He leant back and closed his eyes, thinking he'd counted eight anti-corruption officers in total, but none of them had been DI Duggan.

–

They drove to Lewisham station. 'Thought we would do this as a courtesy,' said Tanner. 'We could have driven you to headquarters, paraded you in front of everyone, but we're not like that.'

'I appreciate it,' said Lambert. His tone was neutral but Tanner would have noted the sarcasm. A second officer joined them in the interview room and introduced herself as Sergeant Maria Whittaker. Tanner ran through

Lambert's rights and reiterated he wasn't under arrest but was entitled to legal representation.

'If I'm not under arrest then why did you drag me out of my house in the middle of the night?' said Lambert.

'We have some pressing questions to ask you. Are you willing to continue without legal representation at this time?' said Tanner, purely for the benefit of the tape.

'Let's see what you want and we can go from there,' said Lambert.

DS Whittaker placed a folder in front of him.

'Would you care to open those?' said Tanner.

Lambert did as instructed, doing his best not to react when he revealed the photograph inside.

'You know who that is?' said DS Whittaker, wiping a loose strand of silver-white hair from her tanned forehead.

'Yes.'

'For the tape, will you tell us who you believe this person to be?' said Tanner.

'I believe that person is Jonathan Barnes, formerly Detective Chief Inspector Jonathan Barnes of the Metropolitan Police.' Lambert elongated each word, speaking to the two officers like they were halfwits.

'You arrested Jonathan Barnes, is that correct?'

'Yes.'

'And because of your investigative work, Barnes was successfully prosecuted. Is that also correct?' said Tanner.

'It is very correct,' said Lambert.

'Can you describe the picture in front of you for the tape?'

Lambert's patience was ebbing away. 'What the hell is this, Tanner?' he said, turning to him. The picture was of Jonathan Barnes and had been taken in prison after he'd suffered the napalm attack. Barnes' face was so disfigured that Lambert struggled to recognise him. 'I'm not playing these games. It's a picture of Jonathan Barnes, that's all I'm saying.'

'For the benefit of the tape, it is a picture of the convict Jonathan Barnes following a so-called napalm attack he suffered in prison. The attack left Barnes severely disfigured as well as causing numerous internal complications. Do you remember the period when this occurred?' asked Tanner, clearly revelling in his job of interrogator.

Lambert couldn't believe he was being questioned over this case again. 'I heard about it, yes.'

'Were you not in fact questioned by this very same department at the time?'

'I was in fact questioned by this very department,' said Lambert, mimicking Tanner.

'And why was that?'

Lambert sighed. 'Let me guess, for the tape?'

'If you wouldn't mind.'

'The convicted paedophile, rapist and murderer Jonathan Barnes had the temerity to accuse myself and a fellow officer of being responsible for the acid attack leading to the disfigurements in this picture. No charges were ever brought against me and, if I am being honest, sir, I can't believe you're dragging me through all this again.'

'And the fellow officer in question?'

'Bloody hell. Detective Chief Superintendent Glenn Tillman, as you well know. This is ludicrous. Of course Barnes would accuse us of setting up the attack but that misses out a number of pertinent facts such as, one, we were never at the prison, and two, refer to number one.'

'Barnes accused you of speaking to his fellow inmates. That they had acted on your instructions.'

'Look, I know how you love putting police officers away so I thought you would have been happy Barnes is rotting in jail. Aren't you being greedy trying to get me in there too?'

'You've got me wrong, son. I don't like putting police officers away. I like putting the corrupt away.'

'Well Barnes was certainly that, wasn't he?'

'Yes, he was, but that doesn't give anyone the right to have him attacked.'

'I agree totally, that's why I had nothing to do with it. Now, if we're quite finished here.'

Lambert stood up and was heading to the door when Tanner spoke. 'Who last questioned you over this case, DCI Lambert?'

Lambert stopped in his tracks. A thought occurred to him, explaining his being there and enduring such questions. 'Inspector Duggan,' he said.

'Sit down,' said Tanner.

'Sir, what's going on?'

Tanner paused, and nodded to Whittaker. 'The body of Inspector Duggan was found in his flat late last night,' he said, staring hard at Lambert, assessing his response.

'Whittaker,' said Tanner.

Whittaker produced a second file and placed it in front of Lambert. Lambert lowered his eyes and prepared for what he was about to see. He opened the file and saw an almost replica picture of the one he'd just viewed. Only this time it was Inspector Duggan's face instead of Jonathan Barnes'. The skin had been torn from his bones, the same eye obliterated, but Lambert could tell it was Duggan.

'Do you recognize the photo?' said Tanner.

Lambert's heart raced; he knew what was coming next. He understood the flashing beacons outside his house and the look of anger and distaste on the faces of the anti-corruption officers.

Tanner's face tensed, the anger palpable. 'After they'd done that to his face, they poured the rest of the liquid down his throat. And guess what, DCI Lambert?'

Lambert didn't have to guess, for he was sure of what Tanner was going to say next.

'Pinned to his chest we found this.' Tanner threw the plastic sheath at him.

Lambert didn't have to look to know the envelope contained a plain white A6 card, with the name DCI Lambert sketched in capital letters on it.

Silence descended. Lambert leant his forehead on the palm of his left hand and forced himself to look at the disfigured face of Inspector Duggan. Finally he sat back in his chair and looked at the two anti-corruption officers. 'You don't honestly think I have anything to do with this, do you?'

'Put yourself in my shoes, Lambert. If you were investigating this case what would you think?'

Lambert accepted the point. He understood he had to be questioned but didn't agree with Tanner's convoluted approach. 'I never saw eye to eye with Duggan but I would never want him killed.'

Tanner ignored him.

'And if I did want him killed why the hell would I go about it in this manner? Why would I leave my name at the scene?'

'You tell me, DCI Lambert, you're the so-called serial killer expert. Why do all these freaks do what they do? Perhaps you were starved for attention – it's been some time since the Manor case now. The press lost interest in you until Mr Beckinsale was murdered. Can you see the irony of that? Your name left at the scene and you become the investigator. It beats me how this was allowed to happen in the first place, but now we have three dead bodies and three little cards with your name on.'

'When was the time of death?' asked Lambert.

Tanner's mouth pursed as if something was lodged in his teeth and glanced at Whittaker.

'We believe it happened sometime in the last thirty-six hours. The acid has done some horrible things to Duggan's body.'

Lambert imagined they had a more specific time for Duggan's death but the timeframe coincided with his visit to Norfolk with Sarah May. When Tanner finally asked him, he said he'd been home at that time. He thought too about the car he'd seen when entering Croydon Road. At the time he'd thought Duggan had been following him but now this revelation suggested otherwise.

'Were you not suspicious when Inspector Duggan didn't turn up for work?' asked Lambert.

Tanner visibly angered. 'Don't try and tell me how to do my job, Lambert, when you're obviously not succeeding at your own. This is how it is, you are suspended from duty and will conduct no further investigation into the murders of Alistair Beckinsale, Lance

Jenkins and Inspector Duggan. You will give over your case notes and files to DS Whittaker and will cooperate fully when necessary.'

Tanner terminated the interview and switched off the recorder. 'If I were you, Lambert,' he said, 'I would get yourself a lawyer sooner rather than later.'

Chapter Twenty-Six

The officers stopped what they were doing as Lambert left the interview room. Lambert didn't recognize any of them, but it was disconcerting having them watch him exit. They would know at that precise moment he wasn't a police officer and he wasn't sure if that was a good or bad thing.

No one offered him a lift home so he left the building into the bright sunshine of early morning. He called Sophie and explained the situation. 'I have somewhere to go, but I'll be back early afternoon.'

Hanging up, he noticed the familiar figure of Mia Helmer loitering by the bus stop. Having been spotted she walked towards him.

'May I have a word, DCI Lambert?'

Despite the early hour she was immaculately made-up, her painted face a mask from which she drew some confidence.

'What can I do for you, Mia?'

'I know about the third body and I know it's one of your fellow officers.'

Lambert hadn't had time to fully process Inspector Duggan's death. Although he'd disliked the man intensely, he'd worked with him in bringing down Jonathan Barnes and, despite working for anti-corruption, he'd been, as Mia suggested, a fellow officer.

'It's tragic news,' said Lambert.

'It certainly is,' she said, not breaking character, her face blank. 'Why are you here, speaking to anti-corruption?' she asked.

Lambert stared hard into the journalist's eyes, searching for a sign of empathy or compassion. Finding none, he said, 'As always, that's none of your business.' He began walking down the road towards Lewisham train station.

'But Michael, it is my business. Your name was found at the scene again, wasn't it? Didn't you have a personal vendetta against Inspector Duggan? This can't be good for your career. Why don't you give me your version of events so I can provide my readers with both sides of the story?'

'You never print my version of the events. You only print your version.'

Mia's rapid steps glided across the pavement behind him as she tried to keep pace. 'All I know, Michael, is you've been suspended and you're possibly under suspicion for a triple murder.'

Lambert stopped and turned towards the journalist. 'You print what you want but I'd be very careful you don't impede an ongoing investigation.'

'Did you have anything to do with Inspector Duggan's death?' she said, not flinching. He could see she was waiting for a comment she could turn to her own ends. He needed to avoid ambiguity.

'Don't be bloody stupid, Mia,' he said, and walked away. He crossed the road at the traffic lights and headed into the shopping centre. He sped through the precinct, towards a shop he'd used many times before. Inside, he purchased four burner phones, paying cash.

Once back outside, he checked he wasn't being followed by Mia Helmer and resumed his journey to Lewisham station. He was under no illusions now the Manor was sending him a message. Few people would know of the attack on Jonathan Barnes, and that Lambert and Tillman had been accused of organizing it. Whoever killed Duggan must have known these two facts.

Lambert hadn't green-lighted any attack on Barnes, but couldn't say the same for Tillman. His superior had contacts at all levels and it wasn't beyond his ability or scruples for him to have staged such an attack. He'd never broached the subject with him. Responsible or not, Tillman would have denied it.

Outside the station, he wasn't surprised to see a car waiting for him. The passenger-side window was buzzed down and through the opening he saw Tillman's bloated face.

'Get in,' said Tillman.

Lambert sighed and did as ordered, Tillman buzzing the window closed and activating the interior central locking as if Lambert would try to escape. 'Morning. I understand you're in a spot of trouble.'

'Yeah, you could say that, Glenn.'

'Well, you're not the only one. AC-10 have been onto me as well – they've been to my place but fortunately I wasn't in. I had to switch my phone off because they keep leaving bloody messages. The sheer audacity of it is staggering.'

'You know what's happened though?' asked Lambert.

'Inspector Duggan,' said Tillman. If anything Tillman's relationship with Duggan had been worse than Lambert's. He actively and openly despised the man. 'Have you been suspended?'

'Yes.'

'Jesus, I'll have to go and speak to them, I suppose. What an almighty fuck-up.'

Lambert took out the package and, making a note of the number, handed Tillman one of the burner phones.

'We're both fugitives now,' he said.

'Hardly,' said Tillman, taking the phone. 'They won't be suspending me, I can guarantee that. I imagine they told you to stay clear of the case?'

'Of course.'

'And I imagine you have no intention of doing so?'

'Of course.'

Tillman frowned. 'You know your ex has been taken off as well?' said Tillman.

Lambert sighed, annoyed by Tillman's turn of phrase. 'Do you mean DCI Sarah May?'

'I do. Sticking her nose in places she shouldn't. Remind you of anyone? Anyway, it's completely MI5's now, we're getting no information. If you've got another one of those, I can pass it on to her,' said Tillman.

Lambert jotted down the number and handed a second phone to him.

'What number should I call you on?'

Lambert looked into the bag at the two remaining phones. 'I'll call you,' he said.

–

There was some power in the burner phone so he called Matilda as he caught the train.

'Who is this?' she said, answering.

'Matilda, it's Lambert. Are you alone?'

'Yes, sir.'

'Have you heard?'

'Yes, anti-corruption were waiting for us when we got in today, they've placed me in charge for the time being.'

'Well, that's a positive at least. Have you been to the crime scene?'

'We were called in this morning when it happened, we were told explicitly not to call you or Glenn.'

'Was he with you at the time?' asked Lambert.

'Yes,' said Matilda, not elaborating.

'OK, call me on this number and keep me updated, but don't let on you're in conversation with me. I'm sure Tillman already knows this but you two need to stay apart until this has all blown over. One more thing, I imagine you're aware but we're going to have to cancel the Christmas break.'

'I understand, sir.'

Lambert hung up and sat back in the chair. It was only a short train ride to his destination. He wanted to be at the office, wanted to know exactly what had happened at Duggan's home but had to trust Matilda and the rest of the team for now.

He left the train at Victoria and walked to the nearby shopping arcade where his final destination lay. From habit, he checked he wasn't being watched. Annoyed by his own paranoia, he assured himself he wasn't being followed by Mia Helmer or one of the anti-corruption team, before opening the door of a small boutique shop.

A suited man greeted him. 'Merry Christmas, sir, how may I be of assistance?'

Lambert reached inside his pocket and took out a glossy piece of paper. 'These earrings,' he said. 'Do you still have them?'

Chapter Twenty-Seven

DS Adams called as Sarah was running. She'd woken before the sun rose and set out in the darkness. She sometimes wished her runs could last forever. It was the only time she was ever truly at peace, her thoughts centred on her breathing and pacing; her only major concern where her foot would fall next. Adams' name appeared on her phone screen but she wasn't about to stop for him. She ran through Clifton Village and across the suspension bridge, recalling a potential suicide she'd managed to talk down from jumping years ago when she'd been a probationary officer.

An hour later she returned to her parents' house, elated from the exercise.

'Fry-up?' said her father, as she opened the front door to the smell of olive oil, bacon and coffee.

'That would be heaven,' said Sarah.

After showering she called Adams. 'I thought you were on leave,' said the DS, with his usual overfamiliarity.

'What have you got for me?'

'The Land Rover belongs to a Brenda Rosenberg, some farm address out in the sticks. Ring any bells?'

Sarah pictured the scene in St Albans, the woman crying and running away from Stuart Pierson. 'No, it was nothing.'

'OK. Ma'am, I was wondering…'

'Yes, Adams, it's not a problem. Take some time off,' said Sarah, hanging up.

She was becoming a slave to her changing emotions. One moment she was desperate to get back to London, the next she was relaxed after taking her run and eating a fried breakfast with her family.

'It does defeat the purpose a bit though, doesn't it?' said her father, teasing her once more at the breakfast table.

'What does?' said her mother, falling for his line.

'Going for such a long run, then eating all this rubbish.'

'You cooked it, Jeff.'

'He's kidding, Mum,' said Sarah, grabbing some extra bacon and sausage off the serving plate.

–

In the afternoon she accompanied her mother to the supermarket, her tension returning as soon as she entered the establishment. Half of Bristol appeared to have also left their shopping until the day before Christmas. Parents dragged screaming children around the corridors as customers fought for dwindling goods from the shelves.

Sarah kept glancing at her phone despite knowing Michael would never call unless it was an emergency. She'd been away for less than twenty-four hours but was already desperate to get back.

'Everything OK?' asked her mother, when they were back in the car.

'Yes, why?'

'For one, you keep looking at your phone every ten minutes. So what's happening with work? Why the sudden decision to come home?'

'I can go back to London if you'd prefer,' said Sarah, hearing the child in her voice. 'Sorry, I didn't mean that. I've been working on a tough case which ended prematurely. I'm just a bit frustrated with things at the moment. Sometimes I can't wait to get away from all the bull… the politics and nonsense of the job.'

'And then when you're away, you can't wait to get back.'

'Something like that.'

'You're like your dad.'

'He was a surveyor.'

'Yes, but he was addicted to work. You sure that's all that's bothering you? You look at your phone like you're waiting to hear from someone specific.'

Her mother was always annoyingly perceptive, but she wasn't ready to talk about Michael yet. Both her parents had met him following their work together on the Souljacker case. They usually asked after him but had stopped since they'd split. Sarah tried to ignore the silence. Her mother was waiting for her to speak and Sarah was sure Michael's name would be mentioned. 'It's fine, Mum. What have you got Dad for Christmas?'

Her mother sighed, unsatisfied with the answer but knowing better than to push Sarah into a question she didn't want to answer. 'You know better than that. If you want to find that out, you'll have to wait until Christmas morning.'

Sarah turned towards her and received a wink.

–

Lambert paid for the earrings, shocked at his extravagance. The incidents of the previous night were beginning to take their toll. After stopping at a newsagent's, he found a local café and acquired his fix of caffeine. From his bag he took out his new burner phone and charged it in one of the café's sockets. He added the two numbers he had for Sarah, as well as Tillman and Matilda. His old burner phone would be compromised now so he removed the SIM card and battery, deciding he would leave it in the shop.

The coffee was hot and bitter and Lambert blinked his eyes as tiredness surged through his body. His access to the System was revoked so he was at a loss to find out what was happening unless he called Matilda or Tillman. He didn't want to call the former again in case it landed her in trouble, and wasn't yet ready for a chat with his superior.

He took out the notebook and pen he'd purchased from the newsagent's and started to try and make sense of the situation he was in.

First he considered the murder of Inspector Duggan. Duggan had been a foe for the last eighteen months but in the main he was a decent man. Working for anti-corruption was a poisoned chalice. Although having such a department was a necessary evil, the majority of police officers despised the division. It was human nature. The AC teams investigated police officers, so the police officers hated them. But Duggan was still a police officer. His death was a travesty and would be mourned by the majority in and out of his department.

Any doubt that the killer was recreating cases connected to Lambert was banished by the mode of Duggan's demise. Duggan had been attacked in the same manner as Jonathan Barnes. The only difference this time was that Barnes had survived his attack while Duggan hadn't. Was this a slip-up on the part of the attacker? Had he meant to keep him alive, a recreation of Jonathan Barnes, or was his death deliberate? He imagined Duggan had been alive when the killer left him in his room. Had the killer expected someone to come to Duggan's rescue? He would have been in horrendous pain, and Lambert could only hope he'd slipped into unconsciousness.

He remembered the sense of being followed as he returned to Beckenham. He'd seen a car, a black Audi, disappear down Beckenham High Street and thought it had been Duggan. Had the killer stolen Duggan's car? Chief Superintendent Tanner hadn't mentioned Duggan's car being taken, but Lambert hadn't asked the question.

Lambert played with his personal mobile phone, deciding whether or not to call Tanner. The information would sound so circumstantial Tanner would see it as a desperate plea to get reinstated.

He winced as he finished the dregs of the coffee. He didn't care what Tanner thought of him. The most important thing was finding the killer. He picked up his phone and called AC chief.

'Lambert?' said Tanner, answering.

'Sir. I had a question about Inspector Duggan.'

'Go on.'

'I was wondering if his car was missing?'

Tanner took a sharp intake of breath. 'Why would you ask that, Lambert?'

Lambert explained about Duggan tracking him and how he thought he'd seen Duggan's car in Beckenham High Street the other evening.

'What time was this?' asked Tanner.

'10.32 p.m.'

'That's exact.'

'I logged the time when I saw the car. Unfortunately I was distracted before I had time to confirm the number plates.'

'That is unfortunate,' said Tanner, deadpan.

'Was Duggan's car taken?'

Tanner didn't respond, which was response enough.

'I take it his car doesn't have a tracker.'

'Unfortunately not. We'll look into the CCTV for that time. Why didn't you volunteer this information earlier?'

'It just occurred to me. Did you know Duggan was following me?'

'I appreciate you calling, Lambert. Is there anything else I should know?' Tanner wasn't about to divulge any information to him.

'You'll let me know if you track the car?'

'No. Goodbye, Lambert.'

Lambert glared at his phone, and considered slamming it numerous times on the café's table. Tanner had purposely not used his rank when addressing him, a subtle reminder he was suspended, was technically no longer a police officer.

He called Matilda and told her about Duggan's car.

'Tanner was here an hour ago, sir. He told us the car was missing.'

'OK, now they have a lead to where the car was last seen. AC-10 will be checking the CCTV image for the high street and surrounding areas. Obviously you didn't hear it from me, but you should try and find out that information as soon as you are able. You find the car, you may find the killer.'

Lambert hung up and called Sophie as he waited for his taxi to arrive.

'Can you pick up some extra sprouts?' she said, after he explained he was on his way back.

Lambert laughed and Sophie asked him what was so funny. 'Nothing, it's just good to know what my priorities are.'

–

Jane was still too young to fully understand what was happening but it was a joy to watch her as she busied herself around the house: hanging up Christmas stockings on the fireplace and preparing treats for Father Christmas and his reindeer.

'Are you sure you've been a good girl this year?' said Lambert, furrowing his brow.

Jane frowned and gave him a threatening look. 'Daddy,' she warned.

'Just checking,' said Lambert, holding his hands up in defence.

Jane rolled her eyes.

'Right, get here you,' said Lambert, jumping from his seat towards the girl who ran screaming through the hallway, giggling as she went.

'That will help her sleep,' said Sophie, pushing herself against the wall as Jane rushed past.

'It's Christmas,' said Lambert, giving chase.

Later, they watched a short animated film together, the three of them cuddled together on the sofa as Sophie's mother prepared some dinner.

'Santa,' said Jane, eyes wide as an animated Father Christmas appeared on screen.

'Better get off to bed, then, or he might miss you,' said Lambert.

'Daddy, it's not time yet.'

'Soon will be though, pumpkin. Five more minutes, OK?' said Sophie.

Jane smiled and snuggled into her parents.

It was at least twenty minutes later before they left the sofa. Jane was doing her utmost to stay awake as Lambert carried her upstairs and placed her in bed. 'Is Santa here?' she asked, as he kissed her goodnight.

'Soon, darling, go to sleep. Lambert turned around to see Sophie, video camera in hand, recording the moment. 'Hey, I haven't brushed my hair.' He took the camera off Sophie as she kissed Jane goodnight. 'That reminds me, I need to go and do something.'

Upstairs, he wrapped the earrings he'd brought Sophie and the other presents he'd managed to buy earlier that day. Unable to resist, he attempted logging onto the System only to be denied access. He ran some Google searches on Peter Saunders, and even resorted to searching his own name. Mia Helmer hadn't yet covered any of the latest developments on his case. She was either waiting for the Christmas period to be over to create greater impact, or wanted to see the fallout from Duggan's death.

It was beyond frustrating being out of the loop and it gave him an insight to what life would be like without the job. There was nothing else he could do on Christmas Eve. He picked up the pile of poorly wrapped presents and headed downstairs.

Chapter Twenty-Eight

Lambert kissed Jane goodbye as he placed her in the child seat. 'I'll see you later on,' he said clicking it into place. 'And you, Glenda,' he said, to Sophie's mother who sat in the front seat.

It was the twenty-seventh December. The Christmas period had gone better than Lambert anticipated. Sophie had been surprised and delighted by his choice of present, and the time had been relaxed in part because Lambert had been unable to attend work.

He hadn't told them about his suspension. He'd explained away the sirens and police cars by saying they'd needed his urgent help but couldn't tell if Sophie believed him.

He waved them goodbye as Sophie drove her mother back home, happy to have some time to himself. Since his questioning by anti-corruption, he'd come as close as he ever had to taking his mind off an active case. He'd exchanged messages with Tillman on the burner phone, and listened to Matilda Kennedy's updates, but had taken no further part in the investigation. Now, left alone, it would be harder not to get involved.

He took a walk in the park at the end of his street, watching the families with their young children, playing with the new bikes and scooters they'd received for Christmas. The friendly community spirit was the main positive about the area. Matilda's investigation into Duggan's death had not progressed well. That his body had been found on the day before Christmas Eve did little to help matters, but neither had AC-10's continuous involvement. Matilda had been questioned on her working relationship with Lambert and Tillman; Lambert concluding they were putting a case together against him.

Despite his best attempts he was still frozen out of the System. He'd requested a secret access code from Tillman, who was yet to grant it and was not answering his calls.

Lambert didn't know what to do with his time. In the high street, he bought a newspaper and took it to one of the local coffee shops. He sat by the large bay window watching the pedestrians still caught up in their seasonal good cheer. He checked through the sports section first, a habit he'd formed as a child. The passion he'd felt then for reading football scores and reports was absent now. Flipping the paper over he skimmed from the front and stopped short on page six when he saw his own face looking back out at him.

Lambert folded the paper, scanning the room, the customers with their coffees and marshmallow-topped hot chocolates, for potential threats and returned to the article written by Mia Helmer. It was buried away from the rest of the news, a quarter-page article with the headline 'Hero Cop Under Suspicion'.

Lambert cursed under his breath. It appeared Helmer was close to getting what she wanted. With his suspension and the growing list of bodies connected to him, his career and reputation were being destroyed.

He'd made lots of enemies over the years, Mia Helmer being a prime example, but all his thoughts were still directed to the Manor. He read the article three times before closing the paper, the other customers glancing his way at his evident anger. He took the burner phone from his pocket and held it in his hand. His first thought was to call Sarah. In many ways she was in the same situation as him, and was so because of him. They could help each other but it would be difficult. He had no access to the System and he wasn't even supposed to be talking to Matilda and Tillman. Similar restrictions had been placed on Sarah. He juggled the phone from hand to hand and considered his options before finishing his coffee.

On the way home he stopped at the supermarket. Even this small act filled him with guilt. How could he bother about what he was going to eat when some two-bit journalist with a grudge was out there trashing his name? He should be investigating, finding out who was responsible for Beckinsale, Jenkins and Duggan, not wasting his time in the bakery aisle choosing which bread he wanted for his lunch.

He walked back through the park, noticing a customer from the supermarket was trailing him from thirty metres away. Lambert had first spotted him in the coffee shop and thought his appearance in the supermarket a coincidence but was now on alert. Lambert slowed his pace, forcing his pursuer to shorten the distance between them. As he reached the playground he stopped and leant on the metal railings. Pretending to use his phone, he turned to face the approaching man. His pursuer hesitated, the slight movement enough to confirm Lambert was right to have been suspicious. The pursuer looked at him, realizing he'd been caught, and began walking over. Lambert put the phone back in his inside pockets and tensed. As always, he was prepared. He reached inside his pocket, his right hand touching his canister of pepper spray.

The figure stopped ten metres away. 'DCI Lambert,' he said.

Lambert kept his hand where it was. He didn't recognize the man and thought by his gait and the easy way he'd been caught out that he was another journalist feeding off Mia Helmer's story.

'What do you want?'

He took a few steps forward. 'Sir, I have a message for you from Glenn Tillman.'

Lambert was surprised at how easy he'd caught out one of Tillman's men. 'Why hasn't he phoned me?'

'He says he wants no record, even on the burner phone.'

'Tell me.'

The man took another step forward, scanning the area for eavesdroppers.

'It's Jonathan Barnes, sir. There are plans to transfer him from his current prison on the twenty-ninth December.'

Chapter Twenty-Nine

Sarah must have run close to a hundred miles since returning to Bristol. She'd managed twelve miles on Christmas Day between opening presents and lunch. It was like an addiction, and she was pushing herself harder today, aiming for close to twenty. She ran along the Portway, her tempo fast but evenly paced, the smell of the muddy river in her nostrils.

It was only the twenty-seventh December, but already she ached to be back at work, her feeling compounded by her frustration at being taken off the Saunders' case. She hadn't heard from Michael, though a burner phone had arrived at her house via courier delivery late on Christmas Eve. Michael's boss, Tillman, called her on the phone and explained Michael was suspended following the suspicious death of Inspector Duggan from anti-corruption. She'd wanted to phone him but he would be home with his family and she couldn't intrude.

Although she was less than two hours from London, she may as well have been in another world. She had no access to the file on Saunders, and Partridge wasn't going to volunteer any information. Part of her wanted to put it behind her, to find another case or even department within the NCA, but until there was some resolution she wouldn't be able to rest.

There was no fried breakfast waiting for her when she returned home. Her parents were visiting relatives, the house desolate without their busy presence. After showering, Sarah took out her case and began packing the few clothes she'd brought from London. She'd enjoyed visiting her parents but was going stir-crazy from the predictable routine.

She checked the train times while eating lunch and flicked through her parents' newspaper, stopping when she reached the article on Michael. Even though she was biased, the journalist appeared to have done a hatchet job on him. Nothing in the article had any substance. It was true Lambert was suspended, but Helmer painted a picture of a corrupt officer. She was too clever to be explicit but the subtext was clear: Michael was under suspicion for the murder of Inspector Duggan and the other two victims.

She held the phone in her hand. Even if she called him, he wouldn't talk about it. Instead, she checked the train times to London and was about to call a taxi when her phone rang.

–

Lambert waited for Tillman's messenger to leave the park before returning home. He took the long route, alert to the possibility of attack. At home he tried Tillman's burner which was either switched off or dumped. Pacing the house, he read the note the messenger had given him once more, memorizing the address before tearing the paper into little pieces.

He'd told Sophie he'd make dinner but needed to prepare. He sent her a text, apologizing for having to go to work and retreated to his office at the top of the house. From the safe he retrieved two sets of keys.

He made a sandwich, watching the clock as he ate. He was still worried that Tillman had gone silent. He wanted to meet at 6.30 p.m. Lambert checked the address on his laptop, not surprised to see the rendezvous was in a side street half a mile from Woolwich prison. He accessed an aerial view on the web, the street surrounded by the backs of towering office buildings. Lambert scanned the road and determined the exact spot where Tillman would wait for him: the dead zone where they wouldn't be viewed.

That Barnes was being moved wasn't in itself a great surprise. Prison transfers were a matter of routine, the reasons for them numerous. What troubled Lambert, and presumably Tillman, was the timing of the move so soon after Saunders' escape and the fact that Barnes was headed to Luton, the same prison where Saunders had been heading when he'd escaped. As the exact details of Saunders' escape were still being kept secret by MI5, the proposed transfer wouldn't have raised many concerns. Lambert found it inconceivable the security services would allow a second prison escape. If Barnes was to be moved, he was sure security would be at its maximum.

Then why was he so troubled by the thought of Barnes being transferred?

He was drawn back to Waverley Manor, the quiet of the underground dungeons, the fact a senior police officer – Barnes – had been partly responsible for the atrocities. He couldn't let him get free. It was hard enough to stomach Saunders' escape, but suspended or not he would not allow Barnes to follow in his colleague's footsteps.

With Tillman not answering, he called Sarah, hoping Tillman had got the burner phone to her. She answered after one ring as if she'd been holding the phone in her hand.

He hesitated, not sure where to begin. 'Jonathan Barnes is moving prisons,' he said, the first of many thoughts in his head demanding to be voiced.

'I see. When?'

'The twenty-ninth, and he's being moved to Luton.'

'I guess they have a spare room there now,' said Sarah with a laugh.

'My concern is it will stay vacant.'

'You don't think they will try to spring Barnes as well? They could never get away with that.'

'Something is happening, Sarah.' He explained about his meeting with Tillman that evening.

'You want some assistance?' she asked, taking her cue from his voice.

'Are you sure?'

'Yeah, I'm going mad here. I haven't put so many miles on the road in a long time. Anything to get out of the house. What time are you meeting Tillman?'

'6.30.'

'I should be able to get back to London in time. Send me the address and I'll meet you beforehand.'

Michael was relieved he hadn't had to ask. He went silent, conflicting thoughts in his head.

Sarah rescued him. 'Tillman told me what happened. About your suspension.'

'Did he now? Yeah, I guess I'm operating without a licence here. It's all nonsense, of course, but I understand if you don't want to get involved.'

'Don't be stupid. I'll call you when I arrive.'

Lambert hung up, thankful Sarah still wanted to help him. Although he trusted Tillman, it would be good to have a second set of eyes to help him. He left the house and made the short journey to a lock-up he used in Orpington.

He reversed the car up a gravel driveway and parked facing the roadside so he would be able to get away quickly. He was always careful, but recent events had created a burgeoning paranoia. He used the lock-up due to the lack of surveillance and was pleased there was no one around. Checking about him, he opened first the chain guard then the metal door securing the area. The space within was similar to a car garage. Lambert had filled it with random pieces of junk, an old table and chairs, a beaten sofa, and cardboard boxes full of books. At the back of the room he shifted a panel in the floor, revealing the digital controls of the floor safe he'd spent a long weekend installing many years ago. From the safe he took his burn bag containing cash, photo identification including a passport, and finally his Glock 22 handgun. Although he was licensed to carry a firearm, such a privilege was subject to heavy scrutiny and did not extend to the use of private guns. He risked jail if discovered, but in the circumstances it was a risk worth taking.

He placed the gun in the leather holdall strapped to his chest and replaced the safe covering. Thankful he was still alone, he locked up before heading to his destination, wanting to arrive before Tillman.

Three hours early, Lambert stopped for a late lunch at a nondescript sandwich shop near the town centre. He ordered a baguette: the bread soft and chewy, the sandwich's fillings flavourless. Restless, he searched through his notes on his laptop, hoping for inspiration. He thought about the body he'd found with Sarah in Norfolk. Had the prison guard, John Prine, been helping Saunders under duress or had he been one of the Manor, betrayed at the last by the organization he trusted? One thing he could not accuse the Manor of was a lack of loyalty. Of the eight men they'd arrested, only Barnes had broken his silence. Convicted mainly through forensic evidence, each of the men had remained silent about the organization itself.

Not that there was anything admirable about such silence. The reasons for it were deep rooted. Each man had family, and Lambert was of the opinion each feared retribution for talking. It was this forced loyalty which made it so difficult to investigate the organization. As a group, Lambert was convinced there were much more than the eight imprisoned men. The Saunders' breakout was proof enough. He estimated the organization numbered into the hundreds. The code of silence adopted by the eight appeared to be ruthlessly enforced by the rest of the members. For such a code to work the members would have to trust one another implicitly. Lambert had seen such loyalty before in organized crime and paedophile groups. It made him conclude on balance that John Prine hadn't been one of their number. That Saunders would not have eliminated a fellow member in such a manner.

That didn't mean Prine didn't work for them. He'd seen from his investigation into Waverly Manor that they were not beyond using, and eliminating, hired help.

Lambert rubbed his face, not sure if his conclusion helped him in any way. With Prine dead, was there another guard on the payroll who would help Barnes escape, or did it go higher? Was Saunders simply the first escapee? Did the Manor somehow have the audacity to believe they could spring all eight from jail?

Lambert shuddered, swearing to himself no more of their number would see the light of day again.

Sarah called. She was already in London. Lambert agreed to meet her in twenty minutes. The clouded sky was pregnant with rain and he feared a deluge as he made his way to the tube station where he'd agreed to meet Sarah. He scanned the crowds, suspicious of everyone who looked his way, his gun heavy inside his knee-length overcoat. Everyone was a potential threat. Anti-corruption were investigating him and were probably attempting to track him even now; everyone he passed could be one of their team.

A scrawny youth, the damp remains of an extinguished cigarette hanging from his mouth like a growth, stood next to Sarah outside the train station. The youth was speaking to her and stopped mid-sentence when Lambert arrived.

'All right, mate?' said the youth.

Lambert ignored him, his attention focused on Sarah. 'Nice hat,' he said, nodding to the flower-patterned beanie hat covering her dark hair.

She smiled and Lambert laughed as the youth tried unsuccessfully to light his limp cigarette.

Lambert led her back to the car where they deposited her luggage and then to the rendezvous point where Lambert was supposed to meet Tillman in two hours. As the online map suggested, office buildings flanked the meeting place. Only now could Lambert see they were derelict. The entrances were boarded up, many of the windows smashed. Five cars lined the road, each with a yellow permit sticker on the windshield.

Together they searched for a vantage point where Sarah could wait undetected. 'Are you in contact with Tillman?' Lambert asked her.

'I haven't spoken to him since he told me about Duggan. I don't have a direct number for him.'

'When was the last time you spoke to the MI5 team?'

'Not since they took me off the case. It was made pretty clear there would be no more contact. I have no idea how the Saunders' case is progressing.'

'Through here,' said Lambert, jamming open one of the office building's doors. What appeared to be a year's worth of post covered the musty-smelling foyer like a second carpet. 'Who's the agent in charge again?' he said, surprised to see the doors to the staircase were open.

'Charles Partridge. I don't think they ever wanted our involvement. I was assigned to the case almost as an afterthought. I could tell from the outset Partridge didn't want me on board. They sidelined me at every opportunity, even when I took them to John Prine's body.'

They moved up the concrete staircase, their footsteps echoing in the cavern of the stairwell. 'You ever get the impression they weren't surprised to see Prine's grave?' asked Lambert, breathless as they reached the tenth flight.

'Hard to tell. As you'd expect, they're professional to a fault. Sharing information was not in their mandate. If anything, I felt under suspicion when they arrived.'

'Did they have any inkling I'd been there?'

'Your name wasn't mentioned but Partridge didn't fully believe my account of events.'

Sarah pushed open the swing doors to a large vacant space, what must once have been an open-plan office. Abandoned furniture, coated in dust, lay strewn on the damp carpet. The same musty smell they'd noticed in the stairwell filling the stale air. Lambert picked up one of the plastic telephones and held it to his ear, hearing nothing but static. 'Over here,' he said, moving towards the windows at the other end of the office. He pulled at the blinds, his fingers coated in a moist grey substance he wiped on the wall.

'Good spot,' said Sarah, gazing down at the road where Lambert had agreed to meet Tillman. 'You think this is necessary?'

'I hope not, but you never know with Tillman. He's loyal but unpredictable.' He handed her his car keys and a plastic fob with a code inscribed on it. 'I've got a tracker on my phone. If Tillman pulls away, or something else happens, use my car to follow.'

Sarah opened the tracking app on her phone and entered the code on the fob. 'Best of luck,' she said, taking her spot by the window as Lambert exited.

It was dusk by the time Lambert left the building. He edged along the street towards the meeting spot, making sure he was in Sarah's eyeline. He was probably being over anxious but, as he'd told Sarah, Tillman could be unpredictable. He was no longer using his burner phone and had sent a messenger to summon him, so Lambert surmised Tillman's paranoia matched his own.

Lambert pushed himself back against a brick wall, merging into the shadows as a woman entered the alleyway. A high-pitched whistle reverberated around the surrounding walls as lights on one of the parked cars flashed twice, the woman opening the doors and driving off. Lambert looked up at the office building but couldn't see any sign of Sarah.

'Waiting for someone?'

'Fuck's sake, Tillman, where did you come from?'

Glenn Tillman was standing behind him wrapped in a heavy knee-length coat and, for the first time Lambert could ever recall, wearing a hat. 'You're getting sloppy, Lambert. You fell for my decoy like an amateur.'

Lambert was pleased the man was in good humour. 'Bullshit. She wasn't a decoy, that was blind luck.'

'Believe what you will. This way,' said Tillman, heading back into the main street.

'Where are we going?' said Lambert, glancing up as Tillman turned his back.

'We're getting picked up on the main street in five minutes,' said Tillman. He paused before adding, 'She can't come with us, but feel free to tell DCI May she can follow.'

Chapter Thirty

Lambert sent Sarah a text from the back of Tillman's car. She had the tracking device activated so would be able to follow with little trouble. 'Where are we going?' he asked.

'I've arranged for us to visit an old friend.'

Twenty minutes later, the car pulled into the staff entrance of Woolwich prison. 'Barnes?' said Lambert.

'The very same.'

'You realize I'm on suspension. I can't be seen visiting a convict.'

'No need to worry about that. It's not an official visit.'

The car stopped in front of a wire-meshed gate which began to open. Through the windshield Lambert saw a lone guard standing in a doorway, light shining behind him like a halo.

'Best if you don't give your name. Davies, turn this car around and keep the engine running in case,' said Tillman. 'You carrying?' he asked Lambert.

Lambert nodded and gave him his gun.

The haloed prison guard greeted them. 'Glenn,' he said, ignoring Lambert. 'This is the last time,' he added, as he shut the door.

'Understood,' said Tillman, as they followed the guard through the bunker-like corridor running beneath the prison. The guard stopped by a cast-iron door which he unlocked with an oversized rusted key.

'I can give you fifteen minutes, max,' he said, ushering them through.

Inside the room, chained to a fixed metal desk, sat Jonathan Barnes.

Lambert shivered as the door locked behind him. Barnes shuffled in his chair, the chains rattling in the hollow confines of the room.

'Great to see you again, Jonathan,' said Tillman, dragging one of the two metal chairs opposite the prisoner.

Even in the poor light, Lambert could see the injuries to Barnes' face were horrific.

'What do you want?' said Barnes. The words were slurred, almost incomprehensible. He appeared to be in pain as he spoke.

'I heard you're getting out of here,' said Tillman.

'So?'

Tillman leant forward and Barnes shrank into his seat. 'So, I was wondering how that was arranged.'

Lambert reminded himself of Barnes' crimes as he experienced a stab of sympathy for him. The man before them had been responsible for the abuse and deaths of tens if not hundreds of children. Some of those poor souls had never seen the light of day, had been confined to a life beneath the ground at Waverley Manor. Directly or indirectly, Barnes had been involved. His suffering, in comparison, was irrelevant.

'I don't know,' said Barnes, shrugging. Lambert sensed the fear and confusion in his slurred voice. If someone was masterminding his escape, it wasn't the remains of the man before them.

'You know about Saunders?' said Tillman.

'Yes.'

'Who organized his escape?'

'How the hell should I know?'

'I know you have your means of communication, Barnes.'

Lambert reminded himself again of Barnes' crimes as Tillman leant in closer and started putting pressure on the cuffs securing Barnes in place.

'This is not an official visit, Jonathan, and I'm not DCI May. What do you know, Jonathan?' whispered Tillman.

It was hard to imagine Barnes had once been a DCI like Lambert. He shook as Tillman continued bombarding him with questions and Lambert was concerned the man would pass out before giving them any credible information.

Sharing his concern, Tillman released the pressure on the prisoner. He sat back on his chair, the metal legs scraping across the stone floor.

Barnes took the opportunity to glance at Lambert, a hint of a smile forming on his lips. 'Wipe that off,' said Lambert, realizing it was the first time he'd spoken since entering the room.

Barnes lowered his good eye but Lambert could still see the amusement there.

Tillman used the break in conversation to speak, his tone gentler than before. 'If you think you have a chance of escaping during your prison transfer then you're sorely mistaken, Jonathan. Whatever security there is in place at the moment, I will double it. I will shoot you myself if I have to. So rule that possibility out. What I can offer you is a better standard of living.'

Barnes snarled, his disfigurement distorting his features into something monstrous. 'I've heard it before and I'd be better off dead,' he said, spittle flying from his mouth.

'We can get you to a better wing. You can remain secluded but I can make sure you get some luxuries. A television, some books. I can even get you a kettle so you can make your own tea. Think of that.'

It sounded like a poor bargain but Barnes was on partial suicide watch at present so wouldn't be allowed such privileges.

'What is it you want?'

'Who is trying to set up DCI Lambert?' said Tillman.

The same distorted smile appeared on Barnes' face and Tillman glanced at Lambert a second too late to stop him attacking.

Lambert grabbed Barnes by the throat, venting all the frustration of the last couple of weeks. 'You think what they did to you is painful? You wait,' said Lambert, enjoying the tension in Barnes' neck as he struggled. 'Three men are dead, one of them a police officer. You think you're going to escape retribution for that?'

Tillman rested his arm on Lambert's as Barnes began struggling for breath. Lambert held on for a few more seconds before letting go.

'This is your last chance. What do you know?' said Tillman.

Barnes coughed, and expelled something bloody from his mouth. He struggled with his breathing but managed a parting shot before the prison door opened. 'I know you know less than I thought.'

–

'Thanks, Jack,' said Tillman, once they were back in the car park.

'That's it,' said the guard. It was supposed to be a statement, but sounded more like a question.

Tillman nodded as Lambert climbed into the back of the car. 'What the hell did Barnes mean by that?' he said.

'He's pretending to know something,' said Tillman.

'I don't think he's pretending. What is the security procedure for his transfer?'

'Our friends in MI5 are handling it. Unless they're involved, I can't see anything happening. They couldn't risk it, and there will be so many of them there.'

'But your team will be there too?'

'Yes, but I think you're missing the point somewhat. You're suspended and implicated in the death of a police officer. And Barnes has given us nothing.'

Lambert was pleased by Tillman's concern. The man wasn't one to openly show his emotions: this was as close as he got to sentiment. 'They could take your badge for this, you realize that?'

'If they're prepared to take my badge because of this then they're welcome to it.'

'Easy to say,' said Tillman.

The driver dropped him back at the derelict office building. 'Stay out of things for the time being,' said Tillman, as Lambert left the car. 'I'll be in touch.'

'My gun?' said Lambert.

Tillman sighed and left the car. From the boot, he retrieved a Glock 26 pistol. Not the gun Lambert had given him. 'I've signed this out. Davies, you're a witness to this. I'm assigning it to you despite your suspension.'

'And my own gun?'

'Sometimes I wonder at your stupidity, Lambert. Walking round with a private firearm while on suspension. Do you want to lose your job?'

It was a good question, one he wasn't sure he knew how to answer. Lambert watched the car depart. Everything had occurred so fast in the prison he'd yet to process it. Barnes had been like a different person, the change in his personality a mirror of his disfigurement. The confidence and authority had all but vanished until that last second. The policeman Barnes had been had disappeared; in its wake was the creature in the shadows, its only power the malevolent way he smiled at Lambert, as if he knew a secret.

Lambert tried to explain this to Sarah when she arrived to pick him up, but failed. 'He certainly didn't mastermind anything but I'm sure he knows something about Duggan and the others,' said Lambert.

'He could have picked something up on the prison grapevine?' suggested Sarah.

'It was more than that.'

'Why don't we interview him in an official capacity?'

'I certainly can't. Neither can you, I imagine.'

'DS Kennedy?'

Matilda had the fourth burner phone. The team appeared no closer to finding a suspect, Duggan's death clouding rather than clarifying the matter. Matilda had called him after seeing Duggan's father, who'd raised him alone. It was tough on her but was also a great opportunity to prove she could manage such a difficult case. He reminded himself he was potentially putting her career in jeopardy by asking her to update him.

'I'm not sure we can justify Matilda seeing Barnes. There doesn't appear to be any reason for it and Barnes could refuse.'

'Or mention you've already paid him a visit,' said Sarah.

'There is that.'

'I could speak to Matilda. Do you think she would let me help?'

'You outrank her. It wouldn't really work procedurally.'

'It doesn't appear any of you pay much attention to procedure.' Sarah kept a straight face but Lambert saw her amusement.

'Very droll. I'll speak to her tonight and see if we can arrange something for tomorrow.'

Sarah parked outside her house. 'Better swap seats,' she said, not moving.

Feeling like a teenager on a first date, Lambert didn't answer. He didn't know what to say, or what Sarah wanted him to say. In the back of his mind, he thought about Sophie and Jane waiting for him at home as Sarah looked at him, the car engine still running.

The moment passed. 'I'll get my bags,' said Sarah.

Lambert left the car and helped her with her luggage. Sarah hesitated as she took the bags off him, as if she too was nervous about the situation they found themselves in. 'Speak tomorrow?' she said, eventually, as they stood facing each other in silence, a world of history between them going unsaid.

Lambert watched her shut the front door. Starting something with Sarah again would be one complication too far, and he owed it to Sophie and Jane to try and make things work at home, yet he couldn't help thinking he'd made a mistake as he made his way home.

Unable to find a space on his own street, he drove to end of the road and parked on a side street next to a local school. It was after eleven p.m., and he decided to wait until morning to call Matilda. He locked up the car and began walking home in time to meet a hailstorm, forcing his walk into a run.

He was out of breath by the time he reached his front door, his breathing becoming more laboured as he noticed the front door was ajar.

The procedure at times like this was not to panic. The door didn't appear to be forced but was off the latch. Lambert withdrew the gun from inside his jacket and moved inside.

The familiar view of the hallway leading to the kitchen, the staircase and side door to the living room, looked normal yet Lambert sensed something irrevocably alien about the place. He wanted to call Sophie's name, to scream out Jane's, but he maintained his professionalism, moving from room to room, gun held in front of him. He cleared the bottom floor and moved upstairs. The building was empty.

Controlling his mounting panic, he called Sophie's phone. His heart fluttered when the phone went straight to voicemail. Not missing a beat, he called her mother.

'Michael, why are you calling so late?'

'Sorry, Glenda, I had to go into work and haven't managed to reach Sophie. Her phone is off. Just wanted to check they got home safe.'

Lambert was desperate to hear they'd decided to stay for the night, that they were safely upstairs in Glenda's house, asleep. 'Oh yes, I'm sure they have. They left at about five. Are you sure everything's OK, Michael. This isn't like you to call me.'

Guilt overcame him. He couldn't tell Glenda what was happening, though she would never forgive him later for lying. 'Sorry again. I was supposed to be in tonight, so I was just a bit worried I'd upset Soph as her phone was switched off.'

The explanation placated Glenda. 'It's good to see you're taking things seriously, Michael. Good night.'

Lambert hung up and took a second look around the house. He'd been alone here hundreds of times before but his family's absence weighed heavy. The ceilings appeared higher, the walls further apart. He made his way through each room in a daze, nauseous at the possibility they'd been taken.

Desperate, he searched for explanations. That Sophie had needed something from the shops, and in her rush had left the door open. Or, more plausibly, one of them had been taken ill and had gone to hospital. He went outside, confirming what he remembered: Sophie's car was parked outside.

Somehow that made things worse. He was about to call Sarah when he noticed something he'd inexplicably missed before. The nausea rose all the way this time as he reached out for the note pinned to the top of the coat hook. He vomited on the wooden floorboards, his hand on the folded note. When he stopped vomiting his hands were trembling.

His name was on the front of the note. Like before, his name was stencilled in black ink. However, this time there was a written note on the back. Also stencilled in black ink, it read:

IF YOU EVER WANT TO SEE YOUR FAMILY
ALIVE AGAIN

ALLOW JONATHAN BARNES TO ESCAPE.

TELL THE POLICE AND YOUR FAMILY DIE.

Chapter Thirty-One

After he'd stopped vomiting, Lambert collapsed on the floor, every part of him aching. In denial, he retreated to a few hours ago in his mind. The guilt he'd felt outside Sarah's house believing Sophie and Jane were waiting for him at home. He would have done anything now to return to that time and place, to be secure in the knowledge that he would see his wife and child again.

Fighting the negative thoughts, he called first Sarah then Tillman, and with a trembling voice told them what had happened.

Sarah arrived first and found him prone on the floor next to the puddle of vomit. She placed a cool hand on his forehand and picked up the note. 'We'll find them,' she said. 'Come on, you need to get up. We have work to do.' She made coffee and told Lambert to change his clothes.

He moved in a void, his limbs pieces of lead he dragged up the stairs. He muttered to himself as he took a cold shower, trying to banish the negative thoughts threatening to derail him. The cold water washed over him, taking his breath. It was painful to endure but he wanted to suffer more. Whoever killed Beckinsale, Jenkins and Duggan had taken his family and it was all because of him. He deserved to suffer and he made a promise to himself as he turned off the shower. That one way or another he would pay for his mistakes. But for now, he had to stop feeling sorry for himself. Sophie and Jane needed him and he was prepared to do anything to find them.

Tillman was waiting downstairs. The look on his face was as close to sympathetic as the big man got. 'We'll find them,' he said, repeating Sarah's words.

The three of them drank coffee and created an incident board in the dining room. They worked through everything logically. The assumption had to be that the card was from the killer of the three men. The card was the same type, the stencilling identical. They hypothesized that the three victims had died as a warning or message to Lambert. That everything had been leading to this point.

'Reading the note, there's no suggestion you need to help Barnes to escape, only you don't hinder it,' said Sarah.

'Which suggests everything is already planned out,' agreed Tillman.

'But how? MI5 are all over this now following Saunders. It would take something momentous to get him free. This could all be a smokescreen for something else,' said Sarah.

'Unless they're going to break him out before the transfer,' said Lambert.

'Someone internal from the prison, like John Prine?' suggested Tillman.

'Even then it would be some feat to break him out,' said Sarah, still unconvinced.

Lambert looked at Tillman, remembering how easy it had been to access the prison early that evening. 'You met with the prison Governor in Luton, Sarah?'

'Stuart Pierson. Not the most pleasant of characters. I told Partridge and MI5 about my concerns. I don't know if they took it any further but Partridge noted it. I took it upon myself to carry out some surveillance.'

Tillman smiled. Lambert imagined Sarah's ignoring authority appealed to his nature. 'What did you discover?'

'He lives alone. He met three separate women during the period I followed him.'

'Bit of a player.'

'That, or he was internet dating. One of them was different though. They knew each other very well. They got into some sort of argument. She followed him out of a restaurant, and became hysterical. It was quite full on, crying and screaming.'

'What did he do?'

'He was embarrassed. He grabbed her by the shoulder at one point and she calmed down for a bit before it went into a full blown argument.'

Listening to Sarah talk, Lambert somehow put to the back of his mind that Sophie and Jane were missing. Remembering hit him hard. He sat at the kitchen table, hoping the other two hadn't noticed the tremor in his body.

'Description?' asked Tillman.

'Five-eight. Brunette. Brown eyes. She looked quite athletic, slim and well-toned, like she worked out. I didn't get that close but I would have put her between forty and forty-eight.'

The description sparked Lambert's memory, something from the hours of trawling through the System assimilating facts and figures. The description corresponded to a person he'd seen in his file, someone he'd seen more than enough of during the Waverley Manor trials.

Sarah took out her phone. 'I had her plates checked. Brenda Rosenberg.'

That was enough for Lambert. 'Can you get me access?' he asked Tillman, opening the laptop on the kitchen table.

Tillman typed his access code into the System, and Lambert ran a search while his superior, intrigued, looked on.

'Was this her?' said Lambert, turning the screen to Sarah.

Sarah pulled the screen closer to her. 'Yes, how the hell did you know?'

Lambert scrolled the screen down, revealing the woman's maiden name.

Sarah frowned. 'Oh, I see.'

–

The woman's previous name was Barnes. Brenda was Jonathan Barnes' ex-wife. Tillman had a special team, a legacy of his time heading up a secret Met division called The Group, he could use to monitor Brenda. The operatives were undercover and even Lambert didn't know their current roles. Tillman made some calls and assigned a car to be sent to the woman's address. They agreed it would be inadvisable to rush in, so the officers in the car would stand guard until they were sure. First they wanted to see the Governor, Stuart Pierson.

Sarah drove them to his address, a new-build block of flats in St Albans, and parked up. 'He'll recognize you,' said Lambert. 'Best I go in with Tillman.'

Lambert didn't want to give anyone orders – at this point, he was running on adrenaline and emotion – but it was logical for Sarah to wait behind.

It was three a.m. Pierson lived on the twelfth floor. Lambert counted twelve rows up and saw four out of twenty lights were switched on. Tillman pressed the buzzers for the lower levels until a disgruntled voice swore at him and buzzed them in.

The smell of fresh paint filled their nostrils as they made their way into the lobby. They took the lift to the tenth floor and made their way up the two flights of stairs to Pierson's flat. Lambert tried to keep calm. He wanted Sophie and Jane safe, but rushing things would only have a detrimental effect.

They'd agreed in the car they would break in. They had no idea of Pierson's involvement but couldn't take the risk of him alerting anyone. Lambert bent down and checked there was no light beneath Pierson's door. Tillman spent a minute analysing the lock before producing a rolled-up toolkit. 'My alternative career,' he whispered, picking the lock with expert ease.

Lambert drew his gun as Tillman eased in through the doorway.

The darkness enveloped them, the sound of a clock ticking in the distance piercing the silence.

Lambert had glanced back at Tillman for a split second when the man attacked.

It was amateur at best, the movements of a panicked house owner. Pierson screamed as he lashed out at Tillman. There was a deadening thud as an object made contact with Tillman's chest. Still holding his gun, Lambert reached for the light switch. The light flickered on to reveal a fully naked Pierson, a baseball bat held over his head ready to crash down on Tillman.

'I wouldn't,' said Lambert, pointing his gun directly at Pierson's chest. 'Drop the bat.'

Startled, Pierson did as instructed, receiving a sharp punch to the nose from Tillman as a reward.

Pierson grabbed his nose as Lambert placed a hand on Tillman to stop him causing more damage.

'What the actual fuck! I know you, you're that dodgy cop. The one in the papers. Yeah, DCI Lambert.'

Lambert expelled air, regretting he'd prevented Tillman from causing more damage to the man. 'Sit down, Pierson.'

'Fuck off. You're suspended, you can't do this.'

Tillman picked up the baseball bat and made a couple of air swings, the second narrowly missing Pierson's head. 'Sit the fuck down.'

'Let me put some clothes on first.'

'I won't tell you again. Sit down.'

The prison Governor did as instructed, though was clearly not used to receiving orders. 'I'll have your badges for this.'

Tillman edged closer. 'You'll be lucky if you don't leave this room in liquid form. I can have you disappeared as simple as anything. Now you tell us what we need to know and I'll consider your chances of survival.'

'Do I know you?'

'You soon fucking will do,' said Tillman, striking the man full force on his right arm with the baseball bat.

'What the fuck?' screamed Pierson.

Lambert didn't care about the breach of protocol; his thoughts were focused on one thing. 'This woman,' he said, showing Pierson the picture on his phone.

'What about her?'

'You know her?'

'Yes.'

'You were seen arguing with her outside a restaurant called The Bistro.'

'Jesus Christ, have you had me under surveillance? Is this to do with Saunders? I bet it is.' Pierson clicked his fingers. 'That bloody lady cop.'

Lambert glanced at Tillman who swung the bat at Pierson's other side, striking the man's shoulder blade. The blow made him double up, his face crashing down on the glass table.

'What did she want?' said Lambert.

'You know who she is, right?' said Pierson, straightening back up, a line of saliva dripping from his mouth.

'Brenda Barnes.'

Pierson smiled. 'Yeah, B.B. One of yours, wasn't she?' The question was rhetorical.

Jonathan Barnes' wife Brenda had been a detective sergeant at the time of Barnes' incarceration. 'I know who she is. What I want to know is what she was doing with you.'

'It goes no further?' asked Pierson, his earlier bravado gone.

'It goes as far as I want it to,' bellowed Tillman, excelling in his role of bad cop.

'Fine. I don't know how but she'd heard about your detective visiting me. And about Peter Saunders. Like DCI May, she had put two and two together and had come to the mistaken conclusion I had something to do with Peter Saunders' escape.'

'And you didn't?'

'Of course bloody not.'

'What did she want from you, then?' said Lambert.

'She wanted me to help Barnes escape. Jesus, you guys are dense.'

Tillman raised the baseball bat and Pierson held his hands up. 'Sorry, sorry. She thought I would, or could, help her. She'd been tipped off he was moving to Luton. I'm not sure how as I didn't even know at that time. When I told her I couldn't help she freaked out.'

Lambert had no way of verifying this. As if reading his thoughts, Tillman moved towards the man.

'It's true, I swear. I swear.'

Tillman moved away and walked over to Lambert. 'We can't let him go now. He'll talk.'

'What do you suggest?'

'I can detain him. Until we've found Sophie and Jane.'

Lambert had spent the briefest time in one of Tillman's detention areas, another throwback to his days in The Group. Lambert wasn't convinced of the legality of the place but could only hope Tillman still had permission from on high.

'Go with Sarah and question Brenda Barnes. I'll get a team in here to sort out Pierson. Best if you're not involved.'

Chapter Thirty-Two

Lambert explained the situation to Sarah. 'Are you sure we should just leave him in there?' she said.

'He knows what he's doing.' They punched in the address they had for Brenda Barnes and set off.

'How are you dealing with all this?' said Sarah.

'I need to focus on the case, treat it like any other. If I let my thoughts wander I'm going to be of no use at all,' said Lambert.

'You think Barnes has the wherewithal to stage something like this?' asked Sarah.

Lambert remembered going through Brenda's file at the time of her husband's arrest. She was a serving officer and had been brought in for questioning. But she'd appeared shocked by the revelations of her husband's activities. Even now Lambert remembered her face as he showed her the pictures of Waverly Manor, the disbelief that a loved one could be responsible for such atrocities. Had that all been an act?

'What I still don't understand is why she would eliminate Beckinsale, Jenkins and Duggan just to get to me.'

'Perhaps it was a warning,' said Sarah.

'Perhaps,' said Lambert, though he feared something worse, that the three victims were just warm-ups. That Brenda Barnes had been exploring the limits of her powers, building up her tolerance for unspeakable acts, until she reached the point where she was comfortable abducting Sophie and Jane.

The sun was rising by the time they reached the Hertfordshire countryside. Every time he closed his eyes, Lambert pictured Sophie and Jane alone in the dark. He clenched his fists together, fighting the swelling sense of despair.

The smell of silage and manure invaded the car, snapping Lambert out of his reverie. Brenda Barnes lived in a farm cum smallholding in the countryside. Tillman's teams had been deployed in the surrounding areas. They had eyes on the farmland but had yet to approach. Lambert studied the sat-nav, counting down the distance to the house. His heartbeat increased as the metres dwindled. Could it be this easy? Could Brenda be responsible for the killings? Were Sophie and Jane less than a mile away?

Sarah parked up and they moved towards the farmhouse along a single track road. Hedges on either side towered over them making the track seem even narrower. 'I'm carrying,' said Lambert, opening his jacket to reveal the Glock.

Sarah sighed but she made no comment. A gated drive led towards the Barnes' residence. A number of guinea fowl screeched as they approached.

They continued past the entrance to the side of the property, protected by a perimeter of hedges five foot in height. 'There,' said Sarah, pointing to a narrow gap

Lambert poked his head out through the clump of shrubs and trees running across the side of the farmhouse. He dragged himself through on his hands and knees, Sarah close behind. They stayed low as they edged forward, their eyes focused on the farmhouse and the lone woman throwing feed onto the grass for the guinea fowl.

As Brenda retreated behind the house, Lambert scrambled down the slight incline, his legs slipping on the damp grass, until he caught the sight of her again in an open field behind the farmhouse feeding a horse.

Lambert kept low in the wet grass, Sarah behind him, and watched Brenda stroke the animal before picking up a silver bucket and walking to a barn to the rear of the field. He closed his eyes and pictured Jane and Sophie sitting within the building, chained in the darkness. He signalled Sarah, and they ran across the field, passing the horse, until they reached the outside of the barn.

Lambert's heart was racing; maybe it was the distraction of Sophie and Jane being within touching distance but he was slow to react. He was about to open the barn door when cold metal struck the back of his neck.

'On your knees,' said Brenda. 'You as well,' she added, to Sarah. 'On your fronts, hands behind your back.'

Lambert did as instructed, looking up to see the cold, blank stare of Brenda Barnes. In her hands the gleaming metal of a shotgun pointed directly between his eyes.

Once they were both on the ground, Barnes began pacing, the rifle aimed directly at Lambert. Lambert strained his neck, wondering if Tillman's team had eyes on them.

'I know you both. We've met before. DCI Lambert and DCI May. What are you doing trespassing on my property?'

'Do you have a licence for that gun, Brenda?' asked Lambert.

'I'm asking the questions. What the hell are you doing here?'

'We have some questions over the disappearance of Peter Saunders,' said Sarah.

'Peter Saunders? What's that got to do with me? Sit up,' she said. 'But keep your hands where I can see them.'

Lambert pushed himself up. He considered reaching for his gun. He was sure he could get off a shot before Brenda had time to respond but he needed information from her.

'Why would you come here unannounced?' said Barnes. 'It doesn't make any sense.'

'We've spoken to Stuart Pierson. He told us what you requested, Brenda,' said Lambert.

Genuine puzzlement came over the woman's face. 'What did that shit say?' she demanded.

'That you asked for his help to free your husband.'

Lambert was surprised when the woman started laughing. 'I've met some men in my time,' she said, 'my husband being one of them, but I've never met a man so full of shit as Stuart Pierson. He's lying to you, protecting himself.'

'I don't think so,' said Lambert. 'He was pretty convincing.'

'Oh yes, he can be.'

'And I saw you, Brenda,' said Sarah.

'You saw me?' said Barnes.

'Outside The Bistro in St Albans.'

Barnes furrowed her brow. 'Was it just coincidental or were you following me?'

'I was following Pierson, working on the Peter Saunders' case.'

Barnes paused, before surprising them by lowering her gun.

'It wasn't even loaded,' she said. 'Now tell me why you're really here.'

Lambert got to his feet, confused by Barnes' reaction. 'Pierson said you were crying and pleading for his help,' said Lambert.

'And I saw you, Brenda, you were crying.'

'Oh Christ, you saw that. Not my finest hour, I agree, but it wasn't because of my husband. Believe me, do you really think I'd want him back in my life? I told you when you interviewed me, everything that happened in that godforsaken place was a shock. Well, a shock doesn't fully describe it. It was like a death. The man I thought I loved, the man I had children with, was not the man I knew at all. He was worse than an animal. All those deaths, all those children. It was like I was responsible. That's why I came here, I left the force, brought my children out to the countryside in the hope we could somehow put the past behind us, put all that animal had done behind us.'

'So why the tears?' said Lambert.

Brenda puffed out her cheeks. 'Because we were lovers. I can pick them, can't I? I knew Stuart from before. We worked in the same patch. I'd taken prisoners into him. I regret to say it but I was having an affair, even before Jonathan was arrested. I kept it quiet at the time, and now I couldn't care less, obviously.'

'And you were crying because?' said Sarah.

'Because he'd broken it off. I knew he was seeing some other women. The worst thing is it's all Jonathan's fault.'

'In what way?' said Lambert.

'Stuart couldn't accept I'd been married to such a man, that I had his children. He deals with perverts on a daily basis and though he handled it to begin with, it slowly ate away at him until he wanted to see less and less of me. That's why I was crying that day at the restaurant, one last pathetic attempt to get a man to stay with me, the man who thought I was a monster. How pathetic is that?'

'We need to check the barn,' said Lambert.

'Be my guest.'

Lambert kept his hand close to his gun, as Barnes opened the barn door.

They searched the space but it was empty. 'It's just haystacks. All we have is the horses and some poultry. I'm not a farmer, my kids up and left me to go to university in September. So I'm all alone, apart from the odd volunteer who comes to help.'

Lambert had sympathy for the woman; her life had been destroyed by the actions of her husband but it didn't explain why Pierson had lied to them.

'Do you think Pierson had anything to do with Peter Saunders' disappearance?' said Lambert.

'I have absolutely no idea. I was wrong about Jonathan and I was wrong about Stuart. What I can say is the only person he truly cares about is himself. For that reason, I'd be surprised if he had anything to do with Saunders escaping. It's ruined his career.

'I'm not stupid, DCI Lambert. There must be more to you coming here than the word of Stuart Pierson?'

They explained about the murders, missing out the details of Sophie and Jane's abduction.

'I'm sorry. I'd help you if I could,' said Barnes.

'Why would Pierson lie to us?' said Lambert.

'You'll have to ask him. He's not stupid though. I imagine incriminating me diverted your attention from questioning him?'

Lambert grimaced, thankful Tillman still had the man in custody. He called his boss and reported back what Brenda had told him.

'Don't worry, we'll get the truth from him,' said Tillman, hanging up.

–

They reconvened back at Lambert's house. Sarah was pouring coffee as Tillman arrived. 'We've questioned him again. He admitted he was lying about Brenda Barnes wanting to get her husband out of jail.'

'Why the hell did he lie about that?' said Lambert.

'Claims he was nervous. Not thinking straight. I've left a team watching Brenda and will release Pierson later in the day. We can see if they arrange to meet.'

Lambert drank the offered coffee, guilty at enjoying the taste. The three of them sat in silence. Lambert imagined the other two were thinking the same as him: they had so little to go on.

Despite which, Lambert had far from given up hope. There was an explanation out there and he knew if he could relax his mind the answer would come. Whoever had taken Sophie and Jane would not leave it at this. There would be an endgame, even if it was a failed attempt to spring Jonathan Barnes from prison.

'Log me onto the System again,' he said to Tillman.

Tillman wrote down his passwords on a piece of paper.

Lambert took the paper and sprinted upstairs with his laptop, past photos of Sophie and Jane and Chloe. He would always blame himself for losing Chloe and refused to allow the same thing to happen again.

He would save Jane and Sophie.

In his office, he dragged up every piece of information he had on the three killings. Using Tillman's passwords he logged onto the System and opened the files on Waverly Manor. What was he missing?

One of Lambert's strengths was determining patterns in a seemingly random order of events. The only downside to such an approach was a lack of methodology; it happened, and he had no way of forcing it.

He studied each victim one by one on the large whiteboard above his desk. He wrote Alistair Beckinsale's name first and listed the potential suspects, repeating the process with Lance Jenkins and Inspector Duggan.

He went back to the beginning and wrote Thomas Powell and Dominic Webster. Last, he reluctantly wrote the name of the disgraced former officer Jonathan Barnes, circling the name as if it tainted the others by its presence.

He stood back from the board, stared hard at the six names and the list of smaller names beneath. He scrubbed out Jonathan Barnes to aid his concentration, and looked again.

He was reaching for something: a word, a phrase, a witness, something explaining or linking the five men on the board. He tried to think logically, starting with the basic facts he knew. Each of the five victims were male; three were under thirty, two over thirty. Beckinsale and Jenkins had suffered some form of abuse either by family members or from outside the family. There was a potential link to the Manor, but it was conjecture at best.

Could the victims be linked somehow? Inspector Duggan had his part to play in the arrest of Jonathan Barnes. So Lambert ticked his name. Next to Beckinsale and Jenkins he made a smaller tick: both had suffered some form of ordeal as a child, though he had no clarification of this yet. Next to Webster and Powell he put a question mark. Powell had been killed by his aunt but there was no suggestion of abuse. Webster was the anomaly. He was an abuser, not a victim, but there was a reason for him being there.

The frustration increased. It was like having a word on the tip of his tongue, something ordinary and everyday he inexplicably couldn't remember. Lambert concentrated, reading the names on the board out loud, adding extra ones as files and snapshots from Waverley Manor scrolled past on his laptop.

He added Brenda Barnes, Stuart Pierson, Peter Saunders and the MI5 agent, Partridge. He closed his eyes and pinched his forehead; he needed to clear the clutter of information scrolling through his head. There was a pattern there, he was sure of it.

He clicked on Inspector Duggan's file, the first time he'd had access to it since the man's death. The picture of the murder scene flashed up and Lambert froze it on the screen. At times he'd hated Duggan, but he'd not deserved this. It was an extraordinary replica of Jonathan Barnes' injuries, almost perfect in its accuracy.

He scrolled through some more pages, the answer beginning to unravel.

Inspector Duggan was survived by one elderly relative, Frank Duggan, an eighty-seven-year-old retiree who lived in Wales.

He went through the other victims. Alistair Beckinsale was survived by his mother and father, Lance Jenkins by his parents. Of the old cases, Thomas Powell was survived by his mother, his father having committed suicide. The only anomaly was Dominic Webster, murdered by his family.

But wasn't that the point? Everything centred around the family.

Lambert turned to the sixth victim, the one he'd scrubbed out, the one still alive, the former DCI Jonathan Barnes. Incarcerated, he'd left behind a wife, a daughter and — most importantly, Lambert was now convinced — a son. He rushed downstairs. 'Parents and their children,' he screamed at Tillman and Sarah.

'Slow down, Michael,' said Sarah.

Lambert took a deep breath and explained his theory, listing the victims and those who survived them.

'Brenda Barnes doesn't want her husband back in her life. It's the son, Edmund Barnes. He's the one we're after.'

Chapter Thirty-Three

Sophie reached out in the near-darkness, her hands grabbing her daughter. Jane didn't respond so she pulled her nearer, tearful as she felt the steady heartbeat of her child. 'Jane, can you hear me, baby?' she whispered into the child's ear, but Jane didn't open her eyes.

A bottle of water rolled away as she adjusted her position on the stone floor. Sophie unscrewed the cap and sniffed the contents. It was odourless but she replaced the cap without drinking.

Her head was a thick sponge, her thinking muddled. She searched for a memory but her amnesia was total. Her last memory was parking the car. She couldn't even remember leaving the vehicle and entering the house. A vague memory of raised voices was just out of reach. It was like the worst ever hangover magnified by a thousand. How could she have let this happen? She was supposed to protect Jane.

She let the child slip from her grasp. Removing her pullover she used it as a pillow for Jane's head. Maybe she would sleep through all this; Michael would arrive any minute and Jane would never know.

Sophie stretched and paced the room. She calculated the dimensions by placing one foot in front of the other, the space approximately fifty metres by thirty. There were no windows, only a locked door with the thinnest shard of light slipping through the opening at the bottom.

A memory of falling down stairs came to her and she winced, her hand reaching for the tender bruise on her left shoulder.

They were in a basement. 'Hello?' she screamed, pulling at the edges of the door, the noise reverberating in her head. She tried to blink away the pain but it was worse than any migraine she'd ever experienced.

'Think,' she said to herself, but it was much easier said than done. She wasn't herself. 'But at least I'm aware of that. They've drugged me,' she mumbled, glancing at the bottle of water.

Dizzy, she sat next to Jane and blinked her eyes, fighting the fatigue. 'Must stay awake,' she said, falling asleep.

Chapter Thirty-Four

The last time Lambert saw Edmund Barnes he'd been a gangly teenager sitting next to his sister in court listening to the heinous crimes being attributed to his father. Lambert had felt sorry for the pair. Both stared ahead as the sentence was read out, hardly reacting as Brenda Barnes hugged them. Why had she brought them to the courthouse? Had it been to support Jonathan Barnes, or a means to explain to her children what their father really was, the monster he'd become?

If Lambert's theory was correct, whatever the reasoning behind taking her children to court, its effect on Edmund Barnes was detrimental.

Lambert explained his thinking to Tillman and Sarah. If they thought he was grasping at straws they didn't give it voice.

'How old is he now?' asked Sarah.

'Nineteen, I believe. In his first year of criminology at the University of Kent,' said Lambert, accessing the boy's file on the System.

'Criminology,' said Tillman, full of disdain.

'We have an address for him. Canterbury.' The photo on his file didn't remind Lambert of Jonathan Barnes. The boy was stick thin. In the picture at least, his eyes looked vacant and dull. Could this really be the killer? Lambert drummed his fingers on the dining room table. He was desperate to move, to find Sophie and Jane. His colleagues noticed his tension.

Sarah moved towards him. Lambert sensed she would have touched him had Tillman not been there. 'There's one more person we need to speak to. I spoke to Paul Guthrie from Woolwich prison when Saunders escaped. If Pierson isn't involved then maybe Guthrie had more of a role to play. He'll be in charge of Barnes' transfer, so we should question him.'

'Glenn, you know that guard at Woolwich. Any information on the Governor?' asked Lambert.

'He's less hands-on than Pierson, that's why it was easy to get access the other night. We could question him but I think our resources are best directed to tracking Barnes junior.'

Lambert looked at Sarah. 'I'll speak to him,' she said. 'You two get to Canterbury.'

Tillman drove, refusing to allow Lambert behind the wheel. 'Try to rest, Michael,' he said, knowing his words were redundant.

Lambert was painfully alert, as if he'd drunk a litre of coffee. His mind replayed the information he'd scrolled through back at the house, verifying the conclusions he'd reached, searching for vital clues he and Sarah had missed while thoughts of Sophie and Jane overran his mind.

Hard as he tried, he couldn't help but imagine them suffering. He pictured narrow corridors, dungeons, darkness and chains. He came close to sobbing as he pictured Jane separated from her mother, alone in the darkness, confused and terrified. It was his fault, and although he vowed to do anything humanly possible to find them, a pessimistic part of him worried he would never get the chance.

They made good time to Canterbury, driving against the traffic to the cathedral city in east Kent. The roads and pavements on the outskirts were coated in rain. Edmund Barnes lived in the student area and, it being Christmas, most residents were at home with their families. They decided not to contact Brenda Barnes in case she warned her son, and so far had kept Matilda out of it. Lambert didn't want to give Sophie and Jane's abductor the slightest reason to fulfil his threat.

'This is it,' said Tillman, driving past a three-storey Edwardian house.

They parked down the road and moved back towards the house. Lambert peered through one of the downstairs windows where the curtains were drawn. Inside he saw a communal room. It was typical student digs, a beige carpet strewn with discarded dinner plates and cutlery, empty beer cans and brimming ashtrays. Posters of female celebrities Lambert didn't recognize adorned the walls, suggesting Edmund Barnes shared the house with other males.

A porch was tacked onto the front of the house, an ugly modern addition. Lambert tried the door, surprised it was open. The second internal door was locked. Lambert looked at Tillman, who took out his toolkit from his jacket without speaking.

Lambert waited until they were inside to withdraw his gun. He risked spooking one of the students but was beyond such concerns. They secured the living room and the kitchen before moving towards the bedrooms.

There were two rooms to the side of the downstairs hall, both empty. The first contained nothing more than a bare double mattress, ancient looking and resplendent with various dark stains, and a lone desk and chair. A large double bed took up most of the second room, its mattress covered by a thick duvet. Paintings and posters lined the walls, arranged in perfect symmetry as if the occupant had a mild case of OCD. A montage of photographs covered the noticeboard by the desk. Lambert studied the photos while Tillman kept guard. Smiling youths beamed back at him, so young Lambert thought it incredible they were at university. He searched for a glimpse of Edmund but couldn't see the boy's dark eyes in any of the photos. Lambert signalled Tillman, pointing upstairs.

Both of the rooms on the second floor were vacant. The first room contained a single bed, its only other contents a weights bench and a bumper pack of man-sized tissues. The second room contained two beds, each with duvets and pillows. The room had posters but no photos. The wardrobes were all but empty, two pairs of trainers in one, a pack of unopened cornflakes in the other. If Edmund was staying in either room then he'd gone home for Christmas. He regretted not asking Brenda Barnes at the farmhouse.

Lambert led the way up the third staircase to the loft area. He baulked on opening the first door. An airless bathroom was covered from floor to ceiling in some form of green fungus. Tillman pushed the door to the last room and Lambert burst through with his gun raised. Damp, flowered-patterned wallpaper drooped from the walls. A sturdy wooden desk heaped with pamphlets and books sat next to a metal-framed bed covered by a single beige sheet. Lambert sifted through the mess until he found a letter addressed to Edmund Barnes. 'Looks like his room,' said Lambert.

Lambert checked the wardrobe and a small wood-panelled chest of drawers. If Edmund had left he hadn't packed, as both items of furniture were full of clothes'

They looked through the books on the desk, mainly criminology textbooks. Lambert flicked through a couple of true crime tomes. There was nothing unusual about the books. They could be picked up easily online or at a local bookshop, but Lambert wondered if Edmund had bought them for other reasons.

'Over here,' said Tillman, who was bent down by the wardrobe. He stood aside so Lambert could see the wooden box nailed to the base of the wardrobe. 'Get my gear,' said Tillman, pointing to the thick metal lock securing the box in place.

Tillman forced the lock off without trouble. 'Oh shit,' he said, reaching inside. 'Looks like father like son.'

Lambert shut his eyes, for the briefest of moments lost in a haze of red swirling images. He wanted to stay there, to allow sleep to steal him from his present reality, but fought the sensation.

Tillman placed the material he'd found on the bed. Lambert was as hardened as it was possible to be to such images from his work on the Waverley Manor case, and similar cases throughout his years on the force. Yet every time he was forced to view such material he felt tainted, as if he was somehow colluding with the sick perverts responsible.

As Tillman surmised, Edmund Barnes, only just turned nineteen, had the same proclivity as his father. They searched through the images in silence, sickened by the sight of the children, trying to find a clue as to Edmund Barnes' whereabouts – to where he was hiding Sophie and Jane.

The last thought kept Lambert going. He'd convinced himself Edmund wouldn't do anything to Sophie and Jane until his father escaped, and he had to cling on to that hope.

They searched the house from top to bottom. There was no garden save for a few metres of weed-strewn concrete to the back of the house. Wherever Edmund was hiding it wasn't here.

Back upstairs they made a final check of Edmund's room, collecting his photographs from the wooden box. The images were emblazed onto Lambert's mind and he feared he would never be free of them. He scrolled through them in his memory. He froze on one image and instructed Tillman to tip out the pictures again. He shuffled through them, saddened at the lost souls staring back at him, until he reached the one that had jogged his memory.

'There,' he said, pointing to the background of a grainy image. 'I know where that is.'

Chapter Thirty-Five

Sarah sat in the lobby of Woolwich prison desperate for some news from Michael and Tillman. Michael was doing his best but she'd seen the change in him. He was strung as tight as piano wire and she was concerned what would happen when he snapped. They'd agreed to keep it between the three of them. She'd not argued. Despite every tenet of her training and procedure telling her they needed to involve the authorities, she agreed it was impossible to know who to trust. Even involving DS Kennedy at this point would alert others. She trusted Michael, and to a lesser extent Tillman, and if they agreed this was the best plan she was inclined to agree, at least for the time being.

Paul Guthrie's assistant, a middle-aged woman with a dour, unreadable face, led her into the Governor's office. 'DCI May, this is a surprise. Please take a seat.'

The Governor didn't rise from his seat or offer her a hand to shake. He stayed behind his desk, arms folded. 'Can I offer you a tea or coffee?'

'Black coffee, please.'

'Two black coffees, Linda.'

Sarah recalled her previous meetings with Guthrie, his willingness to assist her and his jovial countenance in stark contrast to Pierson's manner.

Now he was behaving in the same alpha-male manner as his fellow prison Governor, but Sarah was not convinced. Unlike Pierson, Guthrie's behaviour appeared out of character – like he was acting a part. Sarah had seen it in other people of authority. Talented individuals who were naturally introverted, acting out of character as if they expected that's what others expected. Guthrie gave the impression of being in control, but his gestures were defensive. He stared at her as they waited for the coffee but his arms were folded, his legs crossed. The big desk was meant to make a statement, but to Sarah it looked like it was there to protect him.

The Governor waited until his secretary delivered the drinks before speaking again, glancing at the door as she shut it before opening his mouth. 'So how can I help you this time?' he asked, appearing to burn his lip as he drank his coffee too soon.

'I wanted to talk about John Prine. We haven't spoken since his body was discovered, and I imagine it came as a shock to you and your staff. Do you have any idea why he would have helped Peter Saunders escape?'

The Governor scowled, his look suggesting he'd already answered the same question from Partridge. 'As I've told your colleagues on more than one occasion, I have no idea why he would have gone with Saunders. I can only imagine he was there under duress.'

'What makes you say that?' asked Sarah.

'Why else would he go? Saunders killed him, so to my mind that suggests he didn't want to be there.'

'Maybe he was helping Saunders, and Saunders betrayed him.'

Guthrie shook his head. 'John Prine worked here for eleven years. Long before Peter Saunders was incarcerated. I struggle to believe his head was turned by a category A prisoner.'

'I imagine it was a relief when he left?'

'Saunders? Not really. There's plenty more of them. Makes no difference.'

'Such as Jonathan Barnes?'

Guthrie didn't try to hide his anger. 'Why are you here, DCI May?'

'I believe Jonathan Barnes is being moved on the twenty-ninth December?'

'That is privileged information.'

'Are you concerned Barnes will abscond like Saunders?'

'No, of course not.'

'You sound convinced.'

'As I said, DCI May, Peter Saunders' escape was terrible, but it won't happen again.'

Sarah changed her line of questioning. 'Jonathan Barnes was attacked in prison, was he not?'

'Unfortunately these types of things occasionally happen. The type of person he was... Well, you know, he was a target.'

'Was Saunders?'

'They were in separate blocks, but both high risk.'

'Anyone attack Saunders?'

'No.'

'You sound sure.'

'I'm sure he received some threats but there were no reported incidents.'

'Getting back to Jonathan Barnes. Have you had any contact with his family?'

'No, why would I have?'

'His wife, perhaps.'

'As a rule, I tend not to speak to the inmates' families. We have special liaison teams for that.'

'I understand.' Sarah thought about Brenda Barnes' relationship with Stuart Pierson and wondered if it would lead to the man losing his job.

Guthrie was holding something back. She'd felt it the first time she'd met him, and it was more obvious now. It was the way he'd said 'duress' earlier. 'If there's something you need to tell me, now would be the time.'

Guthrie paused. 'I really don't know what you mean, DCI May. Now if you don't mind…'

Sarah remained sitting. She gave the Governor her card. 'If you're in trouble, I can help. No one needs to know.'

Guthrie took the card. 'As I said, I don't have a clue what you're talking about.'

–

A car was waiting for her outside. She tried to call Lambert to warn him but the door flew open before she had time to enter the digits. 'DCI May. A word.' Agent Partridge stepped out of the car, holding the door open.

Sarah scanned the surrounding area and decided running was pointless. She brushed past Partridge as she took a seat in the back of his car, the warm leather upholstery squeaking as she sat.

'Care to tell me what you are doing here, DCI May?' Partridge asked the question with a wry amusement, as if he wasn't used to being disobeyed.

'Making myself useful.'

'Useful? The last time we spoke you were heading to Bristol for some well-deserved annual leave. What brings you back here?'

'I had some more thoughts.'

'Thoughts you didn't care to share with us?'

'It didn't seem significant enough to trouble you with.'

'Everything is significant, DCI May. You know that. What did you want with Mr Guthrie?'

Technically, Sarah hadn't done anything wrong. She'd spoken to Guthrie on legitimate police business. Partridge couldn't stop her asking questions, but he could make life difficult for her. 'There were some questions I hadn't asked him before. I wanted to clarify things.'

'And did you?'

Sarah matched the agent's stare, refusing to be intimidated. 'Yes, I got what I was looking for. How close are we to finding Peter Saunders?' she asked, trying to change the subject.

Partridge ignored her. 'What was it you found out?'

The word duress sprang to Sarah's mind but she wouldn't be sharing that with the agent. 'I checked Saunders' movements during the day of his escape. Nothing that needed reporting.'

'Oh really, you feel qualified to make that decision?'

Sarah took a deep breath, the smell of the leather and the lingering hint of Partridge's aftershave hitting her. She glanced at Partridge's driver who kept his head straight, gazing into the distance. 'I'm a Detective Chief Inspector in the NCA. Of course I'm qualified to make that decision.' She omitted 'you patronising bastard', but was sure he got the message.

'This would have nothing to with the upcoming transfer of Jonathan Barnes, would it?'

'I've told you my reasons for being here.'

'Because if it is, I would suggest you forget it. Barnes is being transferred under our supervision.'

'Is that supposed to make me feel reassured?' asked Sarah, provoking a glimmer of annoyance from Partridge.

'I would feel reassured if I were you. The professionals are handling things now.'

His smugness was intolerable. Sarah reached for the car door, and was stopped by Partridge placing his hand on hers.

'I don't care who you work for. Get your hand off me,' said Sarah.

The driver turned around, his glare focused on Sarah. She shrugged his intervention off. 'I'm leaving this car now,' she said, shoving Partridge's hand away.

Partridge didn't try to stop her. 'Have it your way, DCI May. But if I find you interfering once more in this case, you'll find yourself in a similar establishment to the one you've just left.'

Sarah left the side door open and walked to her car. She kept her gaze ahead and tried not to hurry despite her desire to put as much distance between herself and Partridge as possible.

Chapter Thirty-Six

How could they have been so stupid? Where else could he have taken them? For Edmund it started with Waverley Manor and would end there.

'Fuck, haven't they concreted that place up yet?' said Tillman.

'No,' said Lambert, recalling his recent visit to the site. 'The entrances are under lock and key, but they can still be accessed.' He fought the visions of Sophie and Jane imprisoned underground. The tunnels had been cleared since the investigation, the chains and torture devices recorded and locked away, but there was no undoing the atmosphere of the place. It was a prison, a torture dungeon, and the thought of his wife and child being kept there for even a second was unbearable. A chill ran through his blood, seeping into his bones. Every living minute was torturous as it meant another minute of suffering for his loved ones.

He called Sarah, her burner going straight to answerphone. He left a coded message, hoping she would decipher their destination.

Tillman made some calls as he drove. A legacy of when he'd led a secret department within the NCA known only as The Group, his superior occasionally called on the services of a secondary team, the full details of which were not known to Lambert. Lambert listened as Tillman arranged for his officers to cover the surrounding areas. He didn't elaborate on the details, and stressed no one was to go anywhere near Waverley Manor without his permission. Lambert trusted him, and knew his covert team would follow his orders.

'We'll get him,' said Tillman, as if reading Lambert's thoughts.

Lambert had experienced fear before, had been seconds from death on too many occasions, but nothing could have prepared him for this. He'd been in an induced coma when Chloe died, and waking to news of his daughter's death had been unbearable. Now Sophie and Jane's fate was in his hands, and all he could do was will the journey to end as he sat impotent and useless as a passenger. He glared at Tillman, willing him to drive faster.

The big man saw his pained look and floored the accelerator. 'Do you think Edmund plans to break his father out of prison?' asked Tillman.

Lambert presumed Tillman was trying to divert his attention. 'Do I think Edmund killed Beckinsale, Jenkins and Duggan? Yes. Do I think he has Sophie and Jane? Yes. Do I think he masterminded the escape of Peter Saunders and is preparing to do the same for his father? No, I don't.'

It was good to air his thoughts. Edmund was able, had learnt or inherited some twisted skills from his father, but Lambert didn't believe he had the capacity to spring Peter Saunders. Lambert was sure he was working alone. He'd seen him at the courthouse, and had seen his pitiful room. Edmund Barnes was a loner. And although he was sure he wanted his father back, he didn't have the resources to get it done. That didn't mean it couldn't happen. Someone was still pulling strings for the Manor. And with Peter Saunders free, it was not inconceivable more of the eight would follow, even if MI5 were in charge of security.

'Here we are,' said Tillman, pulling into the all too familiar lane and parking up. Memories came flooding back, none of them positive. Cutting through the woods to reach the deserted area where they'd eventually uncovered the trapdoor to the underground prison; the metallic, decaying smell of the tunnels. It wasn't enough to concrete up the dungeon. If Lambert had his way, the whole area would be destroyed, the woodland burnt to a cinder along with the memories of all who had suffered within its perimeter.

They pulled on their coats, Tillman retrieved a gun from a hidden compartment within the boot, and headed through the foliage to the pathway. Moving like soldiers in a war zone, they edged through the foliage in silence, attuned to every sound. Lambert dragged his arms on a set of brambles as he reached an area of clear ground. There was one last path to trek through before they reached the Manor.

'You're going to have wait here,' he said to Tillman.

Tillman held his gaze, for the first time in many years displaying a hint of emotion. 'No way.'

'I don't want to take the risk, Glenn. If Edmund sees me alone he could talk. It may give me a chance, an opportunity to put him down. If you're there he'll think I've involved the police.' Lambert shuddered as he remembered the threat on the note.

Lambert typed a message on his burner phone and showed it to Tillman. 'If I send this, you have my permission to come running.' He left the message on his screen and placed the phone in his jacket pocket, heading alone into the woods before Tillman could object.

He remained focused, banishing thoughts of Sophie and Jane. He had a job to complete and couldn't afford emotional distractions. His mission was to find Edmund, eliminate him and end this once and for all.

Waverley Manor existed in a place out of time. Lambert smelt the place before seeing it. It was hard to believe months ago the area was swarming with diggers and machinery, hundreds of personnel trekking through every last ounce of mud, accounting for every lost body. Nature ignored such intrusions. The holes and footprints were covered over now. He'd been here only a few days ago but already it was a different place. The branches of the trees appeared heavier, the undergrowth deeper, as if the ghosts of the manor were telling him to stay clear. Lambert edged along, keeping to the side of the path to avoid detection until he reached his destination. The place he hoped he'd never see again.

He had no plan. Edmund Barnes had told him not to interfere. The gun was in his inside jacket. He could draw and fire in one to two seconds on a good day. Would he be able to do the same now? If Barnes emerged with a screaming Jane in his arms, Sophie gagged and blindfolded, would he behave with the same dispassion he prided himself on, or would he ultimately be betrayed by emotion?

He edged towards the entrance. Darkness covered the place as if Waverley Manor belonged in its own dimension. It sucked out the light and returned Lambert to last year and the first time he'd stepped into its depths.

Lambert was proved right. The steel cage used to block the entry was prised open, the entrance uncovered. Lambert took a deep breath and peered into the darkness stretching on forever into the underground depths. He looked around him, waiting for Edmund to pounce. Was his family down there? The thought shook him into action. He climbed into the small opening, grabbing onto the cold metal of the ladders connected to the side and made his way down, doing his best not to hurry, until he hit the concrete floor.

He illuminated the area with his torch, his chest tight as he sucked in the stale, cold air. In all his nightmares, he never thought he'd return to this place. The terror of the discoveries he'd uncovered last time rushed back to him. He fought the panic and claustrophobia. From this point he had two choices, left or right. Last time he'd chosen right and he made the same choice again. He was already at a disadvantage, his eyes adjusting to the gloom. The Glock led the way, pointing in front of him. He gripped the handle, too tense to risk placing his finger on the trigger, and moved towards the first corner, waiting for the ambush.

It didn't arrive and he understood why a fraction too late.

Adrenaline surged through his body as he stared open mouthed at the body blocking the space in front of him. It was arranged in a perverse recreation of a crucifixion, the arms and legs chained to the walls diagonally, the body caught as if mid-star jump. Lambert held his gun in front of him as if the corpse could do some harm, and retreated at the sound coming from behind him.

He'd been duped by Edmund, the threat on the note tricking him into coming to Waverley Manor on his own. He sprinted back up the tunnel, banishing the thoughts of the last time he'd been here. The sound of metal on metal echoed through the chamber and he shouted out, 'Edmund, stop.'

He reached the ladder in time to see a shadow above the gated doorway. Something akin to laughter filtered down the tunnel as the padlock was snapped shut. Lambert wasted no time, firing into the opening, the sound of the bullets ricocheting off the steel gate echoing in the tunnels, until the light started fading as the opening was covered.

Lambert tried not to panic. Tillman was nearby, and even if something happened to him, sooner or later someone would think to look for him. He had two phones but no signal. He pointed his torch at the walls of the tunnel, warding off feelings of claustrophobia.

The corpse he'd seen in the tunnel was Peter Saunders.

Had Lambert been wrong all along? Had Edmund Barnes been responsible for Saunders' escape?

A second thought crossed Lambert's mind; he'd taken the right tunnel from the junction but there was still one more tunnel to explore.

Sophie and Jane could be down there after all.

Chapter Thirty-Seven

Sophie woke with a shudder, enjoying a split second of confusion before reality assaulted her. 'Jane,' she screamed, dragging her body across the stone floor to her daughter.

Jane was still not responding but her breathing was strong. Sophie couldn't tell how long she'd been asleep. Her slip into unconsciousness was dreamless, a dark void which could have lasted hours or minutes. What could Jane have been given to affect her so?

Sophie moved to the corner of the room and placed her fingers in her mouth, cursing herself for not doing so earlier. She gagged, a weak trickle of vomit coating her fingers. She could only hope the poison had left her. Her body was lethargic, her limbs weak, but that could be down to dehydration. She wouldn't let it defeat her this time.

She began edging along the wall, using the thin shard of light as a guide. She checked as best she could the density of the wall, stretched high on her tiptoes. The walls were smooth, plastered. After making a lap of the room, she started again along the floor, searching for anything that could help, finding only the bottle of poisoned water.

Closing her eyes, she held Jane close, refusing to panic. If their captors wanted them dead, they would have been killed by now. Manic thoughts hovered on the periphery of her mind, trying to gain traction. Pictures of Waverley Manor, the descriptions she'd heard from the trials Michael attended. Each time they intruded she held on to something else: Christmas Eve, Michael carrying Jane to bed. Jane learning to speak, her scrunched-up face as she took her first taste of broccoli. And her other darling girl, Chloe. The two were similar in so many ways, and she couldn't let the same thing happen again.

Michael.

It all came down to him. She began crying, worried her thoughts somehow betrayed her husband. She blamed the dehydration again, but wasn't it Michael's fault? She'd never blamed him for Chloe's death, but he'd been the one driving the car. And now? Now, they were here because of him. It had always been his career, and she'd known what she was getting into, both the first time and the second, following the split, but she had to face the truth. If it wasn't for him they wouldn't be here.

He rarely shared, but his latest case had reached the newspapers again, a killer leaving a card with Michael's name on it. That was why they were here, that was why her baby girl was in danger.

She picked up the bottled water. Heavy in her hand, it was still stone cold. She unscrewed the cap again and sniffed. In the end, she glanced at Jane and the soft lift of her chest and decided she couldn't risk either of them taking a drink. There would be a chance, a moment where she would need to be alert, and she could survive for the time being with the dryness coating her mouth and throat.

A noise came from outside the door and she jumped, clinging tighter to Jane. Was it voices? 'Hello!' she cried, rushing to the door. 'Hello!'

Chapter Thirty-Eight

The sound of Lambert's gunshots reached Tillman. Three loud blasts breaking the stillness of the night. He didn't immediately break cover. He checked the burner phone to see if Lambert had contacted him, and sent word to the team controlling the perimeter, instructing them to move in.

Both of Lambert's phones went straight to voicemail, so he moved off. If he'd been dealing with a civilian he'd never have followed this procedure; it had been madness sending in Lambert on his own but he understood his reasoning.

'I'm too old for this shit,' he mouthed to himself, his foot sliding on a covering of ice as he followed the path taken by Lambert. He could only hope the gunshots had come from Lambert and that they'd proved fatal.

He couldn't hurry despite his desire to reach Waverley Manor. Loud footsteps would alert his presence and the ground was unforgiving, jagged and layered with ice. Instead, he edged forward, his gun poised for the slightest movement. This was not the way it was supposed to play out. He moved to the edge of a copse of trees, the broken remains of the Manor visible through the vines and bushes. He lay down on his front surveying the area, searching for the trapdoor Lambert had made for, wondering if his friend had been foolish enough to enter the tunnels alone.

Time was his enemy. His chest heaved against the ground, his laboured breathing threatening to reveal his presence. He tried moving along the ground on his hands and knees, commando style, but his bulk and age betrayed him.

'Fuck it,' he said, using his hands to push up off the cold hard ground. From his crouched position he sprinted into the darkness, semi-tensed, in case someone was ready to shoot him. He rushed over to the shattered remains of Waverley Manor and through the brickwork and frosted foliage searched for the opening.

–

Lambert screamed, the noise echoing in the cavernous space. He viewed the current situation from Edmund's perspective. Lambert had been responsible for his father's conviction and, some people believed, for the attack on him in prison. Lambert could only guess the extent of Edmund's involvement in his father's world, though the material they'd found in his house gave some indication.

Edmund wanted revenge, and every muscle and sinew in Lambert's aching body told him it was waiting for him around the corner. It wasn't déjà vu overcoming him as he headed back to the junction, more a sense of impending doom. The last time he'd journeyed down this tunnel he hadn't known what to expect. But now he could picture it, and if his worst fears came to pass it would be his undoing.

He shone his torch on the walls as he tiptoed down the tunnel. The cavern held its history in its walls. Bloodstains and scratch marks decorated the porous rock, and Lambert shone the torch away, holding it directly in front of him instead.

The first room he came to was clear. The last time he'd been here he'd seen a blood-soaked mattress and tools of torture and incarceration. Now it was just an empty space but Lambert remembered, would never forget, the heinous crimes committed here.

He moved forward, daring himself to hope as the second room matched the first. Room Three was empty and he sprinted onwards, eager to confirm his optimism that he was alone. He reached Room Four in a rush of movement, and realized he'd been holding his breath. He gasped for air, discovering that, like its counterparts, Room Four held nothing but bare stone and memories.

At the end of the tunnel was a larger room, where during the investigation the real horrors began to reveal themselves. He moved forward once more, hoping against hope as he walked into the high-ceilinged room.

The police had done their best to clear the place but the past lingered. Names were still chiselled onto the walls, holes carved into the stone where chains had hung.

And in the corner was the hatch, the trapdoor to a second level worse even than this first circle of hell. Lambert shone his torch on the padlock holding the door in place and was almost sick with relief when he read the inscription: 'Property of the Metropolitan Police'. He lowered his gun, the tension in his arm easing, until he heard the sound of someone screaming, reverberating down the tunnel.

–

'What the fuck is going on?' said Tillman, his foot catching on the thick slab of concrete. Had this been Edmund Barnes' plan all along, to entice Lambert to Waverley Manor in the hope of finding his wife and daughter, only to trap him underground forever?

Tillman bent on his haunches and pushed at the concrete, grunting with the effort, the slab barely moving more than a few centimetres. Tillman filled the air with obscenities and pushed again, screaming at the exertion. Once he had the slab moving it took on momentum and soon the covering was open. He pulled at the chain gate covering the opening only to find it was padlocked shut. He shone his light down the vertical tunnel, illuminating the ladder, and screamed Lambert's name. Footsteps echoed up the concrete walls and Tillman edged back from the opening, his gun at the ready.

A period of silence followed until Lambert's voice said, 'Glenn?'

'Jesus Christ, Michael,' said Tillman, ashamed to hear the emotion in his voice. 'Can I stick my head down or am I going to get it shot off?'

'He's gone, Glenn. Peter Saunders is down here, what remains of him.'

Tillman shone the torch again, the pale, tired face of Lambert staring up at him. Tillman took out his toolkit and undid the padlock, and waited with heart pounding for Lambert to make his way up the ladder. He stuck out his right arm and pulled Lambert to the surface. Both men embraced, the contact fierce and momentary, before each pulled away.

Tillman didn't want to say it but had to ask. 'Sophie and Jane?'

'They're not down there.'

A wave of tension left Tillman's body. 'OK, let's find this sick bastard.'

Chapter Thirty-Nine

Tillman updated his colleagues, who'd spread out on the perimeter of the forest. Whatever the legality of his secret team, Tillman wasn't about to let Barnes escape. They took different routes, Tillman heading further into the woods, Lambert back the way he'd come.

Lambert ignored the memory of being underground, fighting off thoughts of claustrophobia and nightmares of being buried alive. His only goal now was finding Edmund Barnes and, from there, locating his daughter and wife. He sprinted through the undergrowth, oblivious to loose branches and uneven ground. If Barnes escaped now they might never see him again.

The boy may have expected Lambert to have come alone so hopefully hadn't planned for his escape. Lambert continued running, ignoring the fatigue seeping through his body. He sprinted into the clearing separating the two dark pathways, glancing in every direction, fearing Edmund could have taken multiple exit points. He continued along the second pathway towards his car, regretting having taken this route.

Lambert reached his car without seeing any sign of Barnes. He screamed hysterically into the night air and rained his fists down on the roof of his vehicle, only stopping when the sound of a gunshot filled the night air.

—

Seconds later, Lambert's phone rang. It was Tillman. 'Tell me you've got him,' said Lambert.

'Actually, we have. He's suffered a gunshot wound to the calf but he'll survive. We're about to question him. Get here immediately,' said Tillman, hanging up.

Seconds later a GPS location appeared on Lambert's screen. Lambert didn't hesitate and resumed sprinting back the way he'd just come. He'd been only seconds away from Barnes, who'd run to the south-west corner of the clearing stretching for half a mile behind the clump of oak trees.

Edmund Barnes was lying on his back, his head resting against a tree trunk, flanked on either side by Tillman and two of his men. Edmund was in considerable pain, his body frozen, his face contorted into a rictus mask.

'Edmund,' said Lambert, his breathing rapid and visible in the frosted air, as he waited for Edmund to respond.

The boy stared at him like he was a ghost. 'You?' he questioned.

'If you mean the man you tried to bury alive, then yes, it's me,' said Lambert. 'Now I'm sure these fine officers have already told you, this is only going to work one way. I'm going to ask you some questions and you're going to answer, do you understand?'

Edmund forgot his pain. He smirked as if Lambert had told a joke. Lambert bent down and looked at the wound from the bullet which had entered via the back of

Edmund's right calf and out again to the side, missing his bone.

'You've been quite lucky there, haven't you?' said Lambert, pressing down on the wound, eliciting a howl of pain from Edmund.

'Just so we're clear,' said Lambert. He had no qualms about his actions, couldn't care less if they were against procedure. The teenage boy had killed Peter Saunders and had tried to trap him underground. As far as he could ascertain, he'd kidnapped his wife and daughter, and killed at least three innocent men, so the rule books meant nothing. 'Where are Sophie and Jane?'

'I don't know,' said Barnes.

Lambert kicked the teenager in his stomach with enough force to cause him to cough and splutter.

Edmund started laughing. 'Is that the best you've got, Lambert?' he said, with a cold hostility reminiscent of his father's.

'What's this all about?' said Lambert. 'Why have you thrown your life away like this? Your dad was an evil man and did some monstrous things. Why have you followed in his path?'

'You think I'm going to speak to you? You're the one responsible for this – if you hadn't arrested my father and done that awful thing to him in his prison cell then we wouldn't be here.'

'So this is all just about getting your dad back?'

'No,' said Edmund. 'You destroyed my life, my family, so we wanted to destroy yours.'

'That's why you put my name on those cards?'

'That was one of the ways. We tipped off the journalist, we wanted your reputation ruined, to give you a taste of what it was like.'

'But what about all those innocent people? Alistair Beckinsale, Lance Jenkins, Inspector Duggan.'

Edmund grimaced like he'd swallowed something distasteful. 'You see, they weren't innocent, DCI Lambert. Duggan? Well, he was an irrelevance, but he helped put my father away. But Beckinsale and Jenkins, they were already known to us.'

'You keep saying we and us,' said Lambert. 'Who are you working with?'

Edmund looked confused, as if he'd been caught out. His face was deathly pale, and Lambert wasn't sure how long he would remain conscious.

'Beckinsale and Jenkins have experienced us before,' he said, with a sense of pride.

'You mean the Manor?' said Lambert.

'Yes, the Manor.'

'So you're one of them? What are you, nineteen?'

'I've been one of them all my life.'

Lambert looked hard at the nineteen-year-old, could tell he was telling the truth. How hadn't he seen it before? At the trial there'd been a darkness to the teenager's eyes. Lambert had put it down to confusion, even depression, when it had been a lack of empathy he'd shared with his father. The boy was only nineteen, not yet even a man, yet only God knew the monstrous things he'd experienced during his short time upon the earth.

'So the Manor wanted my reputation destroyed?' said Lambert. 'So they staged these three killings and the kidnapping of my family?'

Edmund smirked and shook his head.

'Well, what then?' screamed Tillman, reaching down to Edmund's shirt and grabbing the boy by his throat. Spittle flew from his mouth as he raged at him. 'Tell me what happened and what you want or I swear to God I will beat you to death with my own hands. You think anyone here is going to stop me?' For emphasis Tillman jabbed the boy sharply in his nose which erupted with a popping sound, a fountain of blood spraying out onto the ground.

Edmund clenched his face, convinced of Tillman's intentions. 'They didn't sanction it, it was all me.'

'Why did you kill Peter Saunders?' asked Lambert.

'Peter betrayed me, they all did,' said Edmund.

'Your dad was supposed to be freed from prison, is that it?' said Lambert.

'Very good, DCI Lambert. Maybe you are the star detective the papers always said you were. I went to them with a plan to free my father and they used it, but to free Peter Saunders instead.'

'Who are they?' said Tillman.

'You wouldn't believe me, even if I could tell you.'

Tillman punched the teenager again, this time to the temple. He closed his eyes, momentarily knocked out.

'It's all over now, Edmund,' said Lambert, bending down and slapping the teenager awake. 'Just tell me where Sophie and Jane are, we can get you some help.'

The boy smirked again. 'They've got them now. Even if there was something I could do, I wouldn't.'

Lambert had seen darkness in his time. Soulless psychopaths with no remorse for the crimes they committed, but the darkness in Barnes' eyes was something far worse. The boy had been destroyed from within. He was devoid of empathy and compassion. Lambert would go so far as to say he was subhuman.

'You said "us",' said Lambert again, searching for a hole in Barnes' story. 'What I don't understand is why the Manor would go to all the trouble of springing Peter Saunders from prison only to kill him.'

'I told you, that was my doing.'

Lambert shook his head. 'No,' he said, convincing himself. 'Who are you working with, Edmund?'

Edmund stared back with those dark blank eyes and spat on the ground.

'When did it start, Edmund?' asked Lambert, nonplussed. 'Were you just a boy? I imagine you were brought here before. What happened, did your daddy take you here as a family outing? Introduce you to his handiwork?'

Lambert had encountered corrupted families before, horrendous abuse starting early in a child's life. The vast majority of abusers had suffered abuse as children. Edmund was either one of them or was something worse. Jonathan Barnes had destroyed his son, one way or another. Lambert had a vague hope that unravelling what happened would help provoke some answers from Edmund but time was running out.

'Did he bring you along to watch? No one is blaming you, Edmund, it's not your fault you're in this situation. Help us now and I promise we will do everything we can to help you.'

There was no flicker of emotion in Edmund's eyes. 'You forget my parents were police officers. You're not going to sway me, Lambert. I know there's nothing you can do. You'll put me away for good, and frankly I don't care.'

Lambert thought quickly, fearing he was losing his opportunity. 'We can put you in the same prison as your father, the same block. You can even share a cell, how does that sound, Edmund?'

It was only momentary, but the boy's face displayed a hint of emotion; with the blink of an eye he banished it, embarrassed.

'What do you say, Edmund? Tell me where Sophie and Jane are and you have my word in front of all these officers, you and your father can be together.'

Lambert stopped speaking, giving the boy time to think. The teenager's thought processes were almost visible, his eyes glazed over, his skin losing its colour. 'I don't feel so good,' said Edmund, collapsing into the soft undergrowth.

Tillman glanced at one of his operatives, who ran over. 'He's in shock,' said the man.

Lambert cursed and moved towards Edmund. 'Stay with me, Edmund, tell me where they are,' he pleaded, as the boy slipped in and out of consciousness. 'Tell me where they are and you can be with your father.'

Edmund's eyes flicked open, large and wide, and he looked at Lambert as if surprised to be there.

'She has them,' he said, closing his eyes once more.

'We need to get him some medical attention, he's lost a lot of blood,' said the operative.

'Who is she?' said Lambert, shaking the boy, but there was no answer.

'Take him away,' said Tillman to the operative, who picked the boy up like he weighed nothing.

'The mother,' suggested Tillman. 'She's ex-police.'

Lambert nodded.

'You've spoken to her. Go there now, speak to her again. We'll take Edmund to a safe place. When he wakes we'll question him again,' said Tillman.

Lambert walked back to the car, still in a daze. He called Sarah and told her to meet him at Brenda Barnes' farmhouse.

'You don't think she had them all along?' said Sarah.

'Either that, or she knows the person who does.'

Chapter Forty

Sophie dragged Jane towards the corner of the room, as footsteps echoed down the stairs. Her initial joy at hearing noises vanished as she considered who might be coming for them.

She scrambled backwards, desperate for something to protect themselves with, her fingers dragging along the floor and picking up the water bottle.

A hatch opened in the door and Sophie caught a shadow of movement behind.

'The water is safe to drink,' said a female voice.

'What have you done to my daughter, she won't wake up.'

'She's had a sedative, a strong one. I thought it would be best for her. I have some food for you. I am going to open the door now and you need to stay where you are. I have a gun, I know how to use it and I will not hesitate to do so. Do you understand me?'

There was a coldness to the woman's voice, but also a vulnerability. 'You don't have to do this,' Sophie said.

'Do you understand?' said the voice, an octave higher.

'Yes,' said Sophie.

The door creaked open, two trays pushed through the opening.

'Please,' said Sophie. 'Please don't hurt my baby.'

The arm hesitated by the door, the elongated fingers gripping its side, before easing it shut. Sophie ran at the door as the locks turned with a metallic clank. Two trays lay on the stone floor, each with small rectangular sections holding unidentifiable mounds of food smelling of nothing. Sophie stuck her finger in one of the warm mounds and placed the substance in her mouth. The taste matched the smell.

Had she been nearer to the door, would she have been able to attack the woman? Nothing on earth would have held her back. She would have torn through the woman like she wasn't there, would have taken the severest of beatings to have the chance of escaping. She pictured the woman's eyes, black and lost, and imagined her hands clawing at them. 'Let us out, you fucking bitch,' she screamed, the noise echoing around the room. She peered beneath the door, blinking at the faint light, before dragging one of the trays back to her sleeping daughter.

How long had they been here? A second bottle of water was on the tray. Unscrewing the top, Sophie sprinkled some of the water onto Jane's lips before taking a tiny sip. It was probably naive of her but she'd sensed a shred of compassion in the woman or at least a hint of uncertainty.

Who had taken them? She recalled the newspaper article about Michael. Three victims, one of them a serving police officer. The dead officer was called Duggan. She recalled the name from before, from the horrendous Waverley Manor case Michael had worked on. Was that the connection? Was that where they were now? She refused to panic and told herself the woman didn't want them dead, at least not yet.

Who would have such a grievance against Michael? She thought of the women in Michael's life. His colleague, Matilda, the poor girl with the horrific facial injuries and of course, Sarah, his one-time lover, but they would have nothing to do with this. What potential enemies did he have? Too many to consider, but she could be methodical. His most recent major prosecutions had been related to Waverley Manor. All men, starting with that scumbag, Jonathan Barnes. Eight men, probably eight wives without husbands. Could it be a revenge thing? She tried to recall the names of those he'd put away. She knew of Peter Saunders, the man who'd escaped. Was he linked somehow?

She took another sip of the water and risked a second taste of the dark mush, and began to plan for when the woman came back.

Chapter Forty-One

Lambert called Matilda as he drove to the farmhouse and explained the situation. 'I need you to do something. Jonathan Barnes' wife, Brenda, or B.B. as she's known to her friends. She's a former Met officer.'

'I remember,' said Matilda.

'Good, then hopefully you remember her children. Edmund Barnes we know about, but it's the daughter I'm interested in now.'

The sound of keystrokes could be heard on the car's speakers as Lambert overtook a startled driver on the back road leading out of Waverly Manor.

'Louise Barnes,' said Matilda. 'Edmund's twin sister, currently at university in Swansea, studying history.'

'Do we have an address for her there?'

'No, but I can find it, though it is the Christmas holidays so I imagine she's back home.'

'Hopefully we'll know soon. Get Swansea CID to go to her university residence anyway and detain her if she's there.'

Despite Lambert's suspension, Matilda didn't argue the point. Lambert hung up, wondering how much Tillman had told her.

Edmund's last words haunted him as he drove. 'She has them.' Initially he'd thought he was referring to his mother. Now he wasn't so sure. Louise Barnes was Edmund's twin sister. Had she somehow been indoctrinated like her brother, the pair of them working in tandem?

Sarah was waiting for him a quarter of mile from the farmhouse. A calmness descended over Lambert as he saw her again. They exchanged updates. Sarah told him about her meeting with Guthrie and Partridge while Lambert relayed the extraordinary events back at Waverley Manor.

'He said, "she has them"?' asked Sarah.

'Those were his final words before he went unconscious. I've asked Matilda to trace the daughter but we can't waste any time. We didn't check the house last time and she could be there. So could Sophie and Jane. It will only be a matter of time before Brenda and or Louise find out Edmund is under arrest.'

They walked to the entrance of the house, hugging the hedges lining the approach. The sky was a sour grey and droplets of rain fell on them as they edged round the back of the house. Lambert opened the unlocked back door and entered, his gun by his side. Sarah followed close behind, as the smell of onions and stale cooking oil drifted towards them. They followed their noses to the kitchen where Brenda Barnes stood chopping vegetables.

Lambert gave her no time to respond. He pointed the gun at her chest and screamed at her to put her hands behind her head.

'What the hell is this?' said Brenda. 'You have no right to be here. If you haven't got a warrant to be on my premises, I swear you're going to regret it. I'll have both your badges.'

Lambert stood firm. 'You have three seconds to drop the knife and put your hands behind your head and to step away from the counter,' he repeated.

'You haven't changed,' said Brenda, a snarl forming on her lips, reminiscent of her husband and son.

'I will shoot you. DCI May here will confirm you pointed a shotgun at me the last time we met and I'm well within my rights to protect myself now.'

'What are you protecting yourself from? A woman chopping vegetables?'

'Three,' said Lambert. 'Two...'

Brenda hesitated, as if she had a plan in mind

'One,' said Lambert, stepping forward, his arms perfectly still as he held the Glock in front of him.

'OK,' said Brenda. She placed her hands behind her head and moved towards him.

'Slowly,' said Lambert. 'On your knees.'

Brenda shook her head like she was unwilling to obey before muttering under her breath and falling to her knees.

'Interlock your fingers, and lie on your front,' said Lambert.

'I bet you get off on this,' said Brenda, falling onto her front with a release of air.

Sarah placed her knee into the small of the woman's back before handcuffing her and dragging her to her feet.

'So am I under arrest or are you guys above the law now?'

'I have reason to believe you're harbouring Sophie and Jane Lambert. Tell me where they are,' said Lambert.

'Oh, don't be so bloody ridiculous. I told you before I had nothing to do with any of this. Jonathan was a monster. I've come to terms with that now, but I didn't know anything about what he was doing then and I know nothing about what has happened since.'

'What about your son?' said Lambert.

The question shook Brenda's confidence. Her eyes opened wide, her lip trembled. 'What about him?'

'Is he a monster as well?'

'Don't talk about my son that way.'

Lambert didn't explain. He wanted to give Brenda time to incriminate herself. 'Are you going to cooperate or not?'

'If you want to look around, be my guest, though it's a big farm.'

'What the hell does that mean?' said Lambert, moving towards the woman.

'I'm just saying, there is a lot of land.'

'This is my wife and daughter you're talking about. If you have them here, you need to tell me.'

Brenda leant forward. 'If I was the kind of person who would kidnap your wife and daughter then I wouldn't be bothered by your threats or pleas, would I? Search the house and the farm. You're wasting your time and you're putting your family at risk.'

'Wait with her,' said Lambert.

The farmhouse was bigger than he'd imagined. With its proximity to London, Lambert wondered how Brenda could afford such a place. He counted six bedrooms, each immaculately furnished. Was it a legacy of Jonathan Barnes' connection to the Manor?

He searched every room inch by inch, pulling up carpets, throwing beds and furniture on its side. He searched for trapdoors and openings but the place was clean. From the master bedroom he scanned the rolling farmland. Were Sophie and Jane huddled together in the darkness, somewhere in a bunker beneath all these acres of land?

He ran downstairs, ready to take a risk. Brenda Barnes sat on the kitchen floor, her arms cuffed behind her back.

'I'm going to come clean with you, Brenda,' said Lambert, placing his gun on the kitchen work surface. 'I've reached a desperate point. My wife and daughter are missing, and I think you and your son are the only people who know where they are.'

'I need to go to the toilet,' said Brenda, unmoved by Lambert's remarks.

'You can piss yourself for all I care, but you're not moving off that spot until you tell me where my wife and daughter are.'

'I can't tell you what I don't know.'

'Then let me tell you what I know,' said Lambert. 'Your son was arrested this morning on suspicion of murder. It appears the father's genes passed straight down to him.'

Brenda appeared genuinely puzzled. 'Don't play these tricks with me, Lambert,' she said, trying to remain calm.

'Suspicion is not really the word. I was there, he was caught red-handed. Your son's not only capable of murder, I would say he's an expert at it.'

Brenda shook her head vigorously. 'Bullshit.'

'How well do you know your son, Brenda? As well as you knew your husband?'

'Who has he killed?'

Lambert glanced at Sarah, who shrugged. 'One of your husband's friends, Peter Saunders.' With time running out, Lambert had no option. He told her about the incident at

Waverley Manor, how Edmund had trapped him underground with the corpse of Peter Saunders.

'I feel sick,' said Brenda. 'This can't be true.'

'You must have had some inkling, Brenda. You were a DI. You must have known your son was capable of this?'

Brenda fought back tears. 'He was always a withdrawn child, very quiet but I never imagined...'

'Was he close to his father?' asked Sarah.

Brenda glared at Sarah as if insulted by the question. 'Yes, they were close but that doesn't mean anything.'

'If you're not involved in this, Brenda, it's time to face facts. Your son murdered Peter Saunders, and I'm pretty sure he is responsible for the deaths of Alistair Beckinsale, Lance Jenkins and Inspector Duggan. He had a vendetta against me for putting your husband in prison and the last piece of that retribution is kidnapping my wife and daughter. And you need to think carefully. You need to help me, Brenda. Where would your son be hiding my family?'

Brenda shook her head again, clearly in denial. She opened her mouth but no words came out.

'What about Louise?' said Lambert, breaking the silence.

Brenda's head shot upwards at the mention of her daughter's name. 'Don't bring Louise into this.'

'When we asked Edmund where he was holding Sophie and Jane he said, "She has them." Now, I'm inclined to believe or at least to entertain the idea you were not involved but if you're not the person he is referring to who else could it be?'

Brenda began rocking on the spot, shaking her head.

'What was Louise like growing up, Brenda?' said Lambert.

'Was she the same as Edmund?' asked Sarah.

All fight left the woman. She slouched, the colour draining from her face. 'Could I have some water, please?' she said.

Lambert poured her some water and dripped it into her mouth.

'I was an absent mother,' said Brenda, her throat coated with the liquid. 'You know how it is in this line of work. I'm afraid my career was my priority. The children were unexpected, not totally wished for. It sounds horrendous to say, but I resented them even before they were born. I begged Jonathan to allow me to have an abortion but he wouldn't hear of it. They told me it would be different when they were born but it wasn't. I didn't even try to breastfeed them, wanted no part of their life. I cared for them, don't get me wrong, but I never wanted them. It sounds awful and it is. I think they realized that.'

Lambert sighed and looked away.

'And Jonathan?' said Sarah.

'He was the go-to parent, spent all his time with them. Obviously, he was busy as well but he always found time for them when I couldn't.'

'And Louise – what was Louise like as a child?'

'She was the same as Edmund, very shy and a little bit withdrawn. They were both quite good academically but not very sociable'

'Do you think Louise was capable of helping Edmund?'

'I still can't quite believe what you've said about Edmund.'

'We can help her, Brenda. We can help both of them but you need to help us. You don't want to have blood on your hands. Where would she have taken them?'

Brenda closed her eyes. Lambert tried to imagine what she was thinking. He didn't believe the revelations about her children shocked her as much as she was portraying. She'd been in denial. However poor her maternal instincts, she would have known something was wrong. He'd seen it before, too many times: a parent turning a blind eye to the abusive partner. Jonathan corrupted his children and her silence had aided him.

'She was supposed to come back from university for Christmas but she never did. She hasn't returned any of my calls.'

'You think she's still at university?' said Lambert.

Brenda paused, struggling with an internal conflict. 'There's one thing you may not know,' she said finally.

'Go on,' said Lambert.

Brenda paused for an age before speaking. 'Peter and Anna Saunders. They were the children's godparents.'

Chapter Forty-Two

Lambert was incredulous. Their godparents? He wasn't religious, but the irony of Peter Saunders being anyone's godparent was staggering.

'Peter and Jonathan knew each other from university. They went to separate colleges but they met at that time. It's probably how Jonathan got involved in...' Brenda stopped, her words trapped in her throat as if understanding for the first time what had happened to her life. 'The twins were christened in a church called St Matthew's. Anna Saunders appeared to be a lovely woman, though I didn't think much of Peter at the time, I guess with good reason. You don't have to say it. I take responsibility for allowing my children to be associated with such people. I didn't know anything but I should have paid more attention.'

'How often did you see the Saunders'?'

'I didn't see them at all but as the children grew older they used to see them quite often.' Brenda faltered again. 'Jesus, they used to see them every month. They were always so secretive about what they got up to and I didn't even try to push them for an answer. What did I let them get involved with?'

Sarah pulled Lambert to the side, reminded him she'd been to Anna Saunders' house, and that Anna suggested they look for Peter Saunders at the farmhouse in Norfolk.

'How far is her house from here?' asked Lambert.

'About fifty minutes.'

Lambert pulled Brenda to her feet. 'We need to pay Anna Saunders a visit,' he said.

–

He drove in a daze, hoping he wasn't following another dead end. He glanced in the rear-view mirror at Brenda Barnes. She was still cuffed and barely moved, her vacant gaze focused on the road ahead. Lambert felt no pity for her. She'd been a serving police officer yet she'd neglected her children to such an extent while her husband had warped them into something inhuman.

He clung on to thoughts of Sophie and Jane as he sped through the London traffic, blinking away thoughts of what he would do to Brenda if anything happened to his family.

'You OK?' asked Sarah.

'I will be when we find them. Any word from Tillman?' he asked, as an afterthought.

'No, still going to answer phone.'

Lambert recalled one of Tillman's holding cells he'd visited during the Waverly Manor case. The place had no Wi-Fi or phone reception; even the GPS locations were masked so once inside you were untraceable. He could only hope Edmund Barnes was now conscious, that Tillman would be able to gain some information from him.

'Here we are,' said Sarah.

'You're coming in as well,' he said to Brenda, after parking up.

Sarah went to the back of the car and grabbed the woman. Together they walked up the stone steps, an unlikely trio, Lambert with his hand on his gun.

Sarah knocked on the door, and shouted through the letterbox when there was no answer. 'Anna, it's DCI Sarah May.'

Light shone from the hallway. 'I can hear something,' she said to Lambert. 'Some sort of music.' She knocked again and turned to Lambert when there was no answer.

'Do you have a mobile phone number for your daughter?' Lambert asked Brenda.

'You can try it but it always goes straight to voicemail.'

Lambert tried the number and got the predicted result. He recalled the gangly teenager he'd seen at the trial. Like her brother, Louise Barnes had looked lost. He would never have imagined at the time she was capable of emulating her father. Filial loyalty was sometimes hard to fathom, and the timid voice suggesting he leave a message threw Lambert further into doubt.

He needed the see what was awaiting them behind Anna Saunders' front door. Lacking Tillman's burglary tools, he went to the boot of his car and retrieved his enforcer, the name given to the police-issued battering ram. He slammed the ram into the door, the lock collapsing after one hit, and led the others into the hallway.

His gun was poised, his patience wearing thin. He didn't recognize the distorted music blaring from the speakers in the living room. At first, the obscure lyrics and heavy bass of the music were out of place in the tasteful surroundings.

Then he saw the body and the jarring music made sense.

Chapter Forty-Three

Sophie didn't even hear the footsteps. The door of the underground prison was flung open, a blinding light filling the space. She blinked rapidly, her eyes first on Jane and then on the blood-soaked apparition in front of her. The woman, or more correctly the girl, was drenched in red. Lumps of matter covered her thin frame and hair. Her eyes were wide, otherworldly. In one shaking hand she held a gun, in the other a set of handcuffs.

Michael had once told Sophie that even at close quarters it wasn't easy to fire a gun with accuracy, especially when under pressure. The girl trembled from head to foot. Was this her chance? She could run, hope the girl either didn't have time to get a shot off or that the pressure of the situation would force her to miss.

'Put these on,' said the girl, throwing the cuffs towards Sophie. And she was definitely only a girl. There was nothing to her. She was a fragile and vulnerable girl; but a girl with a gun.

How could she run? The girl's hands looked unsteady, and one accidental shot could kill Jane. 'You don't have to do this,' said Sophie. 'I know you don't want to be here. Just leave us. Go, get out of here. Escape, but please let us go.'

Sophie glanced past the shaking teenager at the steep staircase. They were metres away from freedom but they might as well have been miles.

'It's your last chance. Do you want to end up like the last woman who disobeyed me?' Something changed in the girl's voice, a steadiness returning to her hand.

Sophie picked up the cold metal cuffs, placed one around her left wrist and clicked it shut.

'Behind your back.'

Sophie placed her hands and behind her and fastened the cuff on her right wrist.

'Turn around.'

Remarkably, Jane hadn't stirred. Sophie turned around, the cuffs still loose.

'Click the other one in place,' said the girl with a high-pitched wail. 'Don't do anything stupid,' she added, moving towards her.

Sophie was surprised by the girl's strength as she grabbed the cuffs and pulled them tighter onto her skin, the metal digging into the bone. It was painful, but Sophie wasn't about to give the girl the satisfaction of hearing her cry out.

'Move,' said the girl.

'No,' screamed Sophie, as the teenager picked up her baby girl and held her in her arms like she was a doll.

Chapter Forty-Four

Lambert rubbed his eyes and stared at the body, at the gaps where her eyes should have been. Carved into the woman's chest was a Latin phrase Lambert knew only too well:

In oculis animus habitat

'The soul dwells in the eyes'. It was the ultimate copycat killing. Lambert had first met Sarah while hunting a serial killer known as the Souljacker. The killer removed the eyes of his victims and carved the Latin inscription into their flesh.

Lambert moved towards Anna Saunders. Next to the inscription, pinned to the bloody remains of the woman's blouse, was a piece of card, his name stencilled onto the front like the others. The three of them stood in shock as Lambert touched the woman's neck.

'Is this Anna Saunders?' he asked.

Sarah nodded.

'She's still alive.'

–

As Sarah called the emergency services, Lambert ventured further into the Saunders' house.

'Louise, are you in here?' he shouted, trying to control his mounting panic. There was no answer but he sensed another presence in the house. In the kitchen, he pulled frantically at the cupboard doors and drawers, sending cutlery, pots and pans crashing to the ground. A side door opened into a larder area where Lambert tore the canned food from the shelves. He lifted the hessian mat on the floor and picked at the floorboards but they were solid.

'Where are you?' he mouthed to himself. He was about to run upstairs when he caught sight of the small opening beneath the staircase. It was a rectangular panel barely big enough to fit through but when he pulled it shifted with ease. He shone his torch through the opening and found what he was looking for: a trapdoor, reminiscent of Waverly Manor.

He pulled the door open, a cold breeze rising from below. 'Louise, are you down there? This is DCI Lambert. Your mother is here, we have your brother in custody. It's all over now, he's safe. Please come out so we can talk.'

He hung back from the opening in case she fired. 'Louise, come out to talk so we can sort this out. I don't care about what you've done, you can go for all I care. I just want to see my family again. Are Sophie and Jane down there?'

It was the faintest of sounds but he caught it, the rumbling of footsteps echoing up the stairs beneath the trapdoor.

'Sophie!' he screamed, dismayed at the panic in his voice.

'Where's my brother?' came a lone voice. It sounded so thin and weedy, a voice not yet matured, a voice belonging to a teenager – to the girl who'd committed the atrocity in the living room.

'He's safe, Louise. He's in custody and he wants to talk to you. We all do. I know it's been hard and I can only imagine what you went through with your father, but it's over now. Let Sophie and Jane come up and we can talk, everyone can be safe again.'

'I want to see him.'

'He's in custody, Louise. I have a second officer with me and backup is on its way. Anna Saunders is still alive. Once the backup arrives, there will be no negotiations. Armed police will be here and they're not renowned for their negotiation skills. Please, I don't want anything to happen to you and I don't want my family to be put at more risk. Your mother's here, Louise.'

'I don't want to speak to that bitch,' said Louise.

Lambert found himself biting his nails. 'I understand. Are Sophie and Jane OK?'

'They are for the time being but they won't be if you don't get out of here.'

'I have a car outside, Louise. Bring them up and we can do a deal. If you want you can take the car and take your chances but there's no other way out for you. You have my word I won't try to stop you.'

Lambert's chest rose and fell, his heart smashing against his ribcage. He was in a desperate situation. He didn't know what Louise would do. He had no real under-standing of why she was in the situation in the first place. Like her brother, she obviously wanted to get back at Lambert. Had she achieved that now with Anna Saunders almost dead? Or was there more to come?

Hopefully Edmund's capture had thrown their plans into disarray. It was conceivable Louise was acting under her brother's instructions. Now he was captured would her resolve fail?

'This is your last chance, Louise.' Lambert tried his best to hide his desperation. 'I can't take the risk any more. If you're not coming up, I'm coming down.'

Sarah followed him into the hallway with Brenda in tow. She shook her head but he was ready to go. What did he have to lose? He scuttled forward and dangled his foot, placing it on the first stair.

'Wait,' said Louise, sounding uncertain. 'Wait, we're coming up. Be warned, I'm carrying your little girl. I have a knife to the back of her neck. You know what I'll do if you try anything.'

Lambert retreated. He was close to breaking, a scream of panic caught in his throat. No amount of training or experience could have prepared him for this. He grimaced, fighting back the emotion threatening to overcome him.

'Stand back,' warned Louise, as footsteps echoed up the stairs.

Sophie appeared first. Ghost-like, she stepped into the light staring vacantly in front of her.

'Sophie, are you OK?' asked Lambert, standing his ground. He was alert now, too focused on events to allow emotion to affect him.

Sophie barely responded.

'She's drugged,' said Sarah.

'Sophie, keep coming,' said Lambert.

She took tiny steps as if she was sleepwalking. She was wearing a soiled nightgown stuck to her skin, but Lambert couldn't see any marks on her. He helped her out of the opening and grabbed her with his free arm. She didn't respond, her body limp in his embrace. Sarah took her hand and guided her away.

'I'm coming up now,' said Louise. 'Remember what I said.'

Lambert closed his eyes, fighting a wave of nausea as Louise appeared at the top of the stairs. As threatened, she was carrying Jane in her arms.

'What have you done to her?' said Lambert. His little girl's eyes were closed. He took one step forward, searching for a sign of life.

'She's alive, she's sedated,' said Louise. 'Stay back.'

Lambert stood firm, energy returning to him as fear transformed to anger. He let out a sigh as he noticed the shallow breaths coming from his daughter.

'Give me the child,' he said.

'What about our deal?'

Lambert reached into his coat pocket with his left hand and held out a set of keys.

He placed the keys on a tabletop in the hall. 'It's outside waiting for you.'

'I need to take the child with me.'

'Absolutely no way,' said Lambert. His right hand was twitching. He was sure he could reach for his gun in his jacket and take her out before she had a chance to use the knife, but how could he take that risk?

'Put Jane down, take the keys and go. They're going to be here within seconds,' said Lambert.

Louise gazed anxiously at the keys on the table, two metres beyond her reach. She looked at Lambert and Sarah, weighing up her options, and appeared to be about to place Jane on the ground when her attention was distracted by another presence in the hallway.

'Louise?' Brenda had made her way into the hallway.

'Mum, what are you doing here?'

'Louise, did you really do this?' Brenda, like the rest of them, appeared to be in shock.

'You don't understand, Mum.'

'How could you do this? Did you do that to Anna?'

'I did it for Dad.'

'You did it for Dad? For that man who did all those awful things to those poor...' She couldn't even say the words. 'Give the man his child back, Louise.'

Something changed in Louise at the request. A spark of light appeared in her eyes, forcing her into action.

Lambert reached for his gun as Louise hoisted a sharp object high above her and held it for a split second, its intended target the gap between Jane's shoulder blades.

Lambert was quick but not quick enough. Louise's movement sparked Sophie into action. Lambert saw it in the same split second as he raised the gun. Sophie charged sideways with everything she had into the teenage girl. The impact sent her crashing into the wall, loosening the grip of her left hand, Jane falling from her arms. Lambert didn't hesitate. He covered the short distance to where she was falling in a millisecond. He was about to lead with his left foot, to kick Louise where she fell, but Louise reacted and swung her knife, slicing Sophie's Achilles tendon with one swift movement.

Lambert grabbed his daughter, still mercifully asleep, and pushed her behind him as Sophie crashed to the ground next to Louise.

Louise held the knife, now coated with blood. Her eyes held the same blank look he'd seen on Edmund and glared at him before bringing the knife down once more, this time towards Sophie's heart.

Lambert wasted no time, four bullets leaving his gun and entering Louise's chest before the knife could find its target.

Chapter Forty-Five

The gunshots woke Jane. Sophie picked her up and stumbled out of the room into the road. Lambert held his arm out towards her but she dodged his touch as if avoiding an assailant.

As sirens wailed in the distance, Brenda crawled to her daughter, wailing. Lambert looked at Sarah, both of them in shock.

The scene resembled a horror movie. Blood splattered the walls behind Louise Barnes, and in the corner Anna Saunders still struggled for life.

Tillman was the first to arrive. 'What the actual fuck?' he said, glancing from Lambert to Sarah, from Louise and Brenda, still in handcuffs, to the mutilated body of Anna Saunders.

'She's still alive, Glenn. Where are the paramedics?'

Tillman looked at him like he was stupid. 'Who is?'

Lambert pointed to Anna Saunders. Tillman was momentarily confused, as if suspicious of being caught in a joke, before springing into life. He began barking orders, summoning his section's medical team and instructing two of his guards not to let anyone else in the house as a third took photos of Anna Saunders as she was lifted out of the house.

'Get her out of here,' said Tillman to his guards, pointing at Brenda Barnes.

'I will get you for this,' screamed the woman at Lambert as she was dragged from her daughter's corpse.

Tillman shook his head, disgusted at the former police officer, compassion far from his mind.

'Who shot her?' he asked, when Brenda had left the scene.

Lambert stepped forward.

'Give me the firearm,' said Tillman, holding out a piece of cloth. He wrapped the gun and placed it in a small plastic bag. 'On the twenty-seventh December we met one another in Woolwich. You raised concerns over your family, and the transfer of Jonathan Barnes. At that time, I authorized the use of your firearm. Think you can remember that?'

'You honestly think that is going to work?' said Lambert.

'You risked your life and found the killer or killers of three men, one of them a police officer. Tanner mistakenly took your badge. If he pushes this I will make sure he loses his job for gross incompetence.'

Lambert appreciated the loyalty but didn't share Tillman's convictions.

'You OK with that, DCI May?' asked Tillman.

'Whatever you agreed,' said Sarah.

–

Sophie was sitting in the back of an ambulance, arguing with the paramedic placing a breathing mask over Jane. 'It's just a precaution,' said the woman, as Sophie watched her every move, her eyes wild.

'Sophie,' said Lambert, stepping into the vehicle. 'Is she OK?'

'She's been unconscious ever since we were taken. Why the hell did this happen, Michael?' Sophie's eyes fixed on him, as if everything was his fault. Blood dripped down his wife's white nightgown, his daughter prone on the gurney. She had every right to blame him, and he had to accept it.

'I'm sorry,' he said, the words meaningless.

'I'll let you know what happens,' said Sophie, holding his gaze.

'OK,' said Lambert, leaving the ambulance. He stood motionless as the ambulance carried his family away.

Tillman and Sarah were talking outside the house as SOCOs moved around him, yet he'd never felt so alone.

–

Lambert spent the night at a hotel. Sophie sent him a single text message telling him Jane was fine and they were going to her mother's for a few days. He called her back seven times, the phone going straight to answerphone, before giving in.

He sat staring at the wall, a glass brimming with single malt in his hand.

–

Sleep must have come at some point. He woke, still sitting on the chair, bright sunshine leaking through the blinds of the hotel room. Miraculously, his glass was still in his hand, the dregs of the whisky swirling around the bottom. It was an effort to move. His mouth was coated in a thick, mucus-like substance, his chest aching as he made his way to the bathroom.

The room moved in and out of focus as he recalled the previous night's events. And despite the horror of Anna Saunders' house, the bullets he'd been forced to put into Louise Saunders, all he could think about was the way Sophie had looked at him. It reminded him of the time they'd split up, when she'd finally had enough of him, but he couldn't see any way back this time. There had been more than accusation in those eyes. She'd given up on him, as if realizing he'd been at fault all along, that her life would be infinitely better without him. She now understood. Everything he'd ever blamed himself for – the days and nights of neglect when he'd worked late, the death of his first daughter, and now the kidnapping of Sophie and Jane – it was all his fault, and there would be no coming back.

He was pulling on his clothes when there was a knock on the door. He checked the peephole, too hungover to care who was there. Through the distorted glass he made out the image of Matilda Kennedy, twirling her red hair as she waited for him to answer.

Lambert didn't recall telling anyone where he was staying. 'Now's not a great time,' he said, opening the door.

Matilda ignored him, pushing past him into the open room. 'Jeez, this room smells as bad as you do,' she said, opening a window. 'Are you OK, Michael?' she asked.

It was surreal to hear Matilda using his first name. 'I've had better nights.'

Matilda glanced around the room noticing the two-thirds empty bottle of whisky, the chair facing the window. 'I'd like to say for the record I don't think this is a good idea but Glenn is waiting downstairs. They're still planning to move Jonathan Barnes today.'

Lambert collapsed on the bed, his stomach lurching. 'How can they move him after all this?' he asked, attempting to keep the contents of the whisky bottle from reappearing.

'The MI5 agent, Partridge, had the final say. They're planning to move him in two hours. Do you think you can make it?' Matilda boiled the kettle, offering him a cup of black instant coffee.

'We'll have to get something better than this,' said Lambert, wincing as he sipped at the coffee.

–

'You just left a nightclub?' said Tillman, as Lambert climbed into the front passenger seat, Matilda sitting in the back. 'You smell like the homeland.'

'I didn't know you were Scottish?' said Lambert, groaning as he pulled the seatbelt across his tender body.

'There's a lot you don't know about me,' said Tillman. He was acting brash, like nothing had happened, but Lambert noted the concern. 'You better take this,' he said, handing him his warrant card.

Lambert tried to hide the tremble in his hand as he took the leather wallet, the alcohol still very much in his system. 'How did you get this?' he asked, his voice a fading croak.

'I spoke to the Chief Constable. I pointed out what a disgrace it was Tanner had suspended you over Duggan and he agreed.'

'But I shot someone four times – I'm surprised anti-corruption haven't taken me in yet.'

Tillman started the car. 'As I told you yesterday, you were working for me undercover. You're the fucking hero here, Michael. You found the killers of three innocent men, one a police officer, and managed to rescue your wife and child for good measure. You really think the Chief wants you prosecuted? That disturbed young woman was going to kill your baby. Every parent on earth would have done what you did, and I'll be pointing that out at every turn.'

Lambert didn't share his optimism but thanked him anyway. He was amazed when the man pulled over and asked him and Matilda what they wanted from the coffee shop.

'You've made a new man out of him,' Lambert said to Matilda, as Tillman left the car.

'If I was you I'd make the most of it. I don't think we'll see its like again anytime soon.'

Lambert managed a chuckle. 'I think you may be right.'

Tillman returned with a large black Americano and a bacon roll, and Lambert thought he'd never tasted anything better. The grease and caffeine ate away at the alcohol and by the time they reached Woolwich his head was almost back to normal.

He welcomed the bitter fresh air outside, welcomed further the sight of Sarah May. She embraced him without speaking, Tillman and Matilda walking away.

'I wanted to call you, but I knew you had to be with Sophie and Jane. Are they OK?'

Lambert recalled Sophie's parting glare, the single text message she'd offered him. Too hungover, he smiled and said, 'I'm glad you're here.'

Jonathan Barnes' transport, a reinforced police riot van, was waiting in the holding area where Tillman had parked. Next to the van were four blacked-out SUVs. As Tillman and Matilda returned to the car, Lambert caught site of the MI5 agent, Partridge, walking towards them.

'No, no, no,' said the agent, striding towards them as if walking on hot coals.

Lambert couldn't help but laugh at the look of disdain on Tillman's face as Partridge stopped two metres short of him.

'Excuse me?' said Tillman.

'Chief Superintendent Tillman... I am—'

'I know who you are,' said Tillman, interrupting.

'How did you get through security?' asked Partridge, momentarily curious. 'Never mind that, what the hell are you doing here?'

'We're here to make sure the prisoner, Jonathan Barnes, is transferred successfully.'

'That's wonderful,' said Partridge, full of sarcasm. 'We always welcome the support of the local constabulary. But hang on, I do believe DCI Lambert here is currently under suspension, and DCI May has been taken off the Peter Saunders' case. In fact, I took her off myself. Furthermore, I have been given full authority over the transfer of Barnes, so if you all don't mind...'

'Finished?' said Tillman, pulling out an envelope from his inside coat pocket and handing it to the agent.

Partridge produced a pair of spectacles and read the note within.

'From Chief Constable Alexander Mitchell of the Metropolitan Police, no less,' said Tillman, mimicking Partridge's tone. 'Let me paraphrase it for you to save you some time. We are to accompany the transfer party of Jonathan Barnes.' Tillman was on his best infuriating behaviour, lacing his fingers and smiling at the agent.

To his credit, Partridge didn't respond to the taunt. 'Fine, the more the merrier. Shall we get this convoy moving?'

And a convoy it was. Three of the SUVs, both containing armed guards, took the lead, followed by the riot van, Tillman's car, and in the rear the last SUV carrying Partridge and his team.

It seemed unthinkable the Manor would try anything after recent events. Even if there was an insider providing information, it would take something on an audacious scale to free Barnes from this motorcade.

The riot van was windowless and Lambert couldn't see the prisoner within. He wondered if the man had been told about his daughter. Her death filled Lambert with a numbness. As Tillman pointed out, she was a murderer and would have more than likely killed Jane had he not stopped her. But it should never have reached that stage. Her father had corrupted her and her brother from birth. They'd never had a chance. She pitied Louise and Edmund for what they'd been and what they'd become. He blamed Jonathan Barnes without reservation. Part of him wished that he had been responsible for the acid attack which disfigured the man. On behalf of Alistair Beckinsale, Lance Jenkins, Inspector Duggan, and even Edmund and Louise, he would happily inflict the same amount of pain again without a second thought.

The transfer went without a hitch. Lambert caught a glimpse of Barnes' melted face as he was shuttled from the van into Luton prison and could only hope his life would be hell within his new home.

The Governor, Stuart Pierson, was under suspension pending investigation into his relationship with Barnes' wife, Brenda. Lambert wasn't sure if it would be enough to get the man dismissed, but with all the surrounding controversy he imagined the man would lose his job. He would also be answering some questions in the near future about how Peter Saunders managed to escape custody, as would many others.

Chapter Forty-Six

Lambert returned home that evening. Sophie and Jane were still at Glenda's house and the house felt empty. Rather than feeling relieved that the case was at an end, tension surged through him. Notwithstanding Edmund Barnes remained to be questioned, it was hard to focus knowing Sophie blamed him for everything. He opened a bottle of red wine, recalling the look of resignation he'd seen on her face. Drinking the copper-tasting liquid, he concluded she was unlikely ever to forgive him. Every time he questioned what that would really mean, he took another sip of wine, in his panic his mind returning over and over to the same question. Would Jane still be part of his life?

Tillman had driven them back from Luton and he'd said an uneasy goodbye to Sarah. She was only a phone call and a thirty-minute taxi drive away, but even now he thought seeing her would be a betrayal. Not only to Sophie and Jane, but to Sarah herself. He would be using her and she deserved better. Instead, he finished off the bottle of red, his hi-fi playing Uncle Tupelo songs on a loop as he fell asleep.

—

It was becoming a habit, one he had to start controlling. He awoke on the sofa, his empty glass of wine on the floor, Jeff Tweedy and Jay Farrar still battling it out on his speakers.

An hour later and he was ready. Showered, breakfasted and changed into a fresh suit, he called Matilda to confirm what time they were questioning Edmund Barnes before walking to the train station, a body brimming with nervous tension.

Tillman summoned him into his office when he arrived, Matilda already waiting there for him. 'Heads-up, I've had Tanner on the phone this morning. He's still pissed you're not suspended. He's not giving up on this, I'm afraid. You're going to have to meet with AC-10 at some point. You remember what happened, don't you?' Tillman handed him a piece of paper, back-dated and signed, stating that while suspended Tillman had asked him to work undercover. Lambert signed it, unsure it would do any good. If he was suspended, he was suspended. He'd killed someone while off duty. He thanked Tillman and pocketed the letter, putting his concerns to one side for the time being.

'You and Matilda will interview Barnes junior. He will know what happened to his sister and I think your presence, Michael, will push his buttons and that is what we want.'

'What can we offer him?' asked Lambert. The boy was facing life without parole and it was hard to negotiate with people in such a position.

'The same as we mentioned before. I have a list of privileges he can receive in prison, and if he comes up with enough answers we'll let him share a cell with his father.'

Although desperate for answers, the last offer was a step too far for Lambert. Neither father nor son deserved such a privilege, though spending the rest of their lives locked away together might not be the privilege the teenage boy thought.

'One point to consider,' said Tillman. 'Edmund asked for a duty solicitor.'

'A solicitor by the name of Benjamin Dale tried to speak to him but Edmund refused,' added Matilda.

'Dale was Jonathan Barnes' solicitor,' said Lambert.

'Yes, and Peter Saunders',' said Tillman.

'You're thinking Dale could be the Manor's *consigliere*?' asked Lambert.

'He represented four of the eight members of the Manor we convicted, so it's more than a possibility.'

That Edmund had rejected the man's representation was promising. Was Edmund about to turn his back on the Manor in return for a better deal? 'Let's find out why,' said Lambert, leading Matilda out of the room.

They questioned Edmund Barnes in Woolwich where he was remanded. He was waiting in an interview room, cuffed, sitting next to his solicitor. He looked much younger than at Waverley Manor. He'd lost weight in the last few days, his face deathly pale and gaunt.

Lambert started the tape and made the introductions. The first words Edmund said were, 'You killed my sister.'

Lambert met the boy's eyes, making Edmund uncomfortable. 'I'm afraid Louise was killed during the course of our investigation, Edmund, you're correct. I can't comment on the actual events but I can assure you we had no option.'

'You had no option?' said Edmund, staring at the ground.

'Let's change the subject, shall we, Edmund? You have been charged with the murders of Alistair Beckinsale, Lance Jenkins, Inspector Duggan and Peter Saunders. I'm sure you've spoken to your solicitor about the charges and the evidence we have to build a successful case.'

Edmund glanced at his solicitor who nodded. Lambert hadn't encountered Kim Morgan before. She was young, and would never have handled anything as high profile as this before, which was all in his favour. He pushed over the list of privileges drawn up by Tillman.

Edmund studied it, his eyes focused on the end of the list, the part offering him the chance to stay with his father.

'This is an exceptional offer, Edmund. One I personally have never seen before. But you need to tell us everything and I mean not just about the murders, do you understand?'

'OK.'

'Let's start with Mr Beckinsale. You electrocuted Mr Beckinsale in his bath, is this correct?'

Edmund looked at his solicitor and began to speak.

He was quick to talk, confessing to the murders of Beckinsale, Jenkins, Duggan and Saunders. Edmund's fingerprints had been found at the scene of each, and DNA analysis would shortly match with the DNA swabs they had taken from the teenage boy.

'Why Beckinsale and Jenkins?' asked Matilda.

When he'd been asked the same question in Waverley Manor he'd claimed the men were known to 'them', not elaborating on what he meant.

'I knew of them,' he said.

'How?' asked Lambert.

'They were on my dad's files.'

'What files?'

'Dad gave me a flash drive before he went to prison.'

'Where is this data, Edmund?' said Lambert.

'I've destroyed it,' said Edmund, a hint of defiance in his eyes.

'If you're lying to us, all deals are off. We're searching everywhere. Your student house, your mother's farmhouse, the Saunders' residence. If I find a flash drive you're not telling me about there will be no privileges. Do you understand?'

Lambert raised his voice and the solicitor opened her mouth to object, only to change her mind.

'It's been destroyed.'

'What exactly was on this list?' asked Matilda.

'It was a list of people known to us.'

'Stop saying that, Edmund. By "us" you mean the Manor?' said Lambert.

Edmund shrugged.

'What do you mean by "known" exactly?'

Edmund whispered something to his solicitor, who appeared shell-shocked by the whole situation. 'I'm not admitting to being part of the Manor,' said Edmund.

'OK, I understand. Why not you use the pronoun "we" instead of the Manor? Then maybe I can understand what the hell you're talking about?'

'Yes. We knew of their existence because they'd visited...' Edmund's face froze as he struggled for the words. 'Our... sites in the past.'

Lambert closed his eyes, his hand reaching for his forehead, the taste of last night's red wine rising up his throat. 'By sites you mean places like Waverley Manor?'

'Possibly,' said Edmund.

Alistair Beckinsale was fifty-four when he died, Lance seventeen. So many lost years. 'But why kill them now?'

'To get your attention.'

'My personal attention?' said Lambert.

'Yes.'

'Why?'

'Because you put my father in jail.'

'He did that himself, Edmund, didn't he? He was guilty of horrendous things, Edmund.'

'You may think so.'

Lambert wanted to get to his feet, grab the boy and scream at him, but managed to control himself.

'And Louise? What was her role in this?'

'She helped. She wanted to get involved earlier but I wouldn't let her.'

'But she did that to Anna Saunders?'

'So I believe,' said Edmund, seemingly proud of his sister's actions.

'OK, let's get back to Alistair and Lance. There must be more to it than that? You got my attention by leaving my name at the scene, getting my name in the press. Why kill those two men, Edmund? Why in that manner?'

Edmund smiled, the blankness in his eyes reminding him of the things the boy was capable of. 'Because no one ever escapes us,' he said, with such pride that Lambert had to look away lest he be forced to attack him.

Let's move on to your two other victims, Inspector Duggan and Peter Saunders,' said Matilda. 'You confess to their killings?'

He shrugged, his solicitor staring at him.

Matilda touched the list in front of him. 'It's up to you, Edmund, but if you want to earn these you better start talking.'

'His issues with Duggan are well known,' said Edmund, pointing to Lambert. 'My father told me about that long ago.'

'So you wanted to implicate DCI Lambert, get him in trouble, is that it?'

'He imprisoned my father, destroyed my family. Can you blame me?'

'You have an interesting sense of justice, Edmund. What about Peter Saunders?' asked Lambert. 'He was your godfather. He was a member of the Manor. Don't you have rules about killing each other?'

Edmund frowned.

'Did he betray you, Edmund, is that it? You said to me before it was your idea, that it should have been your father who was set free. Then along comes Peter Saunders and takes your father's place. That must have been devastating. And John Prine, was he caught in the crossfire?'

'You don't understand the planning involved, the research I undertook,' said Edmund, reacting to Lambert's suggestion.

Edmund's pride was evident. He wanted to share his secrets, to reveal his cleverness. 'I can imagine. How did you stage it, Edmund? How did you arrange for a prisoner to escape? Was it John Prine, was he the key?'

'He was part of it. You have to look for a weakness, a reason to get them to do what you want.'

'And John Prine had a weakness?' asked Lambert.

'He did, but he was a bit player.'

Lambert smiled at Edmund as if impressed with him. They were so close but one wrong word could blow it. 'Who was it, then, Edmund? What did you discover, who had the weakness?'

Edmund lifted his chin, defiant. His eyes started to water, and Lambert feared he'd pushed the boy too far. 'I saw him, you see. In one of the gatherings. No one else had spotted him. He was using an alias, obviously.'

Lambert nodded, not wanting to interrupt the flow in case the boy stopped talking.

'I took videos of him in conversation, and more,' said Edmund, a twisted smile forming on his lips.

'And you used this information to blackmail him?' said Matilda.

'Blackmail is not a very nice word,' said Edmund, turning to face Matilda in accusation. 'I suggested we give him the opportunity to become one of us, and that was exactly what they did. But instead of getting him to free my father, they freed Peter Saunders.'

'Who was it, Edmund? Who helped Saunders escape?'

'My father was right about you, wasn't he? Blinkered was the word he used. Can't see what's directly under your nose.'

Lambert wanted to counter-argue the accusation by pointing out that Edmund's father was in jail but didn't want to antagonize the boy just yet. 'You've definitely got one over us here, Edmund. I'm impressed, but if you want to see your father again you need to tell me who was responsible.'

'They need to go,' said Edmund, pointing to the two prison guards in the room.

'Do you mind, guys?' said Lambert.

The men shrugged, one of them saying, 'You're taking full responsibility, then?'

Lambert looked at the prisoner, a handcuffed teenage boy, and stated the departure of the guards for the tape. 'OK, Edmund, you have our attention.'

'To confirm, if my client gives you the name of the person responsible for Peter Saunders' escape he will receive the privileges stated on this sheet?'

Lambert had forgotten the duty solicitor was in the room. He looked at Matilda and they both nodded. 'Tell us, Edmund.'

'Who do you think? It was the Governor.'

Lambert leant in close. 'You mean the Governor of this prison?'

'Yep, Paul Guthrie.'

–

'I need you both to stay here,' said Lambert to Edmund and his solicitor. 'If you mention what you just told me to the guards, the deal is off. Do you understand?'

Edmund smiled, happy to have Lambert at a disadvantage. If he was telling the truth it would explain many things. Paul Guthrie would have prior knowledge of Peter Saunders' transfer, would have known or could have easily discovered the route he would have taken. With John Prine on board, it would have been feasible to arrange the attack which freed Peter Saunders. It still left unanswered questions, such as which members of the Manor gave the order and supplied the manpower, but at least they had Guthrie.

Lambert rattled the lock and one of the guards checked the peephole before opening the door. 'I need to get permission from your Governor,' said Lambert, to the more senior-looking of the two men.

'For what?' said the man.

'I can't disclose that. Is he in at the moment?'

'I think so. Let me check,' said the guard, using his radio. 'Marge, is Governor Guthrie in his office at the moment?'

'Hang on,' came the reply through a hail of static. 'Yes, he is.'

'The police officers questioning Barnes would like to speak to him. Can I send them up?'

More static. 'Go ahead.'

'Text Tillman,' said Lambert under his breath to Matilda as they were led through the corridors of the prison.

Edmund had mentioned he'd seen Guthrie at a meeting, making Lambert recall the material they'd recovered at Edmund's student digs. Edmund, with or without the help of the Manor, must have used this to blackmail Guthrie. Sarah had been suspicious of the man from the beginning but Partridge hadn't been interested; or if he had been, MI5 had done a very bad job in their investigation.

'Glenn is sending a team over now,' said Matilda once they reached upstairs. Her face was flushed, a thick white line of charred skin prominent on her cheek.

'Good. Be ready for anything when we go in. As soon as Guthrie knows we're onto him he'll become unpredictable.'

They were led through another set of doors by the guard, who didn't follow them through, locking the door from the other side. 'Just through there,' he said, pointing down the corridor.

The prison took on a different appearance through the door. Gone was the grey stone, the claustrophobic narrowness of the corridors and the barred gates. Here, the walls were a pristine white, the floors carpeted. The Governor's secretary greeted them and asked them to take a seat, but both officers stayed on their feet.

'Sir, DCI Lambert and DS Kennedy are here to see you now,' said the secretary, through the intercom.

The machine buzzed with static and Lambert wasted no time.

'You can't do that,' said the secretary, as Lambert opened the Governor's door.

'Matilda,' shouted Lambert, as he burst into the office and ran at Paul Guthrie.

The prison Governor had made a makeshift noose from some electrical wire, and was dangling from a metal girder running the length of the ceiling. The man's face was purple, his swollen tongue protruding from his mouth. Lambert grabbed his legs, his trousers soaked, and pushed his body upwards, taking the strain from the cable.

'You don't get to take the easy way out,' said Lambert, struggling under the man's weight, as Matilda worked with a frantic intensity on the wire until she cut through and Guthrie fell down onto Lambert.

Lambert pushed the body away, as Guthrie made a desperate attempt to breathe, the deep colour in his face fading to white as life returned.

Getting to his feet, Lambert grimaced as he brushed Guthrie's fluids off his clothes. 'DS Kennedy, read this animal his rights,' he said, as Tillman and his team joined them in the office.

Epilogue – Nine Months Later

The smell of stale sweat permeated the interior of the van. The engine was switched off, the five officers within being boiled alive without the aid of air conditioning. Lambert drank his lukewarm bottle of water as he watched DS Bickland on the monitor walking with their suspect to the bed and breakfast.

Following on from the information supplied by Paul Guthrie, Bickland had worked undercover for the last six months. Everything had led to this moment. After surviving his attempted suicide, Guthrie admitted Edmund had blackmailed him. Initially the plan had been to free Jonathan Barnes, but others soon got involved and changed the rules. The figures who'd taken over from Edmund were nameless, but Guthrie had given them enough to work on.

Bickland was chosen due to his anonymity. Lambert and Matilda were known to the Manor but Bickland worked mainly behind the scenes. Not that they'd taken any chances. Bickland changed his appearance for the role, losing twenty pounds of weight, sporting a beard and cropping his hair to a buzz cut.

The man he was walking with was Gareth Hoskins, a convicted paedophile currently on parole. Hoskins had been promising Bickland entry to an exclusive club for the last four months and this morning Bickland received a call instructing him to meet Hoskins at six p.m. That was only four hours ago, Lambert and Tillman assembling the armed team at short notice.

In the time since Bickland had first made contact with Hoskins, Edmund Barnes confessed and had been convicted of the murders of Alistair Beckinsale, Lance Jenkins, Inspector Duggan and Peter Saunders.

Anna Saunders, who had made a miraculous recovery, had confirmed that Louise Barnes had been responsible for the attack on her. Edmund was now rooming at Her Majesty's pleasure in a shared cell with his father in Luton prison, the governorship of which had changed hands following Pierson's dismissal for gross misconduct. All of this served to undermine the MI5 agent, Partridge, whose department had been removed from their investigation into the Manor.

Lambert wasn't sure how it had happened but he'd been appointed to lead a new department, set up with the specific aim of investigating and bringing down the Manor.

'Where are we going, Gareth?' asked Bickland in his West Country drawl, his voice reaching them via the wire sewn into his shirt.

'They're expecting you. You've been cleared, so take it easy,' said Gareth, ringing the bell on the front door of the bed and breakfast.

The scene unfolded on Lambert's screen in the van, cameras having been erected outside earlier that day. Newport House was a four-storey building offering discounted rates and was mainly used by travelling labourers. The sign on the front window suggested there were no vacancies, and it took two minutes before someone answered the door.

With no camera on the inside, they were relying on whatever information Bickland could offer by voice. The interior of the van was hushed; no one moved as the sound of footsteps played through the speakers. 'We're going down here?' said Bickland, for their benefit.

Lambert was taken back to the few minutes he'd been trapped beneath Waverley Manor and the dungeon at Anna Saunders' house where Sophie and Jane were kept. 'Move in,' he instructed, a wave of heat hitting him as he ran from the van.

The armed response team swept through the scene in seconds, the squad leader giving orders as small divisions split up to secure each floor, the main group heading downstairs.

Bickland played along as the response team headed downstairs and instructed the occupants to get to the floor. 'Area secure,' said the commander. 'Ten males, unarmed.'

Lambert took a deep breath and headed inside. His concern all along was the lack of material evidence, but his worries were unfounded. The ten men, Bickland included, lay prone on the ground, as vile images played on a large overhead screen. He turned away, happy to let his fellow officers begin processing the men into custody.

'Good haul?' asked Tillman, who was waiting outside.

'Nine perverts,' said Lambert.

It was merely a start. Hoskins was small fry, and although it was good to get him and his sick friends off the streets, the arrests were the first step in a longer-term plan. Nine men meant nine bargaining chips.

Nine more opportunities to get to the top, to find out who was running the Manor.

Tillman didn't congratulate him. 'We have company,' he said, pointing to a car further down the road.

Lambert recognized the saloon car, and the silhouetted figure within. Chief Superintendent Tanner raised his hand in greeting but didn't leave the vehicle. Tanner and AC-10 had investigated the shooting at Anna Saunders' house and decided not to bring charges against him or Sarah. Lambert would never know what pressure had been put on Tanner to drop the case, but the man had become ever-present in his life since. He was always lurking in the shadows, scrutinizing Lambert's every move, waiting for him to slip up.

'You want to speak to him?' said Tillman.

'And say what? No, if he wants to waste his time let him.'

–

Lambert left Matilda to supervise the processing of the men and headed to his car, with a final glance over to Tanner as he started the engine. It was Friday evening and he didn't want to waste any more time. Cursing the London traffic he called ahead and warned Sophie he would be late.

'OK,' she said, her voice flat, devoid of concern.

He reached Beckenham ninety minutes later and knocked on the door of his former house. 'She should be sleeping, Michael,' said Sophie, holding Jane's hand.

Jane broke from her mother's grip and ran to Lambert who bent down and picked the girl up. It had taken three months to get to the stage where he was allowed to take

Jane from the house. The kidnapping had changed his relationship irrevocably. Sophie, who was still limping following an operation on her Achilles tendon, had told him she no longer loved him, and the truth of her words hit him hard every time he saw her.

Although he understood why, he still struggled with the change in Sophie. All the years they'd spent together, the awful things they'd faced, counted for nothing. She blamed him for her and Jane's kidnapping and nothing would alter that.

'Tomorrow by six p.m.,' said Sophie, kissing Jane on the forehead.

'Bye, Mummy,' said Jane, bouncing up and down in Lambert's arms.

Lambert placed the girl in the back of the car and was reminded of Sophie's mother's words, 'Don't blow it this time, Michael.'

–

Jane had no memory of the incidents at Anna Saunders' house. They'd run numerous checks and met with child psychologists, but she couldn't recall anything. Sophie told him she'd found Jane unconscious in the room before Louise Barnes attacked her. Jane had been injected with a sedative, and they lived in hope that she would never recall the scene.

The girl was asleep by the time they reached the flat Lambert was renting. He carried her to her room, decorated so it matched her room in Beckenham, and watched her for a few minutes as he wondered how he'd so successfully messed things up again.

He checked in with Matilda before opening a bottle of red wine. He switched on the television, attempting to banish all thoughts of the case. Although Jane was asleep, he'd vowed to concentrate on her and her alone whenever they had time together.

The next day went too fast. After breakfast, they went to the park and ate ice cream in the sunshine. In the afternoon, they cuddled together on the sofa and watched one of Jane's movies, Lambert's stomach aching as the time to take Jane home drew nearer.

As he drove her home he told himself this was his deserved penance – for Chloe, and for leading Sophie and Jane into danger – his punishment could have been much worse.

Jane cried as Sophie took her from Lambert's arms. Sophie stared at him like he was an apparition and said, 'Two weeks, no sooner.'

The divorce was not yet finalized so Lambert accepted Sophie's terms. He didn't want to wait two weeks until he saw Jane again, but this was another part of his penance and he had to remain patient.

He drove back and parked at the end of the road next to the local bar. The place was already jumping and Lambert considered joining the revellers within, but no one needed a maudlin figure ruining their evening. He stopped at the off-licence and purchased another bottle of red wine, hesitating as he reached the outside of his flat, a figure waiting by his front door.

Sarah May offered him a lopsided grin as she held aloft her own bottle of wine.

'I thought you might like some company, but it seems you beat me to it.'

'Why don't we ditch these bottles and see what the night has in store for us?' said Lambert. He hesitated before stepping towards her, a sense of calmness and relief coming over him as she reached forward and grabbed his hand.